Sexy at Sixty

By Nina Dockery, Ed.D.

Inner-Journey Press

Acknowledgements

Maggie Honton – I love you! Without your editing, where would I have been? I express utmost respect, gratitude and awe at your abilities.

To Rene Rowe, Debra Wingfield and Pam Arwine: You ladies were wonderful with your ideas, feedback and support. I can't thank you enough! Our laughter made this project great fun!

To reach Nina, go to:

http://intuitiontalesbyninaedd.com/blog/

To the readers: Enjoy!

–

In the Beginning

Today was supposed to be like any other day in Venus Lighton's life: work, meetings and study. But, while driving to the University of California, La Jolla campus, (better known as UCSD) where she was head of the chemistry department, her car began to wobble and make funny sounds. "Damn, a flat tire! Just what I need! I had a feeling something was going to happen with my car, but I just didn't pay attention or ask the next question. Why do I always forget that little step?" She could feel all her defensiveness, fear and sarcasm come to the surface as she accused herself, "All I had to do was ask what's going to go wrong, or something like that, and my guidance could have told me. Yeah, that's a laugh! I'm definitely more psychic with *other* people's dramas."

She called her secretary, and told her she was stuck on the highway and would be about an hour late, depending on how long it took to fix her flat. "Oh well," she thought, "at least there was nothing really important on my agenda. For that, I am thankful." With Venus' work load increasing daily, she was relieved this little distraction occurred on a slow day.

As she got over her embarrassment at being stuck in the middle of the road, and feeling she was regarded as a dumb woman by various male passers-by, she began to get her bearings. "Wow," isn't this perfect – a Discount Tires Store right across the street." After putting on her emergency flashers, she got out of the car, crossed the six-lane road - always a feat in Southern California – and began to breathe again. She walked into the tire store and told them her predicament.

"We need to get you off that road ASAP – before rush hour! We'll tow you in. And don't worry, we'll have you out of here in no time!"

Immediately a tow truck was sent out, and Venus believed she'd make it back to her office within an hour. When two hours later the tire still had not been looked at, she began to mumble to herself, "Damn, what is taking them so long!? Like this is all I have to do, just sit around and wait!"

Venus was not particularly proud that waiting and patience were her weak points, but that was the way things were. She began to cross and uncross her legs and tap her toes. When that wasn't relieving her frustration, she began to shake her legs – at first gently, then with a rapidity that was astonishing. Finally her legs got tired and stiff, so she got up to walk around. Two and one-half hours and still no sign of her car even being looked at!

The waiting room was packed with people. "You'd think they're predicting a huge snowstorm the way people are lined up here to put on new tires. This is quite ridiculous, or did they have a damn fire sale?" Venus muttered to herself. When she finally decided to sit down again, there was only one chair left in the huge waiting room. She walked over with great dramatic flair, and plopped herself down, obviously frustrated. As she looked around, she noticed the gentleman next to her. She grabbed one of the magazines and pretended to read it, glancing ever so often at the guy, thinking, "Wow. Handsome! Sexy! Who *are* you?"

She guessed he was probably in his mid fifties, with a full head of black curly hair, just a few strands of silver weaving in at the sides. He seemed tall even sitting down, maybe six feet plus a couple inches. Broad shoulders, slender, great body. And the killer for her – brilliant green cat eyes. He wore faded jeans and a corduroy jacket with a green sweater under it – incredible! It was hard for her to pull her unwilling eyeballs away from staring. "Damn," she thought, "this guy is a wower. I'm feeling parts of myself I distinctly buried years ago. God! Maybe they're reincarnating! Just what I need! What the heck am I gonna do with that!"

She continued pretending to read while sneaking glances at this gorgeous man until, out of the blue, a soccer ball soared through the air landing between them, hitting both of them on their thighs. Startled, she looked in the direction the ball came from and noticed a boy of about nine sheepishly looking up at them. When she met the youngster's gaze, he hung his head, trying to pretend the whole thing had not occurred.

The gentleman asked her, "You okay? That was a pretty hard hit from the little guy. And so short a throw too!"

"I'm fine but where are this kid's parents?" Venus growled and then began babbling. "Well actually, I am annoyed. This has been an interminably long wait for my tire to be fixed. And yes, I'll probably have a great big black-and-blue tomorrow." Venus knew with each sentence she spoke, her language skills seemed to be going down the drain. There was no sequence to anything she was saying.

"Greg Richards, pretty new to the area. And you are?" Greg rose and extended a hand to her.

"Venus Lighton. Not new to the area at all." As Venus shook Greg's hand, she was aware that her knees were shaking and her face and cheeks were hot-flashing. Worse yet, she was feeling movement in her lower belly all the way down to her toes. Aside from that, she could have sworn there was an electrical charge that ran between both of them. "Oh my God, just what I need."

"What did you say?" Greg asked.

"Nothing, I'm just mumbling to myself – it's a habit I indulge in." Venus laughed, but was mortified that she had actually spoken out loud. "How do you like it here, and where are you from?"

"The East coast, Boston area. I guess I like it here. . . I've been so busy with work I haven't had much time to really explore the area. At this point, I think it has promise," Greg smiled as he spoke.

The next question Venus asked embarrassed even her, "Does your wife like it?"

"No wife. I'm divorced. My kids are grown up but luckily one son, and his family recently moved here with their assorted critters. I get to see them a lot, so that's good. What about you? Married? have kids, critters?"

Before Venus could respond, the mechanic walked over to her, saying the tire was changed and she was set to go. She got up reluctantly, paused in saying goodbye to Greg, and added, "Good talking with you. Hope you enjoy California. Nice meeting you."

When Venus got into the safety of her own car, she began ranting to herself. "Gee, *now* the tire is fixed. If they'd done it right away as they promised, I wouldn't be drooling like I am. Can you beat this, a total body response to a man! Damn! Didn't even have time to pursue it, not that I'd even contemplate that. Hah! Adding insult to injury, almost three damn hours to fix a flat!"

Greg

Greg was completely ready for a change. It was time to move from Boston, even though he was leaving behind his son Ron and his wife Dahlia, two of his grandchildren, assorted dogs and cats, friends, and the main branch of his company. But it was time, and he knew it. Years ago he had bought out the owners of the SeaFoam Company and, since that time, it had expanded seemingly overnight, making him a very rich man. He now had the opportunity to start a western branch – a huge market. He loved the challenge of starting all over again, creating a gigantically successful business. "Yes," he thought, "it is time to begin a new life, and if I don't do it now, I never will. I *am* ready for big-time change."

He was tired of all his old friends giving him mammoth volumes of advice about how he should be in a relationship and their constantly trying to create the perfect 'match' for him. It was all so old and boring. If he heard anyone say one more time, "You need to get married, at least get a girlfriend, how can you not be lonely, it's unnatural to be alone for so long, what are you, gay?" he would probably slug whoever uttered the words. Like *they* were all experts on relationships!

"I am so sick of this. I know what I want and I wish the hell people would stop pestering me. Let them live their own lives," Greg found himself grumbling.

Greg was a few months short of being sixty-years-old, though based on good DNA, he looked much younger. He took good care of himself, eating properly and exercising regularly. It was the exercising that kept him sane and he knew it. "Funny," he thought, "I hated regimented sports and exercise when I was a kid, and now if I don't do something physical, I feel like hell. Ah, the changes we go through."

When Greg was in high school and college, he was always into mischief and having fun. Although not one to "run with a group," or trust many of his peers, he was very popular because of his quick wit and good looks (even though *he* didn't think he was good looking). "On a scale of one to ten, ten being the highest, I'm a six on my better days. I must admit, though, my eyes are a nice green," he assured himself. His interests, even then, ranged from theater to science, from inventing ~~and~~ to writing, all of which he dabbled in and easily managed.

Being so multi-talented and intense, he found many people just plain boring. Some interpreted his stand-offish behavior as being snobby, but he just wasn't interested in the trivial stuff that most teens were into. He attributed his popularity to two factors. Either the rest of the world wanted to get into his creative mischievous schemes or folks felt challenged by his lack of availability. He never could quite figure it out.

Greg was an only child of professional parents who maintained their own lives, separate bedrooms, and cool attitudes towards each other. He sometimes wondered how he was ever conceived, why they ever got married, and whether they maybe, at one time, had ever liked each other. Watching them when they were home together, he observed they were totally disconnected from each other, in ways he didn't even know how to explain.

He was never given much positive attention by either parent. They were too busy fighting with each other, or trying to prove the other wrong, or leaving for one of their many individual business ventures. When he did receive any kind of parental notice, it was to scold, belittle or criticize him.

There was a long series of nannies while Greg was growing up; they ranged from reasonably sane and intelligent to over-the-top crazy. Even as a young child, he wondered, "How in hell did you guys hire *her*?" He guessed it was desperation on his parents' part, so neither one of them had the responsibility for him. *That* was the one thing they agreed on.

Because of his innate intuitive skills at realizing the nannies' weaknesses, Greg found ways to annoy them and to create dramas that made his parents livid with embarrassment and rage and, of course, made the nannies leave. Afterwards, at least, his parents talked to him. He pretended to listen very seriously to what they were saying and silently nod his head, thinking all the while that tomorrow was another day with another new nanny and more mischief. At home, he was in his parents' estimation, an *incorrigible child*. School became his sanctuary and he did brilliantly in all his subjects, social skills and even sports. Greg's fascination with school was, according to his parents, his *saving grace*.

When Greg married his high school sweetheart Judy, he did so out of obligation. She was pregnant and in her junior year of college and he was a senior. Even though his feelings changed the few months prior to her pregnancy, he went through with the wedding. After all, he was a gentleman and his parents, he was quite sure, expected him to do the *right thing*. "It seems like half the married people I know, did so to be responsible," Greg told himself. "I wonder if they are all as miserable as I am," he mused after only their first six months together. After the first year, he concluded his and Judy's marriage was exactly like that of his parent's.

On the one hand, he was fortunate. With the financial help of his parents, he was able to finish his college education as a research chemist. "Are you sure that's what you really want to do? What kind of chemist will you be, and where will you look for a job? What's wrong with the business and investment world? We could help you because of our contacts." His parents seemed united in trying to sell him the world of business, whether they were doing it individually or separately. When he tried to explain the scope of his interest in chemical research, he saw they did not understand what it was he wanted for a career. In his heart of hearts, he wanted variety - to be an inventor, to find solutions, to create. His parents just worried he wouldn't find a job to support his wife and soon-to-be family. God forbid, *they* might have to do it.

He constantly argued with them, "I *will* be able to find an excellent job in this field. Just try giving me some encouragement instead of criticizing! That's all you guys ever do!" He remembered those times like they were yesterday, and they still pained him. His opinions didn't count for much in his family.

Greg did find a fabulous job after college with a newly funded research company that dealt with marine paints and insulation. They not only paid him well, but also paid for his continuing education. He was an essential player in the company's huge financial success, and gradually he worked his way up to the top of the research department - with more responsibility, money, and many inventions to his credit. Eventually, he purchased the SeaFoam Company. He had big plans for it. Being CEO and owner of the company allowed him to use his many qualifications, and the work continually stimulated him. He had learned that if he just invented things or did research, he eventually got bored; he needed the stimulation of people. His ownership of the company provided the many opportunities for change he so needed. It allowed him to stay active mentally and grow in knowledge about business, science, sales and management. Greg did not enjoy being idle.

The invention he was proudest of, and the one that was most lucrative was a marine foam used on the undersides of ships that prevented growth of algae and barnacles (or anything else for that matter) for a significantly longer time then anything previously on the market. Among other things, he was delighted it was not toxic to the environment. His goal to sell it to big shipping companies and navies was rapidly being reached, making him a very wealthy man. There was always someone in the laboratory working on making the foam last even longer, and he knew that soon the present guarantee would be doubled.

Judy and he were not getting along from almost the first day of their marriage. Although they had two children, Ron and Charlie, within the first few years, their marriage was strained and unpleasant for both of them. She wanted out as much as he did, but both were afraid to rock the boat.

Greg constantly mused, "When I was a kid, how did I see the world so humorously? How could I laugh at all the crap I got into? What has changed?"

As the years passed, it became increasingly clear that neither Greg nor Judy were committed to the marriage. Not because they had any other relationships, but because they both wanted to "live a little" and neither had had that opportunity. They actually had nothing in common with each other except the children.

"We were just too young and with no experience," Judy mourned. "Too young to have children without experiencing more of life and even dating others! I want to finish my degree and go to work or I will simply go insane as a house-wife and mother. I suppose I shouldn't feel this way, but I do, especially now that the kids go to school. Even when I worked that part-time job for my father, I came home a much more pleasant person. How can we arrange it so you take care of the kids half time, and I do the other half?"

Greg refused that plan but, because of his good salary, they managed to find excellent after-school programs that both Charlie and Ron wanted to attend. "There will be *no* nannies here," he thought to himself.

Judy finished her degree when the kids were in high school and then spent several years at a job in marketing, even though this didn't qualify as "living a little." Later, she met a co-worker and it was an instant head-over-heels in love situation. When Judy told Greg she had really and truly fallen in love, and wondered if Greg would be willing to give her a divorce, he was delighted. My God, the *two* of them would be free!

Unusual as it was, after the divorce was final, both Judy and Greg were able to communicate better with each other *and* the kids. The kids were actually happier and more secure than they had been during the marriage. Judy and her new husband and Greg lived two houses from each other, so the kids were always wildly running from one house to another.

Greg began to date a variety of women. After all, he was only approaching forty; in the prime of his life, great income, good looking and healthy. Aside from one very short relationship with Emily, a business woman with a local chemical company his firm bought products from, he maintained his singleness. After casually dating her for about a month, with no sex involved, he realized she wanted a relationship and he didn't. When he told her that no relationship was possible and she was just getting too serious, she flew off the handle, crying, screaming at him and calling him names. She even vowed revenge for what he had done to her. He kept calm and repeatedly asked her, "What have I done to you, when I told you all along I didn't want a relationship?" Here he had felt he was being honest and real with her, yet she was not hearing and believing him! "Lies aren't acceptable and neither is the truth," he mused. "Damned if I do and damned if I don't."

Emily felt discarded and worthless when Greg finally said "So long." She could not tell him that, but she seethed inside and vowed to get even. To her, going out with someone four times meant commitment.

From that point on, Greg refused to see anyone more than once. Greg *did not* want any type of relationship that took time from his kids, and he didn't want to introduce his kids to anyone either. He took a woman out, went to her house, slept with her and then left. He was always quite clear about not wanting to be in relationship, but it seemed as if the women just didn't believe him and they kept pestering him. On business trips, which were quite frequent, he always found someone to have sex with, and that was just perfect for him. He managed to live totally "single" at home, and to play when away. That way, he was able to spend more and more time with his family.

He and his boys did almost everything together – sports events, movies, video games, playing baseball, and going hiking. He even became a coach for all the athletic activities they were in, though he never liked playing them himself.

As the boys reached college age and left for their respective studies, Greg sensed a hole developing and growing in his gut. He felt loneliness and an emptiness he couldn't quite get over. He wondered about his choices regarding relationships. "Sure, I've had sex with plenty of women, but I haven't let my heart get at all involved except with my kids. How sick is that? Why? I think I actually was like this before I even married Judy. What's going on?"

As Greg began to look within, he thought with some humor, "When in doubt, blame parents, so I will." Then he heard another part of his mind arguing, "I'm not blaming my folks, but their relationship is so sick – worse than mine and Judy's ever was! They really have no fun, no intimacy, nothing in common except me. What role models! Too bad I'm an only child! I've only known one great relationship and then one of them up and dies. Not good odds!" Greg always viewed his friend Thom's relationship as exceptional, but then his wife Carrie was in a car accident and was killed. Greg's pain was for Thom's family, himself and the ideal relationship he knew was possible but not often seen.

Periodically, Greg came across some new insights – without blaming his folks - as to why he had not been willing to get into another relationship. "They are too much trouble, they don't last, they interfere with my work. I'll never find the 'right' woman, whatever the hell that means, and look at the stats for divorce. If I want sex, I'll find sex. My nannies and my mother were nuts and unreliable ergo; all women are like that. Mostly, you can't count on a woman to be there – she always leaves, just like my mother and even Carrie."

Carrie was married to Thom, Greg's closest friend for at least thirty years. Three years ago, she was killed in a violent car accident. Their marriage had been loving, romantic and filled with fun. Greg and his family, and later just he and his children, often spent afternoons with the family. The shock of the accident was overwhelming. He and Thom's children spent the first year after the accident making sure Thom was able to continue to mourn in safety and with support. Greg mourned with them. After that first year, Greg found ways to actively engage Thom's mind in work. They discussed research-related issues, exercised together, ate together and sailed together. Greg loved him like a brother and to see him so heartbroken was sometimes more than he could endure.

In the following years, as Thom got stronger, Greg once again tackled his own relationship issues. "Okay, so now that I have all the reasons I am unavailable for relationships, now what?" he asked himself, bemoaning his predicament. "Trust won't start in a vacuum. I have to take actions."

It was through these musings and revisiting the pain of his childhood that Greg realized he had not treated his children the way he had been treated, and for that, he was quite proud. Although he could not trust his parents ever to be there when he needed them, he vowed he'd be there for his children. As he reviewed his marriage, he honored himself for having done just that. "Ah yes, I gave them what I never had - trust, honesty and reliability. Now I deserve to be in a healthy, loving relationship. I believe I am ready to risk anything,   including death by relationship." His sarcasm made his laugh.

Greg began dating to see if he was capable of feeling anything towards a woman except the type of friendship he and Judy had. So far, no luck.

On a Saturday morning while Greg was still mulling about his issues around intimate friendships and relationships, Judy dropped by his house with some pictures of the boys. Greg felt as if he had been hit on the head with a new awareness. "She's really not a friend. Friends have things in common other than their children and the weather. I used to know this, didn't I? We are strangers who know nothing about each other."

As Greg continued to look at what he thought was their friendship, he started to laugh. "Oh yeah, this is quite a friendship. We have a comfortable ability to talk about our kids, the general state of the weather and nothing. That's quite profound if I do say so myself. Time to change. Time for action. I want a friendship with a woman as strong as I have with my male friends – of course with some additional benefits," he chuckled.

His son Charlie, wife Sarah, two children, two dogs and three cats moved to the west coast because of a fabulous job offer. As suddenly as they left, Greg too, had a job opportunity presented, to begin a new branch of the SeaFoam Company. He didn't even take a day to think about the decision. "Time to pack up and go. At least I'll have family there and critters to play with," Greg mused. Charlie and family were ecstatic!

"So who am I now" wondered Greg. "I look in the mirror and see broad shoulders, nice hair– yup, I like my hair, great green eyes, deep laugh lines around the eyes. Also a gut not like a twenty-year old, but so what, I'm not twenty." Greg laughed as he sucked in his tiny gut. He continued musing. "Funny, they say the eyes are the mirror to the soul, but I sure don't see my Soul – I just see green. Where and what is my Soul? Maybe the devil took it. I'll continue to ponder that later. But for now, it'll have to be my charm, intelligence and personality that sell me. Yup, age is beginning to show! But then, I'm sure glad I'm not twenty again. With age, *I hope*, comes some maturation and wisdom," and he laughed to himself.

When Greg met Venus at Discount Tires, there was something about her that was appealing, even though she was, in his esteemed opinion, horribly coiffed and more horribly dressed. He sensed there was a lot more to her than her clothing and hairdo: the way she sat, the way she walked, the way she spoke, and the impatient way she had of swinging and shaking each leg. Most surprising of all, when she shook his hand after the little leg hit they had shared; he felt a bolt of lightning run from his arm to his groin. "Curious, unusual, bizarre," he thought. "She is definitely not my type except for the color of her hair. Anyway, I have more important things on my mind right now – like purchasing a building for SeaFoam."

Greg knew what he was looking for and what he was willing to pay for his latest venture. He found a realtor who was recommended, told him what he wanted, where he wanted it and the price point. When the realtor showed him several buildings that had no resemblance to what Greg had described, he could not abide the man's not listening to his requests and immediately told him how he felt. "Either you get me what I want or I'll be glad to take my business elsewhere. I simply don't have time, nor do I wish to waste the effort of looking at places that are unsuitable." Greg could feel the man shrinking; the realtor was clearly upset. "Instead of carrying this arrangement further, I think we ought to part ways. I don't think this is the right match. Thanks for your time."

Greg found another agent and was shown several choice buildings. He purchased a great building in Del Mar within a few weeks of his search. Some of the staff who had been present during Greg's dismissal of his first agent thought he could have used more tact in that particular instance. It was not typical of his behavior, which was almost always kind and considerate, even while totally in charge. Greg was impatient when people he hired deliberately didn't pay attention to what he had requested and ultimately would be paying for. "You don't get ahead in business or in life by being a wimp."

Anyone on the staff of SeaFoam would say that Greg was a man who knew what he wanted and went after it. He did not take no for an answer. The difference between Greg and so many executives was that he had the ability to make people who had differing opinions agree with him and think they were the ones who had initiated his request. He had a superb use of the language, an incredibly quick mind that saw through situations and problems, and an enormous amount of patience when it came to dealing with his own staff and the issues of SeaFoam. He knew when to push and when to be silent. His business expertise, aplomb and creativity were fresh, and up-front. Some said he was not to be reckoned with as an adversary.

Some of his skills Greg attributed with a hint of annoyance, to those genetically inherited from both his parents. "Well, some good comes from them," he rationalized.

Venus and Her Friends

Every day as Venus pulled into her parking space at the LaJolla campus of UCSD, she was awed by the physical beauty of the planted foliage – so unlike the scrub that grew naturally in the area. She particularly loved the very large eucalyptus trees, which must have been planted way before her time. Her favorite was what was called the lemon eucalyptus because, when their leaves were crushed, they gave off a lovely lemon scent. She often walked under the trees while going from building to building, picking up leaves here and there, crushing them and inhaling their wonderful fragrance. For a college campus, this was truly one of the stars. As she walked to her office after her tire disaster, she was feeling excited, fearful and alive. When she was safely secluded in her office, Venus called her friend Sally Parker.

"Oh my God, what am I going to do? I've met this guy and he knocked my socks off! I know he's younger than I am, single and not my type, but good God, he just made me feel stuff I haven't felt for years. I thought after menopause, my sex drive stopped – and it sort of did for many years, but now? This guy just turned me inside out, upside down – and that was just from my looking at him! I am definitely foaming at the mouth – and other places too. What am I going to do? You should have heard me babble! I was embarrassed for myself!"

"Venus, you're still babbling and you sound terrified. The worst you can do is make a fool of yourself and from that, I guarantee you will recover. If however he has any interest, then go, girl, GO! I haven't heard you interested in anyone in ten years. What do you know about him and how can we make it happen?"

"First of all, I already made an ass of myself, and how I'll recover is beyond me! Anyway, I'm not sure I really want anything to 'happen' because I'm just not interested . . . sort of. . . anyway, I'm sure not what I used to be. Yes, I'm babbling. But, back to him, whew! I don't think he's retired because he said he had to get back to work. That's all I really know about him."

"Wait a minute, where did you meet him and how long did you actually talk to him?" asked Sally.

"You won't believe this. I was getting a flat fixed at Discount Tires, and after waiting over two hours, I began to pace – you know the way I do – till I felt more relaxed. Damn, you'd think everyone in Southern California needed new tires today! By the time I was ready to sit down again, there was only one empty chair in the waiting room. It was next to him. I began to read, but I kept sneaking glances at the guy. I think he was oblivious, but then some kid across from us threw a ball and hit both of us on our thighs. We looked up and at each other. My God, I collapsed within myself and was almost inarticulate – and what I did say came out ass-backwards. From that point on, he initiated and carried on most of the conversation. My tongue had been tied and was trying frantically to undo itself, with poor results. Told me his name was Greg and he just moved here from Boston. Asked how the winters are here in California."

"When I finally gathered *some* of my wits, I asked him how his wife liked it here. The question even embarrassed me! How could I ask something like that?

"So what did he say?"

"Told me he didn't have a wife - he was divorced, has a couple of grown kids, grandchildren, grand-kitties, and grand-dogs. After all that information, my tongue once again went into remission. All I could do was nod my head into those beautiful green eyes and feel energy in places that I thought were long ago dead. He asked me some stuff about myself, but frankly, I don't remember what I said! Bottom line: I don't know where he lives; don't even remember if I gave him my name. Anyway, can't imagine a guy like him being interested in me!"

Venus' sense of humor was coming back Sally noticed. "To find him, I guess I could advertise in the paper? Or TV? Radio? I could say, 'Remember the woman at Discount Tires with the auburn hair in a tight bun? You know, the one who was in the beige jumper with the beige turtle neck, brown tights and Birkenstocks?' Yup, that would really turn a guy like him on. Argh! My heart says, BE STILL! Do you realize that this has *never* happened to me – not once in my almost sixty five years of life!"

18

Sally was chuckling as she said, "Going along with your idea, we could describe him and post a reward for him. We could put it in all the post offices and grocery stores. Surely someone in this the sixth, or is it now seventh, largest city in the United States will know him? What do you think?"

"I don't need you to be funny Sally! I'm desperate. This is the first time in forever my body is definitely not feeling over the hill!"

Sally jumped in, "Now maybe you'll consider a make-over, like I've been trying to have you get for the past nine years!"

"*No*! I will not."

"Please, consider it!"

"I will not even discuss it with you."

* * *

Venus, an intelligent, vibrant woman of almost sixty-five, had been divorced for a little over ten years. Alex, her husband of twenty-five years had suddenly decided that younger was better and had traded his old worn slippers, (that is, Venus) for a new look. The new look was Sonja, young enough to be his daughter, with beautiful dark hair and eyes and very, yes obnoxiously, sexy. It was so easy for him, thought Venus. Rich, attractive, totally self-involved and absorbed, he reeked from a sense of elevated ego to which Venus refused to bow.

Although Venus hadn't believed anything like a divorce could happen to her, she knew - intuitively and intellectually that everything was wrong with her marriage. When Alex announced he was leaving her, energetically it felt like a freight train had rammed her. To almost everyone, she insisted that she wasn't terribly surprised. When she chose to think about it, their lovemaking had been boring, infrequent and mechanical, they rarely had anything to say to one another, and didn't enjoy any of the same things. Even their kids knew it; in fact, they were less surprised than she was.

The divorce was, however, the talk of their social circle. It made Venus sick to think how everyone thought Alex was this wonderful, kind, terrific person.

Venus realized in retrospect, that she had gradually changed to accommodate almost every one of his needs. Except she had not given up completing her education, and that was a bone of contention for him. For many years she'd dressed and acted the part of the rich executive's wife when she felt she had to; she wined and dined all his fancy clients, yet the longer she continued to be *that* woman, the more frustrated and intolerant she became of herself and others. Her job at the university was where she went to get away from all the imposed glamour and shallowness. Her mantra was, "Thank God I can go to the students!" When she left for work, she completely dressed down, having decided not to appear like she did at home for her family and Alex's friends. In fact, they probably wouldn't have recognized her on campus, and she liked it that way!

Venus was furious about the way Alex had refused to hear her concerns during their marriage when she tried to bring them up. As a result, she had withdrawn more and more into her work at the University.

Not only was Venus terribly angry at Alex for leaving like he did, but she was furious that Sonja was so readily accepted by the "circle of idiots" (as Venus referred to them behind his back.) "Lucky Sonja! Readily accepted by everyone. I wish they had accepted who I was and what I was into! What a piece of dog poop that is. All those years trying to please, and then a young sexy woman comes by and automatically pleases everyone just by her age and looks. That sucks!"

After the divorce was final, Venus vowed she was *not* going to get involved with anyone else. She'd *never* accommodate to make another person more important than herself. It took her a long time to figure it out, but never again! From now on, it was about taking care of herself and Oliver Munster – OM, her adoring cat. She thought that once in a while she might go to bed with someone, but that hadn't happened, and after ten years, she thought it probably never would. Most of the time she'd found that with a good vibrator she could "come" and go as she wished. Now that was sanity!

Because of anger, and in spite of not loving Alex, it took Venus many years to mourn the loss of her so-called friends, her marriage and her life style, even though she really didn't like any of it. She hadn't realized how she had gradually become accustomed to all it entailed, and the shock of its departure was deep; it made her furious, and in some ways, fearful of the future.

Venus was surprised how married women treated her as a threat. In fact, she was outraged! Single women, she quickly found out, were deliberately and definitely out to get the married or involved man. "God," she thought, "as if I want another little boy to take care of!"

She spent many hours alone resenting the withdrawal of her old so-called friends who thought they had to take sides. She felt isolated and alienated from her female friends and associates of years – except for her friend Sally who had also gone through a divorce, though was now in a loving relationship. Venus vowed never to turn her back on her dear friends if one of them were so lucky (or unlucky) to be in the situation she found herself saddled in.

When Venus had met Alex, they were both twenty. Each was very good looking and the envy of many of their peers. Their courtship was brisk, fun and filled with laughter – mostly laughter about the way things were. It was the 60's, and there was so much to make fun of and so many parentally unacceptable acts to engage in, all of which they did!

Both of them were still in school; he for finance, she for chemical research. His goal was to make his first million by thirty-two. He accomplished that feat and went on to become a multi-millionaire. She went on to get her doctoral degree.

Children came three years after marriage: Toni, a beautiful sensitive child with gorgeous black curly hair and black eyes, and Bret, a robust little athletic demon with auburn hair and brown eyes. Both kids inherited their parents' extreme intelligence, good looks and sense of humor. While the children were growing up, Venus was the good little wife (except for taking those classes!) and performed all the social obligations expected and requested of her. When the children were older, she began to look at her life with a researcher's eye. "Not very good," she thought. "There must be more."

Venus took a job as a research assistant at the nearby university, (University of California, La Jolla or UCSD) where she was thrilled by the opportunities of discovery. She loved her work though the pay was nothing! Alex didn't want Venus to work, and constantly attempted to change her mind, sabotage her plans, and have her resign. Her job and her loyalty to it embarrassed him and became inconvenient when he spontaneously wanted to entertain his big-wig friends. Housework and royal social entertaining were just *not* what Venus had in mind for the rest of her life. She had played Mrs. Alex for many years, but as time wore on, so did the tediousness of their life style.

At the same time as the demise of her marriage, both of her parents died rather suddenly; one from a stroke and the other from a heart attack. Even though she hadn't gotten along with them because of their quite different values, as an only child, she now felt alone in the world. To make matters worse, her children grew up, moved out, and were on their own. Venus recognized she had to let them go too, even though she loved them with a passion. All the loss was a shock to her system. She didn't want anyone to feel sorry for her or think they had to take care of her, but she was experiencing a huge case of empty-nest syndrome. So that's when she got a cat. Now, of course, there was always OM. Every day she'd say, "Thank God for your noisy motor and furry little body. Don't know what I'd do without your fur all over this place," and she'd laugh.

Fortunately, both Toni and Bret and their families lived within forty minutes, and they spoke at least weekly.

Sometimes, when she was feeling down and like a victim, she pondered if anyone could love her, or if she'd ever let herself love anyone again. The most important question was, "Will I learn to love and accept *myself* again?" She wasn't sure her questions could be answered in the affirmative, especially the last one; and she was exquisitely aware that would entail some major transformations in her belief system. It was in issues such as this when her ever-present intuition consistently let her down – probably the only times it did. She knew that her negative beliefs about receiving information regarding her *own* situation blatantly disallowed anything coming in. To receive intuition, she knew she had to be *open and willing to hear*. Though it upset her to the point of tears, was it possible she didn't want to change?

Although her kids loved her and told her how beautiful she was and how she ought to start dating, her defenses rose with thoughts like, "What do the kids know anyway! When I look in the mirror, all I see is a colorless woman getting up in years and, you know what, that's good enough for me!"

Once in a while, she heard quite another voice denying the whole story about how she didn't care what she looked like and how she was just another colorless older woman. When she heard that voice, she got disgusted and countered, "What do you know, anyway? I have my work and the excitement of that, OM, and my trusty vibrator. I need no one, I am fine the way I am. I will not dress for anyone, nor change in any way. Nor will I change my stories!"

Venus became a tenured professor of chemistry and worked up quickly to be head of the department. She loved the intellectual challenges she received, mostly from her students, and the actual research she was doing which had and continued to bring her considerable accolades and even some monetary rewards. She was an outstanding leader in the department. She was constantly grateful how easy it was to listen to her Inner Voice regarding work and others; it was a source of joy, love, inspiration and wisdom for her. Except, of course, when it came to listening about her own life!

It was after her divorce Venus began studying the development of intuition, spiritual growth and past lives. She had consistently used her incredible gifts in her work- related discoveries. Now she wanted to learn how to receive answers to questions she was posing for herself - some on the mundane level, others on the spiritual. She persuaded Sally into attending classes, where they met LuAnne and Rachael, who then became fast friends. Involved in a new life, Venus delighted in her new-found friends, plus her amazing openings that brought both excitement and amazement.

At work Venus told herself all kinds of stories. "I was pretty lucky and stumbled on some important discoveries. That's why everyone likes me or sucks up to me, thinking maybe some of what I did will rub off on them. And they want to stay on my good side because I'm head of this department. Everyone humors me here, but I'm not sure how they really feel about me and how I feel about all this attention. Do I believe it all?" These views were coming from a part of herself that didn't trust or believe in herself, no matter what brilliant discoveries she had made, how intuitive she was or what fun she was to be around. Quite often her mind focused on the negative about herself. Fortunately, though, when she caught herself, she deliberately stopped the thoughts. She was proud of her ability to accomplish that end.

Contrary to her sometimes negative interpretation of her popularity, the chemistry department was full of both professional and nonprofessionals who appreciated and responded to Venus' incredible intelligence, kindness, and delightful sense of humor. Even in her worst days after the divorce, she brought light, smiles, and laughter to work.

She had a way of being dramatically funny and getting her points across. For this, people hung out in her department, waiting for her to entertain and teach them. Her close friends thought it was sad she didn't see that part of herself!

It was a few years after her divorce that she consciously realized how grateful she was for the variety of people who came and spent time near and in her office. Her sense of appreciating and loving to have fun and laughter returned, and it was noticed! Although she moaned and whined about her lack of a social life, inwardly, she knew she wasn't ready or willing to participate in any form of one. But she surely put up a front by complaining and mumbling! She figured no one knew whether she was serious or not; they usually didn't.

With a sense of high drama, Venus would look at everyone with irreverence and say, "Jeez, the social life here at this university is so hierarchal and boring. No one knows how to have fun. You never laugh! It's like all your passion is for your work. Bor - ing! Lighten up folks!"

And the rest of her staff laughed and agreed, even recognizing she was talking about them too.

Her monologue about the university's hierarchy was pretty consistent. "Good grief, if you aren't a full professor, then you can't be with full professors, except to do their grunt work. God forbid you're a grad student, it's like being in the armed services and being a mere private - no fraternizing with sergeants or generals! Why is that, you intellectual snobs?"

Though she never received an answer, Venus came to understand that practically every group of folks had a social-caste system, and the university was not much different from the life she had lived with her husband. It made her unhappy, but she accepted the way it was. It didn't mean she had to play their game and she didn't. She associated with whom she wished, including those who were not part of the university's elite teaching faculty.

As time went on, she began to question the areas of her life that didn't feel very healthy, and those that were definitely southward bound. "Humph, my life's gone south like my boobs. Arg. There must be more than this!"

By gift of birth, Venus was a beautiful woman! She had gorgeous auburn hair framing an oval face, huge hazel eyes, a small turned-up nose and lips that women now were copying by injecting Botox into them to plump them up. Hers were naturally full and a beautiful deep pink. Her skin had good tone, and although she had laugh lines and wrinkles on her face, she didn't even think about having any sort of face-lift (although she'd been accused of it many times.) "Genes," she thought. "I inherited some great genes and I'm thankful for them - must have been from my mother's side of the family. Whatever, works for me! Especially living in Southern California where beauty rules."   She was average height, five feet four with a lithe, well-proportioned body which never lost its gracefulness or shape, even after bearing two children. What she had recently noticed about her body was her breasts; they had grown a bit since menopause and also drooped a bit too, but so what!

Venus became less and less interested in her physical appearance and more and more married to her work. In spite of her new friends constantly wanting to fix her up – both socially and in her attire, she was loath to go anywhere or do anything. Every once in a while, to get them off her back, she attended something they invited her to. Unfortunately, the fight over her choice of clothing, hairstyle, makeup (or lack thereof) and general presentation was simply dreadful.

Sally, Rachael and LuAnne were her three closest friends and they constantly did things together and discussed everything. Venus was delighted with their friendship and discussions, which were sometimes very heated and explosive, then filled with laughter as they reconciled their perceived differences or agreed to disagree. They read books and either rejoiced in the brilliance of the authors or had a field day panning them. The four of them were professional women with a hunger for spiritual experience and learning.

Sally

Sally had been Venus' closest friend for more than twenty-five years. They were the same age. Sally was the first of Venus' group to get divorced, and the event shocked and rattled everyone. Everyone except Venus, who admitted to her that the divorce was about time. Sally's husband Ralph, had been emotionally abusive to Sally with increased frequency. Though never physical, Venus had watched how his cruel words affected Sally's body, mind and spirit. When Sally called her, Venus always lent an open ear, and encouraged Sally to get whatever was bothering her off her chest. "Sometimes," thought Sally, "Venus should consider being a psychologist. How she listens to me moan and complain so much is totally beyond me."

Sally was a very attractive perky woman with medium-brown hair highlighted with golden streaks. She had hazel eyes, a petite frame even though she was five-foot seven, and a slender well-kept body. She was exceedingly attractive. Ralph verbally abused every part of who she was as a parent, her physical appearances, her sense of humor and on and on. She stayed for two reasons: the children and because she felt trapped. Even though she had a career as a writer, she did not believe in herself enough to be able to support herself in the manner to which she had become accustomed. She grew to hate Ralph, looking forward to when he was on one of his many business trips. Sally sometimes wondered what type of business trips they actually were, but never questioned him because his absence made her life much more pleasant.

Venus often told Sally how much she changed when she was around Ralph. Unfortunately, her kids noticed it too and Sally was greatly saddened by it..

The final straw was when she had a birthday party for the one of the children and Ralph began his usual tirade in front of both the kids and their parents. This time the abuse was so substantial, so degrading, so demeaning, she'd had it. When everyone had left, she quietly went to the bedroom and called Venus and said, "I have to get out. If I need to, and he won't leave here, can I bring the kids and come to your house? I'll tell you what happened later, but I've got to do this while I have the nerve."

Venus, horrified, said, "Of course. If I don't hear from you within an hour and a half, I'm coming over. Okay?"

"Okay."

Sally literally had to puff herself up to confront Ralph, but confront she did. In a calm, powerful voice, but blazing with anger, she demanded, "Leave the house now, Ralph. Go upstairs and pack everything you want. If you don't leave now, I'll call the police and have you arrested for domestic violence. I've had it. YOU. ARE. OUT." Ralph attempted to negate Sally further, but she was finished with being powerless. "OUT! And stay OUT! You are NOT to come back here again. If you wish to see the kids, call and we will make arrangements. The locks will be changed. It is enough. We're done."

Sally was surprised that as she spoke, she felt self-esteem coming back. She wasn't afraid, and she wasn't taking no for an answer. She was taking her life back.

By the time Ralph left, Sally wondered why in hell she had waited so long. Was it just for finances? Or was she afraid of being alone? She called Venus, "It's done. He's gone."

"How do you feel about it now?" asked Venus.

"God, I feel great. I wonder why I stayed with that abuse so long. I think it really wasn't financial security, but I was afraid of being alone. The kids are still young, and I guess I felt any help is better than no help, that being alone with someone is better than being alone apart. Not true. It's just as easy to be alone by yourself as alone with another. Lots of lessons here, Venus. I guess I haven't been loving myself very much to stay with the abuse. You know, he mirrored how I talk to myself. I'll sure be stopping that!"

After her divorce, Sally began to socialize, but did not want to date. She knew she needed to heal and pursue her own interests. Metaphysics was one of the subjects she wanted to study and coincidentally, so did Venus. When the two of them met LuAnne and Rachael, all four felt instant connections.

Three years prior, Sally met Joe, the owner of the company she worked for but had never actually met. She had finally agreed to go to a company party at the request of several of her fellow employees, and while there took one look at Joe. That was *it* for her. Apparently, the same thing for him. It was love at first sight. A little less than a year later, they were married.

Rachael

Venus could clearly remember meeting Rachael; they were at a class on past-life regressions. Venus wasn't quite sure she even believed in such things. When she admitted that, Rachael jumped on her, saying, "When you learn more, you *will* change your mind." Rachael was totally right; and Venus was forced to "eat crow" often in the beginning of their friendship. But it quickly blossomed into an intimate relationship.

Rachael, widowed when she was fifty-four, had inherited several million dollars. She was about five years younger than Venus' and was an attractive brunette, about five-four with a good shape, lively brown eyes, and beautiful full lips. Rachael was a real "dresser," and could be the life of the party whenever she chose to be. She was full of fun and laughter, with a quick wit. She and Venus loved to banter back and forth, laughing at anyone who thought either of them was serious. Rachael loved shopping, looking good and playing well - all with class. "I can't help it if I have expensive taste. It feels better that way."

As far as dating, she'd gone with one man for a couple of years, but found out that he just didn't "do" it for her. "If I wanted a friend, I'd get a friend. I want someone exciting in my life - and he isn't." She broke up with him.

Rachael loved the study of metaphysics and was extremely intuitive, often giving psychic readings and teaching classes. Everything was just an amusement to her as she pursued life with a type of diligence. She wanted to experience as much as she could. Her husband had been kind, but with an extremely rigid set of beliefs about religion that was more than Rachael could bear. In order for him to become involved with anything, she had to constantly prod him – another trait not pleasing to her. In spite of it all, she thought she loved him. When he died of a massive stroke, she was shocked – but also somewhat relieved. Intimately and painfully she recognized the sanctity and tenuousness of life while also realizing for the first time in her adult life just how free she felt and how much she loved freedom. She then began to question whether she really had loved him or simply put up with him. Her conclusion: she had married because her parents approved of him. Now, alone, she pushed her life into all the activities she thought she might enjoy. She did all sorts of strange and sometimes daring things: bunjee jumping, white-water rafting, and snorkeling to name just a few. Age was not going to stop her!

She trusted her intuition enough to know that if something were dangerous, she'd get the message and stop, and if it didn't come, she might die. But that was okay. Beyond that, she knew life left when it was damn well ready, and there was nothing anyone could do about it. She believed birthdays and deathdays were mutually agreed upon by the Soul prior to birth. This belief, although contrary to anything her husband believed, helped her enormously when he died. After his death, she allowed herself to go to some invisible line in every new experience, a line that was seen only by her inner being. She loved the thrill. However within the last year or so, she noticed that the excitement of doing new, daring, sometimes even dangerous stuff was wearing thin. "Maybe I'm getting over this phase of my life. What's next?" she wondered.

LuAnne

    LuAnne and Rachael had been friends for years, and as Sally and Venus connected with them on an intimate level, they became a strong foursome: vacationing, going to all sorts of metaphysical functions and enjoying hours together discussing the world.

    LuAnne was also a divorcee. The only word to describe her was cute. She was about five-feet tall, well built, with medium brown hair and huge blue eyes, a small nose with a beautiful smile. She had become a professional psychic/past-life reader/healer ten years prior, and was truly committed to serve humanity. She loved her work and was still constantly studying and taking classes. During one series of classes, she met the man she currently was living with. Well, on and off for the past couple of years. Corey and she got together for six weeks at a time. She'd live there, then he'd move in with her; or maybe there would be six weeks when they were in their own places separately. It was a strange arrangement, but it seemed to work for them. LuAnne had a huge fear of commitment and it seemed that Corey did too, so on they played with their relationship. In spite of their confusing living situation, she considered herself single and available for dating. She often laughed and said in front of Corey and her friends, "Hey, know anyone good to fix me up with?" Her friends laughed, pointed to Corey and said, "We have the perfect guy for you." It seemed both Corey and LuAnne were happy – at least for the time – with the status of their relationship. They went anywhere and everywhere together, but insisted it wasn't really anything of lasting quality. Rachael, Sally, and Venus shook their heads and laughed whenever LuAnne professed their undying non-love for each other.

    In order to keep LuAnne happy, the other three women laughingly referred to her as "in the dating game" although they knew better. Anyone looking at LuAnne and Corey interacting, saw the love and adoration they felt for each other. Too bad neither one of them saw it.

LuAnne and Rachael had studied psychic development together and both had been totally taken with it, begging for more. They then went on to explore the vast number of weird and not so weird offerings available in the San Diego and Los Angeles areas. LuAnne quickly learned to listen to her own intuition about what was legit and what was off-the-wall. The more she learned, the more she found her own spiritual life. She talked to anyone who listened to her about finding her Soul. She was truly a convert from being a strict Baptist to a non-religious spiritual being.

Venus

Venus' friends were a Godsend to her. In spite of that, they were constantly on her case to do something with her physical appearance. One weekend when they were all going away, the argument began again. Venus protested, "What's wrong with the way I look? I refuse to cut or color my hair, and I am comfortable in these empire dresses and jumpers! Beige *is* a color, damn it! There's nothing wrong with my shoes – Birkenstocks are just fine! Damn, I pay enough for them. And for your information, my bras fit fine! Just leave me alone! If you want me to attend your big party, then take me as I am or forget it! Why are you all trying to remake me?"

Rachael, in frustration, gazed at the ceiling and said, "No one is asking you to dye your hair – damn, you're one of the few people I know whose hair hasn't turned gray! But that tight bun has got to go! Get yourself some reading glasses that don't look like they're from the 1400's and wear some color!"

"Let me take you to my hair stylist," Sally begged.

Her friends' arguments fell on deaf ears.

Venus attended every one of the shindigs she was invited to dressed in the way *she* wanted, much to the chagrin of the other women, and probably men too. When she was asked out, most often she refused. When she did finally go on a date, it was a disaster. She just wasn't interested. She became quiet, about as nondescript as any human being could be, and she faded into whatever was around. Though she wasn't happy with her behavior, she didn't seem to be able to do anything about it. "If they wanted a model conversationalist or model beauty, then they should've invited me," was her constant defense.

Sally was upset by the way Venus seemingly had regressed to being a beige twenty-one-year old from the sixties. It seemed as if this time period captured her. Venus looked like something the cat dragged in. Oh, not her kitty, OM. He was very content with her and didn't give a damn what she looked like. He just purred and purred.

Sally was waiting for some appropriate time when Venus might actually listen to what she had been saying for years. But she wasn't sure how much longer she could tolerate seeing her closest friend *make* herself look ugly and blend into a wall, living the life of a social recluse. She knew Venus loved fun, laughed a lot and adored being dramatic. Sally was the one friend with whom Venus was comfortable enough to let her hair down, so to speak. Sally had a feeling she was going to be able to speak her truth very soon. And she didn't have to wait long.

Venus' Makeover

Two weeks after Venus' flat tire, Sally met Venus for drinks at Tiger's Eye, a favorite hangout for business folks, computer geeks and university big-wigs. From there, they were going to go to Sally's for dinner where Joe, Sally's husband of two years, would meet them. The only booth open at Tiger's Eye was one in a dark corner, away from most of the crowd. Sally was thankful because she was going to bring up Venus' obvious self-hatred as evidenced by her outward appearance.

The Gods were with Sally because Venus brought up her meeting with Greg over and over and how she was so affected by him.

"Aha! Now is the time!" Sally said, "You know you might never see or hear of Greg again, but I need to talk to you about your future."

Rather than attack Venus as she had in the past, Sally began to gently question her friend. She wanted her to look within her own psyche to find answers to why she was going backward in time and letting herself "go to pot."

Sally began, "Were those years so happy for you that you're trying to recapture them? Come forward and take a good look at yourself in the mirror without the judgment you have that 'to look good is bad.' Look at what you have to forgive to get through these beliefs you have. It seems as if, since you've been divorced, you have deliberately let yourself go to hell. God knows what type of messages you're giving yourself about why it's not acceptable or desirable to look great. I imagine it has something to do with your parent's telling you how beautiful you were all your life and not appreciating, honoring or respecting your mind. So is this about, 'Now I'll show them? I'll make everyone forget I'm pretty and focus only on my mind!' You are allowing and actually encouraging yourself to look as bad as possible. Look inside Venus! Are you afraid of loving yourself?

Afraid of being loved? What kind of stuff are you holding onto? Do you think your Spiritual Essence wants you to look like a piece of shit? Do you think it's cool? What gives?"

The conversation went on and on, for way longer than Venus could have imagined. By the time they left Tiger's Eye, she had a splitting headache and a huge weight on her shoulders. Somehow, she knew what Sally was saying was right on target. Yes, she finally heard what was being said. Although she wasn't looking forward to it, she knew she had to do something with herself and about herself. When she joined Sally and Joe for dinner, she pleaded a huge headache and went home quite early.

Joe asked Sally, "What did you tell Venus? She looked like shit and seemed so quiet tonight."

Sally shared the conversation and added, "I think she might have heard me. I can only pray so."

When Venus got home that night, aside from her splitting headache which required immediate aspirin, she knew she had work to do and vowed to do it no matter how long it took. For days, she sat alone in her room taking no phone calls. What had she chosen for her life since, and prior, to the divorce? God, she had hated all the parties, entertainment and phoniness during her marriage. She felt she was a show-piece for Alex's business. But, damn, she had implicitly agreed to it just by going along with it. She hated and resented how she had given in to each step of it. She had thought she was being everything her parents wanted her to be, except of course, when she went back to school. Jesus, they hated that. All of them. Alex and her parents tried to stop her, but thank God she wasn't to be stopped. She had to prove she had a good mind and wasn't just pretty. At least at her job, her parents and Alex's values didn't count. *They* didn't care if she was pretty.

After her divorce, she screamed at herself, "Never again! Never again will I give up myself or change in any way to suit another person. I will dress the way I want, wear my hair the way I want, and if no one likes it, screw them! I don't care what anyone says."

As she began to look deeply within herself, she saw how she used beige and loose sloppy clothing as a cover-up so as not to be seen, so no one would ever notice her again for her appearance. She was afraid of opening herself up to loving again, or even getting involved. Being unattractive seemed to be the natural way, and so far, it had worked.

As Venus delved further on her inner journey, she danced with her anger, fear and pain and eventually reached forgiveness. First she'd be furious, only to find that beneath her fury was extreme pain. She sobbed, beat up some pillows, cowered in the fear of being seen, and recycled the same emotions over and over - all based on different memories and feelings in her body and heart. There was so much pain within her body based on stories she told herself, they made her weep uncontrollably. She had convinced herself she was unlovable – it was just beauty that was lovable and acceptable. If she wasn't beautiful any more, then there should be no problems. No relationship. But when she put her natural beauty aside, she put aside a huge part of her relationship with herself. She had to take that back, open it, and see it all. In truth, she really did love brilliant colors, clothing and jewelry.

She realized, "I went to the opposite extreme – it was okay to be smart and study, invent and create, but it wasn't okay to be attractive!"

For days, Venus went in and out of great bouts of tears. Yet as she began to shed some of those old stories, she found herself in deep fits of belly-laughing. She was beginning to find her old ideas and behaviors rather hilarious. . . absurd! She truly was forgiving herself, and in that forgiveness came great joy.

After a good week of soul-searching, it seemed as if her internal slate was much cleaner than it had ever been. She forgave her parents for being human with all sorts of silly beliefs, and herself for buying into many of them. In describing her experience to Sally later, she used the term "a high colonic of the body/mind/soul." She was now ready to re-enter the world feeling that at least, a couple of tons had been lifted from her heart and shoulders. She also knew she was willing to look at whatever might come up. "Hiding just doesn't make it and I am comin' out!"

With that thought, she went over to the telephone and made a call.

"Sally, I need a make-over. Now! Who do I go to?"

"What did you say? What happened to you? Are you okay?"

"I took your advice and went inside where I found little demons of all shapes and sizes ready to bite me if I slipped up. If they didn't bite me, I bit myself. It's all rather amusing in retrospect. However, that is not getting me a make-over. I want hair, clothes, bras. . . Yes, you heard me, bras and lingerie! Everything from top to bottom! I'm going after ME! I'm going after loving me, instead of hating me and I will *be* the beautiful woman I am. So who do you know, and can you come with me?"

Sally was delightfully amazed. "I'll call you right back. How about we call Rachael and LuAnne to come with us? That way, you'll have lots of feedback"

"Sounds good to me, but they have to promise they won't make fun of me," Venus sighed, knowing full well that would never happen.

Sally called Rachael and LuAnne, who were only too thrilled to see the unmovable Venus finally changing her costumes and accepting who she was. Both were excited, anticipating a grand performance.

After she had spoken with the other two women, Sally called for various appointments for Venus and was fortunate to get everything she had wanted for her dear friend. Then she then called Venus. "We have an appointment for your hair and nails in exactly one-half hour. I'll pick you up in ten minutes. You have an appointment at Salon de Belle in Encinitas, so we'll have no trouble making it. See you then."

"Thank you!"

Two hours later, with the other three women watching and giggling the whole time, Venus emerged amazingly transformed. Her hair was shoulder length with natural waves around her face. Highlights of different shades of red and blond were woven in, and the result was spectacular. Her nails were manicured with a light pink pearl polish, her brows were gently shaped and her eyes made up so they appeared even bigger than they were. Venus purchased all the makeup and hair products that were used on her so she could continue with the change. As she looked in the mirror, even she was shocked. "Hey, you three, do my face and hair look as hot as I think they do?"

"That is an understatement! You look fantastic. Holy moley! Now let's get rid of that crap you're wearing. We'll go to Nordstrom's and totally buy everything new!" Sally replied, with choruses of ooh's and aah's from the other two.

"My God, *Yes!*"

The three of them decided the Escondido Nordstrom's and North County Shopping Mall had to be the most fun with the most stores in one place. They could totally outfit their friend from top to bottom and leave *all* her old clothes at the store!

Sally was in charge and began to pull clothes off racks in amazing numbers, and soon the other two women were adding more. Venus watched for a while, then got brave and joined in the fun. She had no idea what was in style or what looked good on her or even what size she wore. "No problem," said the saleswoman, "we'll get you fixed up here."

Venus told the saleswoman, "I want everything new, from top to bottom – all kinds of clothes, from casual to dressy. Can we do that?" The other women agreed with Venus.

"Certainly," she replied, "but first go down to the lingerie department and pick out your bras and panties and whatever else you want. Bring them back here, and then you can try on to your heart's content."

"Sounds like a plan. Let's go."

The four of them traipsed down to the lingerie section where they waited patiently as Venus described what she wanted. Embarrassment - no mortification - was how Venus was feeling as she took off her beige outfit. For there, beneath her unfashionable outer clothing was underwear someone should have died even thinking about wearing. All three of the friends stared in disbelief.

"You're a working woman; *surely* you could have bitten the bullet and bought some new stuff. If you had waited any longer, your underwear and bras would have fallen off you! I can't believe you have been wearing this stuff all day, every day" Rachael stated grimly.

"Safety-pins on your panties?" LuAnne about shrieked.

"My God, what would happen if you got into an accident? You know, my mother always said to wear clean underwear just in case. Oh, I know it's clean, but how *old* is the stuff you're wearing?" Sally chimed in.

Venus defended herself, "I just saw a cartoon debating that very issue. Little kid says to his mom, 'why wear clean underwear in case I get into an accident? I'm gonna shit myself anyway.'"

The other women groaned. "No excuse, Venus!"

"There's no elastic in the underpants to hold them up, but safety-pins are good?" LuAnne said sarcastically. "It's a good thing you wear tights or your pants would have fallen down; your bras are gray with no elastic and they're stretched to their limits. *When* was the last time you bought underwear?"

Sally, too, was appalled and grimaced, "The cup size is wrong, your boobs are overflowing the bra. You look like you have four boobs! Have the saleswoman measure you," she commanded. "Boy, this could not have waited even another day!" Sally muttered. "Whew!"

Venus was, for once, not trying to defend herself when she replied, "I know, it's pretty bad, isn't it? Call the saleswoman in and I'll have her measure my correct size."

The saleswoman measured Venus, telling her both her cup and back size were totally wrong, and then brought her at least ten different beautiful lacy undergarments in beautiful colors. (They all insisted!) All the women waited while Venus tried on new underwear. An emerald green bra-and-matching panties were probably Venus' favorites, but there was a purple bra with matching panties too. When all was tallied, she purchased ten bra-and-panty sets – all of which were different, covered with lace, and very sexy - even to her own way of thinking - plus extra panties in a vast array of colors and styles. She made sure to announce prior to her trying-on session, "No thongs for me, but everything else is definitely grist for the mill – or in this case, for my body."

She left the dressing room wearing a sapphire-blue lace bra with matching panties. "Please put on my account I'm wearing new underwear out of here. And is there a trash receptacle nearby where I can dispose of my old stuff?" Her friends laughed with her as she discarded her ancient panties and bras in the closed wastebasket outside the dressing room.

While trying on the varieties of bras brought to her, the women heard Venus mumbling. "Damn, what in hell was my mother thinking when she named me Venus! Didn't she know what was gonna happen when I got old? Jesus, ladies, come here and just look at me! Venus, my ass! Just *look* at these arms; the bat-wings that flap ever so gracefully! The crepe-paper skin with wrinkles and dimples galore. Cellulite! Argh. Good God, I'm glad I'm not here for a swimming suit. How the hell can I display these arms to the world? Or legs?"

"Are you talking to us?" laughed Rachael. "If so, we're gonna ignore you."

Soon they found themselves all howling at Venus' proclamations about her various body parts and the drama she was emerged in. Then they all then shared how *they* felt when they became aware of their skin changes (among other things.)

Venus, at almost sixty-five, was shocked with the way her body seemed to deteriorate before her very eyes. Or was it that she hadn't looked in a mirror for ten years? "I guess I have to do this for me, not for anyone else. At least I'll appreciate pretty things next to me and on me. I can't imagine anyone interested in a woman of sixty-five with all these physical flaws. At least when I was first married I was a young thing with beauty, firmness, perky boobs and hair where there is supposed to be hair, not where I think it is now – my nose, chin, ears, and who knows where I can't see it! Good God! I know this happens to everyone, but how in hell are you supposed to bare your body as well as your soul to someone new?" She paused as she finally answered herself, "I guess in the dark only."

Everyone laughed at Venus' mumblings because she did have an amazing ability to be a very funny drama queen. There was truth to what she was saying, Sally mused, as she clearly remembered the first time she and Joe made love. "Oh my God, it was a good thing I had a couple glasses of wine or it probably never would have happened." Yet Joe loved Sally for Sally. It was a good thing, too.

"Hey, Venus, you think your arms are bad, let me show you mine," offered Rachael. "And my boobs as well as my belly droop with stretch marks *and* dimples."

"All my skin has lost its springiness," added LuAnne. "And I'm here to tell you my bat wings have specific purposes. Ya know I spread them out to gain both momentum and to balance."

"Yeah, and our eyesight that gets poorer as we age is for a purpose," suggested Sally. "That way we can't see all the wrinkles, saggy skin, and droopy boobs and on and on," she laughed. "No one makes love with glasses on – I think."

The women humorously continued their self-deprecating conversation about how their bodies weren't what they used to be. But they concluded that the wisdom gained in their maturing had been worth all the changes in their bodies. Surprisingly they could, in some ways appreciate getting older.

"After all," said Rachael, "if there were no good to come from all of this, then what's the point? Or is there a point to it all?" she paused and laughed again – for effect. . . .

By this time, they were all in stitches, with tears in their eyes from laughing so much, and several saleswomen had joined them in the dressing room to chuckle with them. They had gained a considerable audience of customers too, with everyone enjoying the mockeries they were indulging in, nodding their heads in agreement.

"*You* all may have bat wings and droopy stomachs, but I have legs with flab between them that rustles when I walk."

"You do not! When was the last time you looked at yourself naked?" asked Sally.

"Oh, probably ten years ago. What a shock this is." Then Venus asked Sally, "How did you do it with Joe that first time? My Lord, I'd die of embarrassment if anyone looked at my body for sex. I think, nah, I know, that part of my life is truly over, even though I'm buying new stuff."

The recriminations about their bodies and how to hide all their flaws continued until they were all yelling, "No More. I have a stomach ache."

"Let's go try on casual clothes," LuAnne said. The women watched as Venus began to pull stuff off the racks. Practically everything she picked out was too matronly for her.

"You sure don't have any idea what you'll look good in anymore," exclaimed Rachael.

"How did you manage to look like a fashion-plate when you were married to Alex?" asked LuAnne."

"I don't know. I guess I just *knew* back then. Now I am self-conscious about everything - my boobs, my arms, my wrinkly skin. You name it. I guess I've been trying to cover up everything. Apparently you ladies don't approve."

"No, we don't. We are what we are. Go for the styles you wore back then," suggested Sally.

"You mean like this?" Venus picked out a bright blue dress with tiny white flowers on it. The fabric was silk, but that's all it had going for it.

"Good God, NO! That is frumpy and old-lady looking. Tiny patterns do nothing for you."

Venus' next selection denied she had any type of body whatsoever. It was a reasonable color, but hung like an old nightgown.

Sally gasped. "We're going to let you try that on, but only to show you how awful it looks. Right, ladies?"

The two others responded just the way Sally expected them to – in the affirmative.

Finally after much coaching, Venus went into a very large dressing room where the other three women could join her. "First try on the "nightgown."

After Venus put it on she admitted, "I guess I have to agree with you. It's just a brighter version of my beige shit."

"YOU GOT IT!" Rachael hugged Venus in excitement.

From there, with the other three helping by hanging up discarded clothes, getting Venus zipped up and fitted correctly, Venus found that she really did know what looked good and what was flattering.

Sally said, "Venus, you still have work to do to get off the shitty wagon, thinking you have to look like you did when you were twenty years old. Ain't gonna happen! I guess we all have to do some of that. Right ladies? Look at who you are! Look at your sense of humor, your depth, your friendships. You, my friend, are still not quite seeing yourself, but you are beginning to. You need glasses for your insides!"

Sally took a deep breath before continuing. "As for the first time with Joe. . . whew! It was no easy thing. I was grateful both of us are far-sighted. I think that's God's way of helping us older folks get into new relationships. You know, if you can't see the wrinkles and blotches, then they don't exist." Sally laughed wryly. "I had to go through tons and tons of fear and questioning. Aside from the body stuff, what if he doesn't like me? What if we're incompatible? What if he couldn't get it up? That'd be my fault for sure – cuz you know, I turned him off kind of thing? What if he was a lousy lover? Nah, actually, that never entered it because by the time we went to bed, I knew how compassionate, gentle and attentive he was. I expected it all and I got it." Sally laughed, "Now what was the question again? What memory problems? Who me?" The women giggled in acquiescence.

Sally remembered as she found herself thinking warm, loving and sexy thoughts of Joe. Wow, she was some lucky lady!

"Now that brings up, or shall we say, tries to bring up, another subject," said LuAnne. "What do you do if a guy you're with *can't* get it up? Have you had that experience, any of you?"

Rachael responded, "Have you ever heard of Viagra and all the other 'uppers' and 'firmers' that exist? They're available to almost every guy," and she chuckled. "Remember the 'Bob' commercial? You know,

42

Bob is always smiling and we all know why... some enhancer product. But what was 'harder' for me was that damn vaginal dryness. Took me months to figure out what worked without having Hormone Replacement Therapy. I refuse to take pregnant-mare urine into my body."

"Me too," chimed Sally. "I take a bioidentical hormone replacement therapy, but what really gets me is my insurance company refuses to pay for it. They'll only pay for horse urine. Bioidenticals are made of plants and are considered food; did you know that"

"No, I didn't," said LuAnne. "When I get home, if my doctor's office is open, I will try to get a prescription."

"So back to the question, ladies," said Venus. "Have you ever been with a guy who couldn't get it up?"

"I have," replied Sally. "In my dating prior to Joe, I went out with a guy who had a very limp dick. I felt sorry for him and also immediately translated his limpness to *my* sexual inadequacy. *I* caused his limpness. Isn't it a hoot how we always bring everyone else's problems back to being ours?"

"Yes to the question, and what happened?" asked Rachael.

"Absolutely nothing. We stopped what we were attempting to do and he never called me again. Of course that made me feel even more inadequate."

Venus said, "I haven't had that problem. . . " She didn't have a chance to finish her sentence because the other women jumped on her, all saying something similar with different words.

"That's because you haven't been with a man in ten years!"

"I know, and if you all hadn't interrupted me I'd have told you that was the reason."

After Venus' major shopping spree and make over, the women went out for drinks and dinner.

"Does this mean you're in the dating game again?" asked Rachael. "If you are, you might want to consider the newest of fads for ladies and actually for gentlemen too."

"What's that?" asked Sally. "I'm not aware of any new fads."

"That's because you're an old married lady, whereas Rachael and I aren't. Does Joe read *Playboy*," snickered LuAnne?

"Probably, why?"

"Have you looked through the magazine lately – like the last several years?" Rachael continued, "If you had, you've noticed none of the women have pubic hair. It's not shaved off, it's waxed off! Called Brazilian waxing," said Rachel with a huge grin.

"Oh yeah, those are the women he refers to as "babies with tits," Sally laughed.

"If that's part of the dating deal, forget about it," Venus about shrieked, grateful for the noise of the busy restaurant. She paused for a moment and then said, "Wait a minute, do you mean to tell me women spread their legs wide open to a complete stranger who then puts hot wax on their labia and ass, waits for it to dry and then rips the hair out? Is that what you're telling me is the fad of the day?"

"Affirmative" answered Rachael with a huge guffaw.

"Count me out. No way in hell! That's masochistic! At my age women do that? That's incredulous. Did any of you ever have it done?"

"You must be insane," they all roared.

"But you both date," Venus said looking at Rachael and LuAnne.

"Yeah but the guys who want *that*" Rachael grimaced, "will just have to look elsewhere. I'm with you, Venus."

Sally chirped in, "I get my eyebrows waxed and that hurts. I can't imagine the pain of having the hair on my genitals ripped off!"

"Well, I just had my eyebrows done today, and again, more fodder *not* to do a – what did you call it?" Venus grumbled dramatically and the other three laughed.

"Gee. Or for a guy to have his testicle hairs waxed sounds like a torture chamber to me," added Rachael.

"Well, I heard from one couple who had it done that sex was just dandy after – I mean after they healed and could once again walk," LuAnne snickered. "The picture in my mind of either a man or woman opening their legs to complete strangers, just about gets me."

"I wonder what they do with the dick and the balls when they do a man," mused Venus.

"I hear they just pick the stuff up and move it away."

"They pick up the 'stuff?'" Rachael howled, trying to catch her breath from laughing.

By this time, all four of the women, along with several other folks who were sitting at tables near them were clutching their sides in laughter.

"One more thing," Sally interjected. "Why do women, or men, for that matter, want to be like babies? Is our society so obsessed with youth that we have to look like four-year olds to have sex?"

44

"Probably. Actually, if we were minus all hair, we'd still look like old women – or at least women with a few years on us." Rachael concluded. "I wonder if men in our age group want that sort of torture."

"I don't know or care, but I grew pussy hair and it's staying there until I die, or until it continues to thin, as it has been doing since menopause," LuAnne added with a smirk.

"Me too," chimed in Venus, Sally and Rachael.

From one of the tables near them, a woman's voice called out, "I'm with you gals. No way!"

After Venus' Makeover

When Venus returned to work the next day, she was dazzling in
an emerald-green silk skirt with a mint-green and cobalt-blue silk shirt that
skimmed both the top of her skirt and her beautiful shape. Her feet, with
polished toenails, were clad in cobalt-blue and green sandals, and she
knew beneath her beautiful outer garments were glorious emerald-green
lingerie! Quite a change from her beige jumper, beige shirt and brown
Birkenstocks! Her hair was beautiful, shiny and free, flowing to her
shoulders. There were a few people who literally did not recognize her;
some asked if they could help her find something or someone. There
were even those who thought she might be a twin sister of Venus. All of
this was so amusing to Venus, she began to laugh as she strolled into her
office.

Glenda jumped up and down in approval and screamed, "Oh My
God, you have a body! You're beautiful! It's about time! Good for you.
I never thought I'd see the day when you even so much as let your hair
down. Praises to the powers that be! What caused this sudden and
dramatic change?"

Venus, who loved the attention she was receiving, but was still a
bit shy about her over-the-top change, answered simply, "It was about
time I started loving myself and showing the world who I really am – in all
ways, not just brains."

Her office staff and those who hung around her office still were
amazed two weeks later and still congratulating her on her "coming out as
a beautiful woman." One of her co-workers, John Paul, suggested - with
quite exaggerated hand motions - that they have a celebratory coming-out
party for her. "We need an excuse to have a big shindig, you know, and
I'll take care of everything. You know how we queens are," he laughed.
"We should have it with lots of wonderful food, sexy lighting and in a
simply *gorgeous* place. How does that sound, Venus?"

John Paul was obviously gay, with a most feminine walk and
gestures all flaunting his sexuality. He was the non-official host of the
department, and most of the staff wondered why he had picked a career
in education rather than something like a wedding planner. Of course,

they all knew his brains and astuteness when it came to both writing and utilizing current theories in nuclear chemistry, but if he could have had another career. . . ?

Venus replied, "Oh no, I couldn't let you all do that. Well, only if you want to. Actually, sounds great. But make sure it's fun and there is lots of good wine and food. *Everyone* comes. I want dancing too."

"You want *what?*" asked John Paul, about swooning in jest.

"You heard me, dancing! And make sure everyone brings their partners, playmates, friends or whoever wants to par – ty!"

One of the other staff who was listening asked, "This from the Head of the Chemistry Department? Since when did you become such a partier?"

"Since two weeks ago. Let's get it moving…. When are we having this affair?"

"We need to do this while the iron's hot – er, that's you Venus," and John Paul laughed as he looked at the department's calendar. He suggested the following Friday night. "We'll send out invites and flyers to everyone in this department, final count by next Thursday. I have a great restaurant in mind – the Endless Sea, and they shouldn't be too busy this time of year. They have a simply fab-u-lous banquet room - I think the best in the area. I'll call them and verify it in the flyer."

That afternoon as Venus was walking through the halls she was shocked beyond words! There was Greg from Discount Tires. "Oh my God! What is *he* doing here?" She thought. Her face immediately turned beet red as she raced by him with her head bent down – hoping he had not noticed her. But he had.

He did a double-take, paused and looked as if he wanted to say something. She didn't stop, just nodded a brief hello. She had two things to do! One; call Sally. Two: find out from those in her department what he was doing here and who he was.

"Sally, answer your phone if you're there. I need to talk to you NOW," Venus almost yelled into Sally's answering machine.

Just as she was about to hang up, Sally picked up. "What's wrong, you sound panicked!"

"I am. I am super-panicked. I am more than super-panicked! Remember the guy I told you about from Discount Tires? Well, as I was walking down the hall, I saw him coming towards me. I bent my head down like a silly teenager because I didn't know what to do. He saw me and nodded, paused and seemed as if he wanted to talk. But in my embarrassment, I simply nodded back and ran into my office. Honestly, I felt like an idiot! Pure and simple *idiot*. No, beyond idiot. Good grief."

Sally could hear Venus' mortification and imagine her body language, a woe-is-me posturing. "So what are you going to do now?"

"I have to find out who he is, what he's doing here and how in the world I'll be able to handle myself if I see him again. Oh Shit. Kill me now and get it over with. I'll talk to you later."

Sally grinned when Venus abruptly hung up the phone. "Wow," she thought, "maybe our Venus will find herself a lover. About time."

Venus, being a woman of action, finally pulled herself together and left her office to inquire casually of Glenda, "Do you know who that guy is I saw down the hall? Tall, about six-feet-two, wearing a green short- sleeve shirt with khaki pants, black hair, green eyes and nice looking?"

"Why, you interested? So is every other single woman in the department. His name is Greg Richards and he's a chemist, researcher, inventor, CEO and mostly owner of SeaFoam, a company from Boston. He's starting up a branch of his company here. From what I understand, he's sharing some information with some of the chemists in the department. Surprised this is the first time you've seen him. He's been coming around for a few weeks and, like I said, every other woman in the building and beyond is aware of him. They're also hot for Thom, one of his employees. But then that's another story. I hear tell Richard's a real go-getter and usually gets what he wants although he's extremely ethical – if the two can go together. The staff here seems to think the world of him. Apparently he knows business in and out and hires only those with considerable expertise in whatever he is looking for. That's all I know, except of course, the obvious. He is one hell of a good looking guy – and those eyes of his!!"

"He's been here a few weeks, huh? Never saw him."

"No surprise, coming from you. What made you noticed him today? Yeah, his company is setting up a new plant that makes some kind of paint or something for boats and ships that prevents any marine life from attaching itself to the painted surface. I think he's trying to sell it to the Navy too. Anyway, he seems to be a nice guy though I know nothing of his personal life."

48

Venus was quiet for a moment before she said, "Yes, I think I'd be interested in him, but please do *not* let anyone know I said that. You know how gossip starts and spreads here. Anyway, I'd just like to meet him, I think."

"We can arrange that. I think John Paul invited him and his group to our party on Friday night."

Venus nodded and left the office before Glenda could see the effect of her comments – a bright red face.

"I am just so brave it blows me away," she told Sally as she called her once again at work to tell her what was planned for Friday night and how Greg and his staff might be there. "Sally, you and Joe *have* to come to our bash. It's my Celebratory Coming-Out Party. What do you suppose Greg will think if he found out it's for me? Do you think he'd still come? *You* have to be there. I don't think I can do this. Oh, listen to me. . . I thought I was sounding like a silly teenager, but it's even worse. I sound like a silly pre-teenager. Oh, the party will be at the Endless Sea Restaurant. Good thing it's one of my favorites. That way, at least there will be good food, though I may not want to eat anything if my stomach doesn't settle down."

Sally listened as Venus chattered away. She knew her well enough not to interrupt because, at that point, Venus was just letting off steam and wasn't listening anyway. A true extrovert.

"I'll call you when I get home and you can let me know more of the details, okay ? In the meantime, why don't you go take a yoga class or go for a long walk on the beach? Do anything, Venus, to work off some of your energy and to ground yourself! You're like a filled balloon with the air being let out, and you're flying uncontrollably all over."

***

The next few days passed quickly and peacefully, as Venus took Sally's advice. She spent many hours walking and running along the beautiful Carlsbad, Encinitas and Del Mar beaches, then she sat and meditated. She became much calmer but still made a bee-line directly from the parking lot to her office, even forgoing the lemon eucalyptus and all the other plants she'd daily admired. Because Venus was afraid of running into Greg again, and she just didn't know what to say to him, she began to rehearse. Then she'd scold herself for trying to control the situation and for not being present. Gradually, as the days past, while Venus was running, walking, and meditating, she was able to stop her mind from panicking. That was a big victory.

On the physical side of her life, Venus was grateful and surprised at how easy it had been to give up her old shorts and Birkenstocks for a pair of respectable shorts and good running shoes. In retrospect, she realized she sometimes even surprised herself. "Thank heavens there is no going back with clothing and makeup; I am so thrilled that part of my life is over. I'm even more ecstatic that I decided to go through the emotional shit to be rid of it all. Pat myself on the back! Yup! It seems as if the old metaphysicians are right: close one door and another opens. Sure seems like that has happened. Imagine a Coming-Out party for me!

Just the idea that her staff thought so much of her to create a huge celebration in her honor was a pleasant shock to Venus' system. She was beginning to look at herself in a less judgmental manner, becoming aware that so many of the old stories were quickly dying. "What a relief," she thought, and was able to laugh at herself and the silliness she had thought was absolute truth, with a capital 'T.'

As Venus gained more confidence she worried less about everything. Aside from possibly meeting up with Greg, which had its pros and cons. She did allow her mind to meander about what she was going to wear on Friday night. Finally, aware that she had so many wonderful new choices, she settled on an emerald-green cocktail dress. "I just love that color!" Venus adored the green dress. It was a simple sheath with three-quarter sleeves and a v-neckline made of knobby-silk material. She would take a black cashmere throw with her just in case it would become chilly. With her auburn hair and hazel eyes that turned green when she put the dress on, the affect was stunning. Having decided on her clothing, Venus thought about the accessories to wear, going over each item to make sure she would not look too lavishly adorned. She finally decided on a crystal necklace and her diamond stud earrings. "That will do it," she approved out loud. "Ah, I guess I will wear a black high-heel sandal; that is, if I can still walk on those things. I know I bought them, now I have to practice walking and dancing." She laughed at herself.

The Celebration

The night of her Celebratory Coming-Out Party was one of those magnificent Southern California nights - full moon, slight breeze and perfect temperature in the sixties. She didn't know how many people might be coming, but was told that the guest list was growing rapidly. Some of the people attending didn't even know her! There had been a department conference that she was unable to attend, with new people from Virginia who were also opening another branch of *their* company. Even they were invited. Venus didn't pay much attention to the details — there were always folks coming out here starting up new businesses and they were always after information she and her department could provide.

***

The Endless Sea Restaurant had a fabulous reputation for its food and ambience, but she'd never been in their banquet room. It was even more lush than the main part of the restaurant, with an elegant wood floor, high ceiling, subtle lighting from a beautiful crystal fixture, with just enough light to make the crystals dance. There were comfortable fully-padded chairs in a brocade-wine material, and a buffet to make any expert on fine food drool. Tables were placed around the buffet in a horseshoe shape, and there was a fireplace in the corner with a real fire going. "How much more romantic could this be?" thought Venus. Then she noticed the windows. "Ah yes, I had rated this banquet room an A, now it's an A+. I see the harbor, the boats and yachts. My, oh my! I haven't felt this romantic since I was twenty. This could be dangerous."

The band was wonderful, playing a great variety of music, and the food was scrumptious: fresh seafood of all sorts, standing roasts, barbequed chicken, fruit, fresh breads, pastry, salads, an ice cream/yogurt bar complete with nuts and fruits, and a coffee/tea bar with an extensive display of lattes, frappes, chais and whatever else one could possibly think of. "I wonder if my new clothes will fit after tonight," thought Venus. In her peripheral vision, she saw John Paul and immediately went up to him.

"John Paul, what a fabulous place! I've been to the restaurant but never here in the banquet room. My hat's off to you. I knew you'd be absolutely the best in setting this up. I am so excited this evening and thank you from the bottom of my heart. What an incredible evening!" With dramatic flair, John Paul asked Venus to dance with him, and as he was swirling her around, she saw Greg.

"John, do you know anything about Greg? What's he like, how long will he be here? You know?"

John Paul teased, "Why, you interested too?" He chuckled, "Seems like every woman I know wants to know about him – even those not in our department. But, to answer your questions, he's providing some useful information to a few of the chemists here, and we're sharing information with his company. All in all, it's a really dandy exchange. But ask Will; if he doesn't know, he'll find out who does. Have you formally met Greg?" He paused a bit and chuckled. "Actually, in my best match-making capabilities I think you two might be fabulous together."

Venus laughed at his overly dramatic flair, "I do believe I met him a month or so ago, but I am sure he didn't remember me." She was thinking, "Damn right he didn't remember me; I was a schoolmarm study in beige, not the woman who is here now, either in looks or any other way."

"Please excuse me, John Paul, I really do need to visit the lady's room. Anyway Simon is going to kill me if you don't pay more attention to him," said Venus. "You know how he is!"

"Of course. Enjoy your restroom experience. In the meantime, you're right about Simon. I'd better dance with him or I'm in bigger trouble than you can imagine. Think that will be too shocking to the new folks?" John Paul said with a smirk. "Don't want to upset their wagons."

"Nah. If it does, too bad. Go!" She took off to find Sally standing at the bar with Joe. "Sally, don't we need to go to the lady's room?"

"I guess so. Is he here?" asked Sally.

"Yup, over there." Venus was almost hyperventilating.

"Okay" said Sally, "just go up to him and say hello. Not bad, if I do say so myself."

"God, you sound like men appraising women," Joe snickered.

But Venus was in too much of a snit to pay attention to Joe's barb and rambled. "What if he remembers me the way I was? Or what if he doesn't remember me? I'm sure he doesn't remember me. Oooh, I don't know which is worse. I want to run towards him and grab him, but that's not gonna happen. Half the women in the building are after him," Venus lamented. "I guess I'll just bite the bullet and go over there, after all it is *our* department party. Obviously he's not in the department. I 'm just doing a good job of hosting; don't you think?"

"Right," said Sally laughing at Venus' approach/avoidance behavior. "You go, girl!" She had never seen Venus so unglued.

"Okay, here I go! Breathe," she silently commanded herself.

Venus slowly walked over to where 'her dibs-on" handsome gentleman Greg was talking to two of her co-workers and several strangers. They seemed to be mesmerized by him and hanging on his every word. Venus could only think, "Wow, me too. You look incredible in that dark- green sports jacket with the mint-green shirt. Who taught you to dress? One thing we both have in common is our love of green. Good God, I'm babbling again."

Venus knew if she had had a few more drinks, those words might have popped right out of her mouth. As it was, she wasn't sure she hadn't made some sort of unintelligible sounds. She carefully took a deep breath and was about to introduce herself to the folks Greg was standing with, when Roy Berrub, a co-worker, playfully grabbed her and said, "This is our very beautiful, wonderful, and smart Head of our Chemistry Department; I'd like you to meet Venus Lighton. By the way, I normally could never get away with that type of sexist talk. So please, Venus, forgive me just this one time for being a male chauvinist and commenting on your beauty. I guess once you're a male, you're automatically a male chauvinist pig. I'm guilty. And you do look particularly stunning this evening!" To further illustrate his point, Roy got down on one knee with a grin and pleaded his case.

"Just this once Roy, but *never* again!" She pretended to be stern.

Venus mentioned she had seen Greg and Thom walking through the department and had nodded to them, but she hadn't been formally introduced. Her mind was actively thinking, "Yeah, I ran away before I made a fool of myself." After her "formal" introduction, Greg proceeded to introduce her to Thom Gordon, his scientific cohort, part-owner, friend, confidant and chemist; Bill Dewart, his accountant and financial advisor; Larry Sorrell, the company's marketing director; and Rita Johnson, who was in charge of the books and business aspect of

SeaFoam. These were the people on his team in California to start up a west coast branch of Greg's company from Boston. Greg was the "mostly" owner, CEO and fearless leader, with Thom a close second. As Venus acknowledged each of them, Greg looked at her rather quizzically and said, "Haven't we met before – I mean before nodding at each other in the halls?"

Venus paused, then rambled, "Possibly, I meet many people at the university who need help for their businesses and certainly many businesses want to settle here because really now, what's not to like - except for earthquakes, fires, mudslides, traffic and freeways to die *on* rather than for? Otherwise, this is a very lovely area." Venus figured she should quit before she lost her ability to speak; she could feel that happening again. "Damn," she thought, "what is it about this guy that knocks my brain into infancy?" She decided to just make herself listen quietly to the conversation and not contribute a thing. As she stood there, she became aware of Rita watching her, which made her uncomfortable. She wondered if Rita and Greg had something going. "The eyes of a woman can't lie to another," she thought. "Before I get involved I will have to check this out."

Pretty soon, Roy commented, "What's happening with you? Cat must have gotten your tongue, Venus. Never saw you so quiet."

With Roy's proclamation and her ensuing discomfort, Venus decided to leave while her legs were still functioning. "It was nice meeting you all, and I wish you huge success here in Sunny Southern California." She felt like she was slinking away with a terrible rash of redness about her face and ears.

Sally joined Venus after her not so very brilliant meeting with Greg and asked her how it went. "It went like nothing! I trembled as I walked away! Brave, huh?"

Greg couldn't stop himself from watching Venus walk away. There was something in the natural sway of her hips, the way she threw her head back, the way her beautiful auburn hair moved, and her very presence that electrified him in all his parts. "I'll ask her to dance," he thought to himself.

Bill Dewart had exactly the same idea; in fact, he was just about drooling over Venus.

Bill

Bill was a fifty-seven-year-old twice-divorced bachelor who had an eye for beautiful women. "Whew, this gal Venus is a babe!" He was close to six feet, had a shaved head, bright blue eyes, prominent nose and cheekbones and broad shoulders. A little paunch was beginning to show but he, like Greg, vowed he'd get rid of it.

Money was his idol and he reeked from his "fine taste" (of which he was quite proud.) He had come to California to rid himself of a relationship that was beginning to tax his freedom. Financially, he was a whiz and seemed to have incredible luck and savvy in anything that had to do with money. Joining SeaFoam in Boston six months prior, he had already made himself, in many ways, indispensable. Often folks found him brusque and even rude, but he knew his business. He joked with the rest of the staff and told them, "That's why you have a marketing director who isn't like I am. Aren't you happy?" He gloated to the others, "I work because it amuses me and I want to, not because I have to. Maybe when you're as wise and knowing and intelligent as I am, you won't have to either."

His knowledge of computers, tax laws and business was amazing. All the major players at SeaFoam acknowledged his expertise and regularly went to him for assistance – in spite of his often brusque manner. He often thought, "If I'd really kissed up to a whole lot of people, I'd have been even more than the multi-millionaire I am! He was sometimes angry at himself for not being able to keep his mouth shut because it embarrassed even him. Most of the time he was reasonably pleasant, except for his occasional pontification about his own intelligence, his wisdom about stocks, law and or anything and everything else he was into at the moment. The staff at SeaFoam appreciated and respected him, yet were somewhat threatened by his huge ego and how it could play out.

With women, Bill became a different sort of person. He was considerate, fun, gentle, witty and generous – until he was tired of them, and that happened fairly quickly. Then he became what the staff experienced – rude, nasty and sometimes downright cruel.

In his years of experience, he had learned long ago never to sleep with someone where he worked. It was a steel rule he kept to, having once not followed it and been fired for his "little" indiscretion. He still burned thinking about it. When Rita came on to him, he explained, albeit sourly, his position. She seemed to understand, and they became work buddies.

There never was enough money for a guy like Bill, and everyone knew that. Some even questioned why Greg hired him; others realized his Midas touch. There was much talk about what kind of salary Bill received or if he had stock in the company. Regardless, Bill worked hard.

Seeing Venus walking and greeting people was a real turn-on for him. He thought he'd wait awhile and then go over and ask her to dance. He chatted amicably with a few of SeaFoam's staff and then was stopped by some of the people from the chemistry department. He got so involved with telling them about a certain stock that he found to be an excellent risk, before he knew it, well over an hour had passed.

Back to the Celebration

Greg continued socializing with his staff and those from the chemistry department while also keeping a close eye on Venus. This was definitely a night of celebration for everyone, his staff included. They were all relaxing, knowing that Monday would bring a whole new series of work-related issues. Rita, who was in charge of the business/office complex and the others on his staff had done a phenomenal job. They had worked their butts off in setting up the new office, and they were finally feeling like there was organization, order and the necessary equipment to really get the business going. Greg was grateful to the chemistry department for their help, their shared information, and their invitation to this Celebration or "Coming-Out Party" as they called it. He wasn't quite sure what they meant by a "Coming-Out Party", but he supposed he'd know by the end of the evening. This event was an easy way to meet new people in the area, which was the reason he and his group chose to attend. It was an added bonus that the woman Venus was attending, too. He found himself watching her throughout the evening, his curiosity flaming higher and higher. When she walked to the other side of the room, he found himself hoping she wasn't leaving. If she left before he got the opportunity to talk with her, he at least knew where to be able to call her and ask her out. He continued to watch for her. "Maybe I'll go over to where I last saw her." As he was pondering that, she suddenly reappeared. He breathed a sigh of relief.

Sally, observing Venus, remarked, "You got it bad, girl!"

The evening continued to be pleasant, but Venus kept glancing at Greg and feeling like a silly school girl. All in all, it made for a great deal of discomfort. She didn't know what to do. God, was she embarrassed! Every so often she saw him glance her way and once or twice their eyes met. She tried to pretend she didn't notice, but, she thought, "Good grief, those eyes just bore right into me, into my soul."

Just when Venus thought she couldn't take much more, from behind her she felt a tap on her shoulder. "Can I convince you to dance with me?" asked Greg.

"Oh my God! What do I do?" As her brain was engaged in thinking, Greg took her hand, and she again felt the electrical charge. He led her to the dance floor where the music was changing from a fairly fast beat to a slow dance. "Lord, what will become of me?" Venus asked herself. She realized how perfectly she fit in Greg's arms and how their sense of timing was exact. She couldn't remember ever dancing with anyone as easily and as in sync. "Breathe," she told herself over and over.

"You dance beautifully," said Greg, obviously smitten. "Tell me about yourself."

Venus' mind raced; she knew she could not speak. He seemed to affect her that way. "Ah, you first."

Greg, though struck with Venus, was still totally capable of carrying on a conversation. He told her about his move from Boston, and how his son Charlie and the family were here too. He amused her with stories about the way the cats and dogs handled the transition, and how their finding a house was a nightmare. She contributed to the conversation by nodding and every so often asking something else to keep Greg talking. "But what about you?" she prompted. "Do you live with them? Have you your own critters?" Her mind screamed loudly, "Stop talking now or you'll put your foot in your mouth." She listened as he responded.

"Well, right now I am renting a place on the water in LaJolla, but I don't think I want to stay there. It's too loud, too much traffic and not the type of property I like. Once the company is up-and-running I'll look for another place. No, no critters at this time. Later on that too. How about you?"

"Oh, critters. Yes, let's see. I have purr machine I call OM though his real name is Oliver Munster. He is a huge, white long-haired semi-cat/semi-lion with lime-green eyes. I have this thing for green eyes – in people and cats." In the paused nanosecond it took for her to end her sentence, her mind hollered, "Quiet!" "Yup," she replied.

"Is that all you can tell me about yourself?" asked Greg, giving her a killer smile. "About cats and eyes, and by the way, do my eyes meet the "thing" as you called it, for green eyes?"

Venus could feel herself blushing and was thankful the room was dimly lit. "Yeah. Can't tell you more, I prefer to be a mystery woman," Venus laughed.

"So, what about my green eyes? Yes or No? Fit the bill or not?"

"Mmm?" Venus shrugged her shoulders, knowing that whatever she answered she'd feel silly. She was astutely aware that Greg knew his way around women. What was worse, he knew it too. "Just what I need to get involved with," Venus thought, "a player."

Thankfully, ("Whew!" thought Venus) the dance ended. Yet Greg kept his arm on her waist and began to guide her to the bar. " How about a glass of wine?" he asked, not removing his hand.

"Yes," she replied, "red please." Another voice in her head was screaming, "NO WINE! Next thing you know you'll take him home and to your bed. NOT ACCEPTABLE! Get his hand off before you melt. Breathe!"

As Greg went to get the wine, Venus took a deep breath and found she acknowledged his quiet but very strong presence. It oozed from him. "Even worse for me," she feared.

Anyone watching Venus and Greg noticed the incredible sexual energy that radiated from each of them to the other.

Sally said to Joe, "Wow, if this isn't something! I never thought I would see the day Venus was even attracted to someone, no less oblivious to everyone here. Those two are energetically glued to the hip. I wonder if they are aware of how they have become alone in this crowd of people."

Joe responded in exactly the way Sally wanted him to, "Just like how I fell for you on that very first meeting. I saw no one else, heard nothing else, and wanted only you."

"Oh Joe, you are such a romantic. I do so love you! I hope Venus gets what she wants and Greg does too. Even though they just met, there sure is chemistry there for our head chemist. Wow! I think the regulars in her department are saying the same thing!" Sally said as she looked around.

Sally was right; she and Joe were not the only ones to notice the intense energy between Greg and Venus. Everyone in her department did. Everyone Greg brought with him from Boston did. It seemed as if there was magic between them, shining on them and reflecting back to everyone else, lighting everyone in their company.

Bill Dewart was especially aware of it and felt his gut churn at the amazing amount of jealousy spiking through him. Not a feeling he was intimately familiar with, and one he didn't like at all. He began to look at ways he could "out woo" Greg.

While everyone else watched, Venus and Greg went onto the dance floor again. Venus could hardly believe this was happening to her, and from the look in Greg's eyes, Venus decided Greg was pretty okay with what was happening too. They just seemed to fit. "I'll worry about his lady-killing tendencies later," a part of her thought.

"Let's go for a walk. The harbor is so beautifully lit, you can point out the sights to a newcomer. Are you up for it?" asked Greg. He paused a moment to acknowledge Venus' nod of her head, then gently put his hand on her waist. Once again she found herself being guided easily and smoothly.

As they were walking out, Bill approached them and said, "Venus, how about a dance with me before you leave?"

"Um, ah, I think Greg and I are going for a walk on the harbor. Maybe later, okay?"

Bill blurted out, "You want another guy trailing along?"

Greg quickly responded, "I don't think that's necessary, I think I can protect Venus from all the giants, killers, and trolls out there. Surely there must be another lady who'd be most flattered to dance with you." Greg took Venus' hand possessively, giving the clear message that "*she belongs to me.*"

Bill forced a laugh and said, "You're quite right. Enjoy your walk." His insides were on fire with anger and humiliation as he turned and strolled inside as casually as possible.

"Later," he thought, "I'll see to him later. For that matter to her too. This sucks."

Venus said, "I believe Bill is mad at the two of us for excluding him, but I guess that's his problem. Now, back to your question. I think I've already answered it with a nod. Yes, I'd love to go for a walk. I can show you the sights. San Diego is so beautiful, the coastline, the city, everything is just magical." As Venus was pointing out and naming all the various shopping areas, restaurants, hotels and ships that could be seen, she began to relax.

"This whole evening is magical," commented Greg as they strolled the moon lit-path where he gently stroked the fingers of Venus' hand. She felt an instant grip within her stomach and all up and down her spine. "Good God," she panicked, "can't remember the last time I felt Kundalini energy by someone's touch. I feel it from top to bottom." Venus became aware of the softness of his hands, in spite of certain calluses on his palm. "I wonder if he knows such soft skin is that of a sensitive man," she mused.

"What are you thinking? You're awfully quiet."

After a pause, Venus replied, "What a lovely evening." There was no way she was going to tell him what was happening in her body!

For both of them all of their senses were magnified. The smells of the ocean, the cooking of many different foods, freshly-mown grass, the sounds of music from the restaurants in the area and of the water lapping against the shore, the brilliant sky and the outlines of the lit-up buildings from downtown San Diego all contributed to the magic.

"It's lovely here; I love to walk near the water. I love that nature always makes me remember its beauty and its power. I don't think I could live in a place that wasn't near an ocean."

"Me neither," said Greg. "I walked along the Boston harbor almost daily, and have a beach house on the Cape. Have you ever been there?"

"No. I was once in Boston, but didn't get to the shore."

"You'd love it there if you love it here. It is different. The Pacific is so unlike the Atlantic. The water's a lot colder here, you know. Took me by surprise! I figured that where palm trees grew, the water would be warm."

"Not true," smiled Venus.

"Boy, did I find that out fast," and Greg laughed.

Venus intuitively knew what he was talking about. She had many male relatives from the East who had problems going into the cold waters of the Pacific: it seemed their testicles shriveled into their bodies. Remembering the term, "blue balls," she laughed out loud and said, "I think I've heard about that problem. She then proceeded to tell him how she had witnessed several male relative's shock at the temperature of the water and been told their ensuing problems.

Greg held her hand tighter and Venus became more aware of the man himself. "Whew," she thought! They continued to walk slowly until Venus became mindful that her beautiful high heels were not for long distance walking. Her feet were killing her!

"I think we better head back. My feet are not used to this type of heel for walking, and these shoes are not very comfortable at this point," she said regretfully.

"I see a bench up ahead, let's sit for a while to rest your toes," Greg offered.

"Okay."

The two of them sat on the bench and talked as if they had known each other for years. Venus finally went through the fears she had experienced and found her voice. She was able to participate in a conversation, for which she was extraordinarily grateful.

"So, how did you get into the business you're in? I mean, why did you research paints?"

"No one else was doing it, and it was a need. Damn pain to constantly paint the bottom of your boat!"

"Do you have a boat?"

"Not now, I kind of gave it to my son Ron before I left. But I'll tell ya, my foam sure made the maintenance less stressful. Instead of having maintenance every two years, it's now up to four years. My boat slept eight comfortably and it could squeeze in ten. Especially when the kids were smaller. Then when they were older...."

Venus interrupted, "Did your wife object to their going out?"

"Not at all. I was, and am, extremely into boat safety, and the kids learned it from the time they could walk."

"Why didn't you bring your boat here?"

"I'll buy another soon. Ron and Charlie practically grew up on that boat. I figured Ron would really enjoy it and use it if I left it behind. I suppose I could have him sail it here. Do you know anything about boats?"

"Not a thing. I've been on a couple here and there but never had any real interest in doing all the work I see some of my friends involved in. Didn't even know about your type of paint."

"Actually it's more a foam than a paint. Easy to put on and spread. I'm hoping to up the time between maintenance to six years."

"I guess that will really help the addicted boat owner, huh? What kind of boat will you get?"

"My preference is the really old wood boats that have been maintained or refurbished. The ones from composite or fiberglass are more common, but I'd just as soon not buy products made from petroleum-based anything. The wood ones are more efficient and better for the environment. If I get another it will be that type again. Yes, to answer your unspoken question, they are still made. I think more are made on the East coast than out here. I guess the old New Englanders value antiquity."

"You mean the stodgy old folks who never let you forget you're a flatlander, no matter how many years you've lived there? Friends of mine from Vermont who have lived there over thirty years are *still* considered flatlanders. How's that for absurd?"

"I agree," Greg laughed

"I thought all sailboats were made of fiberglass except the really, really expensive ones."

"No, you can get a fairly small oldie without breaking the bank. One day maybe you'll go out boat-shopping with me? Huh?"

"Sounds interesting." Venus answered. She was rather surprised that Greg assumed they'd see each other in the future, and was afraid he might be giving her a line.

As they spoke, Greg softly stroked her hand and then her arm. Both of them were astutely aware of the rising sexual tension between them. Each touch of Greg's hand on her arm sent shivers of longing through her.

"Are you cold?" Greg asked gently.

"No." Venus could feel herself blush. She was sure Greg was feeling the same intense of sexual energy she was, and she didn't know how long she could, or would, pretend it wasn't there. For the first time in eons, she could feel herself sexually stimulated and, amazingly, it was just by his holding her hand. "Wow, does this bode good stuff," she thought, "but then there are all sorts of questions about how he deals with women. Guess I'll just have to wait and see. Won't change anything right now." No sooner had those thoughts occurred to her then she knew she had a big decision to make.

"What are you doing when you leave this place?" asked Greg.

"I don't know. You have something in mind? You don't think I have to dance with Bill, do you? "

"No, you don't have to dance with Bill, and yeah, I do have something on my mind." Greg whispered, "How about I meet OM?"

Before her mind could kick in, she replied, "Sounds like a wonderful plan. You'll love him." Venus chuckled out loud, thinking to herself, "Right, we'll be with OM."

Venus stopped chuckling when Greg silently and swiftly bent over her and softly kissed her lips. She gasped and fully responded by running her tongue over his lips and moaning softly. She put her arms around his neck and delighted in his smell, his touch, his lips, his mouth.

Greg felt himself rising in a way that was powerful. He drew away, took both of her hands and arms, pulled her up from the bench and said, "Let's get out of here. Take off your shoes and you'll be more comfortable!" They just about ran back to the restaurant, said their goodbyes and left together in Greg's car. Even as he was driving Venus home, holding one of her hands in his, he could feel his body responding to her in a way he could not even begin to remember. Or control. All he could think about was feeling her, kissing her, getting her naked and aroused to…. "Stop that! You just met the woman," his mind was reprimanding. "Who is talking here? Brains, emotions or dick? You're acting like a seventeen-year-old." The other parts of him that weren't screaming said, "Sure does feel good."

After the Celebration

It didn't matter who in Greg was talking because by the time they reached Venus' front door, the two of them were all over each other. And it had only begun with a simple kiss that glossed over Venus' lips!

"Let's get in the house, please?" panted Venus "Not give the neighbors something to talk about."

They stumbled in, and as soon as the door was shut, Greg took Venus in his arms and then gently pulled his fingers through her hair. He whispered in a husky voice, "You may love green eyes, but I love auburn hair and I've been dying to do this since I saw you. Your hair, as well as you, are…" He never got out the next words as he slowly and thoroughly kissed her lips, her eyes, her neck, and then began to move his way down. Every touch was with just the right amount of gentleness, persuasiveness and passion. Venus felt him tightly against her, and his hard arousal increased her own sense of urgency - wanting all he had to offer. She could feel the growing moisture in her panties and was rather shocked by it. "Long time since that occurred," she mused. All thoughts left her mind as her body became totally enmeshed, entwined, and at one with Greg's.

"I want to taste and touch you, all of you. Now," Greg moaned.

"I want that too, but honestly, I've never done this or anything like this with someone I don't know – or for that matter with anyone I did know," Venus moaned in return.

"We're adults and we both know we want each other. The truth is, I feel I do know you, though I want to know you more. I want to know all of you," answered Greg.

Instead of replying, Venus took Greg by the hand and led him into her dark bedroom where they stumbled against each other and whatever was in the way to the bed. Gradually, Greg came back to being somewhat in control of himself, and in her dimly lit bedroom, he began to undress her. Slowly. After each piece of clothing was removed, he kissed, licked and stroked the area with reverence. Venus was grateful about the soft light, which made her wrinkled skin less noticeable. She realized how very self-conscious she was of her now aging body, even though she had

65

undergone a major outer transformation. All just passing thoughts as her body took over any discussions her mind was attempting to hold.

Greg didn't seem to be aware of Venus's perceived lack of perfection as he made his way down her body, methodically exploring, touching, licking and embracing each part of her. She hadn't believed she was capable of experiencing such heat and passion! It just kept growing in every part of her until she felt as if her belly and genitals were directly connected and needed to move on their very own. As he continued to caress her breasts, she could feel her body screaming for more and her responses to his lovemaking became more self-confident.

"God, you are incredible," he said, "you are so beautiful." As he continued to make love to her, he groaned, "You taste good, you smell good…."

Venus began to feel embarrassed, but he made quick work of that. Sensing her semi-withdrawal, he licked and sucked at her nipples with a gentleness - and then with an intensity - that made her cry out in passion and arch towards him, wanting all of him. She moved her hands so she could hold onto him as much as she could while kissing and licking him, sucking at his neck and lips. There were no thoughts, only bodies moving with each other and exploring. She flipped over so he could not continue to torture her with his caresses. "Stop! I want to taste and touch you too," she groaned. She reached for his erection and began to stroke it gently. When she put her mouth on it as he gasped in delight.

"Stop! I can take only so much!" Greg cried, and he gently turned her over, licking and kissing her stomach. When he spread her legs and began to suck her clitoris, moving his tongue from side to side as well as up and down and pushing his tongue deep within her, she could no longer hold back. Venus exploded into spasms of delight and saw stars.

"My God, you are beautiful when you come," said Greg. Then waiting no time whatsoever, he began once again to touch her all over - her breasts, stomach, legs. Finally with one finger in her vagina and then two, he went down on her again. She felt herself contract powerfully against his fingers, her climax was quick, easy and more powerful than before.

66

"This has never happened to me before. I've never come twice in one night, but please, come inside me," pleaded Venus, "I want to feel *you*."

"Yes." Greg was able to control himself with great effort, stroking her insides deeper and more demanding with each thrust. He finally came in a way he never remembered experiencing, and Venus exploded with him at exactly the same time.   .

The bliss was amazing for both of them.

"I've never ever had sex like this," Venus said. As if to emphasize her point, she repeated, "Never!" She laughed as she asked, "Where have you been hiding? You're scary! Must be all those other ladies you've practiced on."

"Beautiful Venus, the feelings are mutual. Practice only works on the technicalities, not on any emotional connection. I've never had sex like this before either. As to where I was, I'm guessing it just wasn't time for us to meet until now."

Greg and Venus lay together just *being*, enjoying the moment, present with each other, content. Content not to talk, not to do anything other than be. OM jumped on the bed and broke their silence, his motor loud and strong. Venus giggled, "Ah yes, there you are sweetie. OM, meet Greg, Greg meet OM. Chuckling, she said, "He came here to meet you sweetie."

"A handsome cat if I ever saw one. I see your attraction to him and his green eyes." He softly laughed as he gently kissed her once again.

"He's a small lion – just remember that!"

"Okay. Now, my dear, am I allowed to stay the night?"

Venus paused before she answered, wondering how she was might feel in the light of the day. To him she replied, "Yes, of course." To herself she said, "Oh well, I'll worry about that tomorrow. Now is definitely delicious." She curled up to Greg and they snuggled as if they had been together for countless years.

During the night, Venus had a dream that seemed realer than real. She and Greg were in another lifetime – in London in the early 1900's. She saw the two of them: she a teacher and he a merchant. He was very much in love with her and she with him. He had asked for her hand in marriage from her father, who was quite overjoyed with the union, as were all of the other family members on both sides of the family. She couldn't wait for their marriage, she was so excited. But as Venus viewed and participated in the dream, she could feel her stomach turning in fear. The week before the wedding, she watched her love, her fiancé, killed by the daughter of his next-door neighbor, a woman who was so unbalanced and jealous that she thought he should be marrying her instead.

Venus woke with a start, trembling and feeling hot all over her body. Greg immediately awakened and asked her what was wrong. She related the dream. "You know the way you said, 'I know you?' Well, if you believe in past lives, the dream shows we've been together before."

"I'm not sure I do," Greg answered while pulling her tightly against him.

"It was *so* real. I'm still shaking. Even if I sometimes don't believe in past lives, maybe there is a warning here for us." Venus was trying to make sense from the dream.

"The only warning may be one that tells us what we already know: our attraction to each other is huge. You think that could be it?" asked Greg. "Or do you think perhaps I wouldn't marry you?"

"No, the marriage thing is definitely not it," Venus continued, "It's something else. I don't know anything other than my heart is still thumping faster than usual."

"Without trying to make light of your dream, let's make your heart beat even harder but for a more pleasant reason. And mine too." Greg smiled at her, and began to caress her in a comforting manner, stroking her, petting her the way she did her cat. "Let's calm down the fear, and when you're ready we'll go for the fun! Okay with you?"

Venus could feel his hardness against her, and just that feeling aroused her and begged for more, more of him. More touches, more kisses, more hugs, more, just more. It had been a long dry spell.

Greg was very obliging and soon they were both passionately moving in rhythm until their explosive climaxes.

"Four for me in less than twelve hours! Pretty damn shocking, if I do say so myself," Venus laughed. "Never thought I was capable of that. You're good. Very good. Wanna stay around?"

"Damn right. I have every intention of doing just that!"

As they began to cuddle again, Venus felt the need to tell Greg about their first brief meeting. "Greg, I *did* meet you once before – at Discount Tires about two months ago. Only at that time I was going through a very long period of not liking myself very much. To hide, I wore beige and loose-fitting clothing, until one day I decided it was quite enough. Then I spent days and days getting rid of the ghosts from my past that had encouraged me to dress and feel that way. I'm not sure I'm totally done with everything, but I know I'm on my way. You see, the whole celebratory "coming-out" party was begun for me. I used to love to dress until it became what was expected of me in my marriage, and then when the marriage ended ten years ago, I thumbed my nose at everyone and there was a gradual decline from there. I am now back to being who I know I am – accepting my brains and totally knowing it's okay to look good. Hope this doesn't hit you the wrong way. But that's what is true."

"Nothing about you could hit me the wrong way at this point. I may sound shallow being bowled over by your beauty and our attraction, but I guess men are like that. No excuses for that, I might add. And yes, in retrospect, now that you mentioned it, I do remember you. I remember your beautiful face with gorgeous auburn hair that was so tightly pulled back that you probably got a headache from it. I wondered what made you dress like an old hippie. In the Boston area, I think because there are so many schools there, many women dressed the way you were dressed. I often wondered why they took their natural beauty and hid it. But, on the positive side, I'm glad to see you decided to clean-up your act. By the way, you did clean up beautifully," he laughed.

"Oh, I remember one other thing when I met you." Greg paused, then added gently, "When I offered you my hand, I actually felt a spark of electricity go between us."

"Oh my God! You did too? I felt it again this evening when you took my hand to dance with me. Oh dear, this is serious. Too much, too fast, too too…" Venus trailed off.

"No way, *too too*. We'll take this a day at a time and see where we go. I want to learn all about you and be with you, which I might add, has never happened to me before! I want to know you in all ways. Be flattered."

"Humph. I can see how you got ahead in the business world and why you are in charge! Well, just in case you're interested, Mr. All Things, I have never wanted to be with any man either. I guess we've just been too stuck on ourselves," Venus challenged.

"No way! I was never stuck on myself, it's just relationships were not what I wanted. I needed the safety of being by myself – or at least I thought I was safe by myself. Never wanted to bring home any woman after the divorce; just wanted peace and quiet. Didn't want to get trapped again."

"How were you trapped? Venus asked, recognizing too late that she was possibly opening up a can of worms.

Greg told Venus about how Judy had become pregnant in his senior year of college just when he thought it was time for them to break up and see others. How he did the "honorable" thing and married her, staying in the marriage until their kids were teens. How, after that, he never had any real relationships. "In fact," Greg said, "Judy and I as husband and wife, had practically no relationship the whole time. It was pretty empty for both of us. I wonder what type of role model for relationships we gave our kids. That's pretty painful to me as I've thought about it. We didn't even sleep in the same bed for the last seven years.

"So when I was traveling, I screwed around – all one-night stands, women I met through work. I knew what I was doing wasn't the right thing and I can't say I'm particularly proud of myself, but that's what I did and how I handled our lackluster marriage. I have no idea what Judy did – especially after she went back to school. All I know is I brought home money for her to do what she wanted to do, and I played with the kids. It was our unspoken agreement. When I look back at it, it really was sick."

"My marriage was pretty sick too," said Venus. "I became Mrs. Alex, dressing the part, being the social butterfly and the good little country-club wife. After a while I hated it, but continued because it was something that was expected of me – you know, I had to be a "good girl." The only thing I did that challenged the marriage and my parent's values was to finish my schooling. They all hated when I wasn't there twenty-four/seven at Alex's calling. I hated my behavior and myself, and when Alex finally found his young chick, I was relieved, although disappointed. I let myself do absolutely *nothing* to make myself look good or fit into any of his society bullshit. We've been divorced over ten years and it's only six weeks ago that I decided it was time to get rid of all that baggage I was carrying especially about looking bad is something good. In the past, it felt like I was thumbing my nose at all of them. But, in the chemistry department, they didn't care about my appearance. In fact, if I had continued to play the role of auburn-haired Barbie, I wouldn't have gotten as far as I have. I even refused to date anyone or go anywhere. Isn't it

70

amazing how decisions we make from our old beliefs end up biting us in our asses?" Venus muttered.

She continued, "My story was a little different, but in essence, the same sentiment. Never Again! I refuse to give myself away to any man, so just remember, I'm too old to begin to play the role of good girl. Won't do it! Don't ask. That's why maybe we ought to play this out really, really slowly with no promises, no commitments, okay?"

"So, am I the first guy you've actually been out with since your divorce ten years ago?"

"Every once and a while I'd go out with someone, mostly to appease my friends," Venus said. "Never saw anyone more than once or at the most twice. No sex. Didn't even want it!"

"Wait, *you* didn't want sex, *you* the sexiest woman I have ever met didn't want sex?" Greg felt a huge relief when he realized Venus didn't get involved with men. In fact, he felt pretty special that she had picked him, and he could already feel a possessive streak ten miles long.

"Right," laughed Venus, "no other men. Does that qualify me as a born-again-virgin?"

"Um, I'll think on that." Without pausing a beat, Greg smiled and continued, "No, it doesn't. This may sound odd for a guy to say, especially after seemingly just meeting you, but I've been with a lot of women; and you, you're different. Yes, you scare the hell out of me but I want to be with you and see where we go. And, if there is anything to that dream of yours…."

He paused to kiss her gently, then quickly changed the subject by asking, "How about showing me some of the local beaches in the area tomorrow? I really haven't had a chance to do much sight-seeing since I moved here. Beaches are my first priority. I know La Jolla and that's about it."

The Next Day

Venus rolled over to look at the clock and noticed it was just beginning to get light outside. She was quite relieved when Greg left the subject of relationships for the benign topic of sight seeing. "What are your time constraints?" she asked.

"I'm yours for the day. How about showering with me, then we can grab something to eat, get your car, bring it here and then I'll drive us over to my place and pick up some clothes."

Venus went from being calm and relaxed to panicked. "Shower with him!" she thought, "so he can see my lumps and bumps and wrinkled skin? Oh my God, what do I do? Isn't it weird how I just mentioned to Sally how I was so glad I wasn't shopping for a bathing suit, that the clothes were more than enough! Dear Lord, if I have a bathing suit, I haven't put it on in years." Then another part of her chimed in, "Good Grief, we've had sex so much, he's been down on me, and I'm worried about my wrinkles?" The two parts argued, getting nowhere.

After throwing on her robe and feeding OM, who had finally jumped off the bed, Venus went to get Greg a towel. She heard the shower running and knew she was stalling him from seeing her naked in the morning light. Her mind was still telling her, "Forget it" while her body and heart were telling her, "Go for it!"

While Venus spent the next several minutes trying to look busy, Greg, soaking wet, walked to the entrance of the shower and said, "I'm waiting for you. Please come in."

Venus took a deep breath, slowly took off her robe and backed deeply into the shower. Greg turned her to him and pulled her towards his chest and hugged her. Just as Venus began to breathe again, he pushed her away and began to look her up and down, ever so slowly. Her first instinct was to cover herself with her hands, but she dropped her head and just let him stare. "You have a beautiful body, Venus."

"Once I did but now it's filled with wrinkles, crepe paper skin and…." Venus didn't get a chance to finish because Greg again pulled her to himself and began to kiss her passionately. First her mouth, then her neck and - as he worked his way down to her breasts, he moved the shower heads off them both, allowing the steam to fill the room and not get in their faces. Then, kneeling down, he put his fingers in her wet opening, hitting her g-spot with perfection and sucking her clit until she was crazy with desire. Venus stopped thinking – about anything.

She couldn't get enough of him as he touched her with his mouth and hands. Her whole body was on fire from his caresses. When she thought she could take it no longer, she gasped as her body exploded into spasms of ecstasy. He stood up and turned her so her back was to him. Never releasing his touch from her clit, he continued stroking her with his thumb while his other fingers probed her. She was ready to collapse when he entered her. As he began to move his body in deep thrusts, she felt herself moving with him in a rhythm that brought her to another level of ecstasy, another passionate climax.

Venus turned around and kissed Greg in a manner she couldn't remember kissing anyone before. "My God, I thought older men couldn't get it up so much," she exclaimed.

"I'm not most older men. And you are an incredible turn-on. I love it. Nothing like this has ever ever happened to me before! There's something you are, something you have, something that just gets my mind and body on fire. Give me some recoup time and I want more," Greg moaned as he kissed her once again.

"At this rate, we'll never get to those beaches you want to see," Venus murmured.

"All right, let's get dressed and eat. I'm starving. Woman, for the time being, you have worn me out."

"I'll just throw on a pair of shorts; the water's too cold to go in."

"Sounds like an idea to me. All I want to do is find the beaches and walk with this lovely lady by my side."

After Venus made them vanilla-flavored coffee with freshly-ground beans, a wonderful spinach-and-onion omelet and whole wheat toast, Greg asked for a tour through her house.

There were four bedrooms, all brightly decorated; four bathrooms with a huge master bath done in shades of white, cobalt blue and green accessories with a mammoth walk in shower with many adjustable heads (as Greg had discovered earlier.) All the rooms were comfortably furnished and looked lived in. Greg, pleasantly surprised commented, "You know, we have the same taste in furniture, same colors and even the need for bright light. What's that about? I love your house.

Reminds me of the house I grew up in." He hastily added, "Only in the amount of light. My folks sure didn't mix styles like you do. Did I mention I also favor Chinese furniture?"

Venus had always thought her home was furnished in "Venus Eclectic" and no one could possibly have the same taste. After Alex had gone, she redid the whole house in *her* taste. In the living room, she had mixed together very modern furniture with several beautiful antique Chinese pieces, and there were huge live plants all over each of the rooms, many in Oriental containers. The dining room had a very large Asian-style table with ten chairs covered in material of pale multi-shades of greens ranging to blue. Splashes of bright jewel tones livened up the many tones of green. All the windows in the house were treated simply, allowing light to enter. The ceilings were vaulted, with sky-lights in the master bath, walk-in closets and foyer. The house had over one-hundred-eighty degrees of windows for exquisite views of the ocean. Venus thought people who bought a house on the ocean, and then covered up all the windows were a bit out-of-their minds. She herself had shades that blocked out the blinding rays of the setting sun, but even when the shades were closed, they were transparent; the view of the beautiful Pacific could be seen through them. Her floors were a light bamboo with scattered Oriental rugs, some with large modern designs and some with unusual antique Chinese designs. Flowers were always on her kitchen counters, which were soft mint-green granite with dark chocolate specks and there was an abundance of pale-green stained-wood cabinets. She had received the house as a guilt "gift" from Alex after their divorce, a gift she gladly accepted. She knew he didn't want the house anyway, he felt it was way too small for a man of his means. If he hadn't offered it, she would have fought like a tiger for it. She had put so much of herself and her time in it, even before she redecorated. She felt blessed knowing it was paid for and all she was responsible for were the taxes and insurance. "That's enough," she often thought. She truly adored the house, even though it was too big for her. She and OM roamed through it blessedly happy.

"Let me take you outside. That's where the real beauty is, and my sanctuary."

Venus took Greg's hand and led him out the side door to a magically beautiful place.

Because the house was on two lots and there wasn't much of a back yard, except for the Pacific, she had planted magnificent gardens on each side of the house. "I definitely have a green thumb."

First Venus took him to the side that had orange, lemon, plum, apricot and grapefruit trees with rose gardens and beds of flowers. Greg was impressed and then was awed when Venus took him to her favorite place, a gazebo she had made into a serene meditation garden for herself. There were hanging plants all around the periphery and large potted plants placed strategically around the sitting area. It was quite a large gazebo and Greg could see how, when she had been married, it was a perfect place to entertain. But now it had a peace, beauty, and tranquility that was breathtaking.

"This is truly exquisite, Venus. You did all this yourself?"

"I did. When I was married, Alex made fun of me for wanting to create an outdoor place that was peaceful and beautiful. He wanted only the gardeners to work around the house. Didn't look good if his wife had her hands in the dirt. God forbid I wasn't *the perfect wife* and beautifully dressed and coiffed all the time. Most of the time I gave in to his wishes. After he left, I felt like I'd gotten out of my own self-sentenced prison and immediately set forth to create my magic space. I love it here." Greg took Venus' hand and they walked back into her house together.

"Your home reflects you, and is beautiful. I love everything in it.

"Thank you. I never thought anyone liked what I did to the house after Alex left. You know - my taste, never mind the colors. I feel blessed to have this home. I've loved the peace and tranquility the ocean provides, and I adore my gardens." Venus asserted.

"Greg, if you look out to my back yard, you'll see cliffs and more cliffs. Sometimes they are unstable and people get hurt walking on them. and also hurt the habitat. As you can see, there is special fencing there to protect the habitat, with lots of plants to hold the soil down. The fence also protects our property from people climbing into our back yard. I don't particularly like having it there, but it really is important."

"Yeah, that makes sense. I think I like this area better than LaJolla to live in. It's much more peaceful."

"When do you think you'll buy a place?"

"Once SeaFoam is really up-and-running. I guess within the year."

As Greg roamed about, he was more and more impressed with this lady named Venus and told her so. He laughed, "I'm kind of in shock about our compatibility of values, amazed at the beauty you've created, your concern and caring for the environment, your sensitivity, and how great we are together in bed!'

Venus took Greg's hand as she said quietly, "Me too."

By the time they ate and finished the tour, then went to Greg's house where he was going to change his clothes, it was late morning.

"Good God. How can I bring you into this place? It's so cold, so unappealing. Please don't judge me on the house I'm in now. This isn't me. It's so unaesthetic and too. . . "

"Hey, I know it is temporary. You've already told me that. But it does serve your purpose for now, doesn't it?"

"Well yes," he paused, "but I want you to be in more elegant surroundings and more warmth, to match who you are. None of this is my furniture. The only stuff I've unpacked are the books and things I need for work, and a few towels. The rest of my belongings are in storage. Actually, I didn't bring much because I wanted to start with a clean slate. Only some dishes and stuff ya need in the kitchen. Jeez, I sound like an interior decorator or some wuss."

"Honestly, Greg, I'm not judging you on your house and you don't sound like a wuss. After all I've heard about you and experienced, I know you're not." Venus laughed as she continued, "To have picked me, I know you have excellent taste. Anyway, what do you expect from a rental? Just because it's in mighty LaJolla on the beach doesn't mean a damn thing. So now let me see the rest of this place, okay?"

When they reached the kitchen, Greg grabbed Venus and hugged her, then quickly added a deep kiss that knocked both of them for a loop. "We keep getting better, huh?"

As Greg was returning his attention to their plan of visiting the various beaches in the area, he noticed a long white envelope half in and half out of his door. "That's curious," he mused, "I thought this house was too tight to have something shoved in the door. And who would put something in the back door anyway?"

As Venus pulled away, regaining her lost composure, Greg went over to the envelope and put it on the counter unopened.

Venus sighed, "Yes, we do keep getting better. But now, about getting to our tour," she sighed, "what beach do you want to visit first?

76

My favorites are north of here. Guess that's because I live north of here. I love Carlsbad for walking, parts of Solana Beach for rocks and sounds and Yogananda's Beach in Encinitas for surfing and the gardens above it, and the hominess of Moonlight Beach."

Greg grinned, realizing how they were both affected by their kiss. "Doesn't matter to me. You pick."

"Well, let's just go up the coastline and stop at each of them or until we don't want to stop anymore. How's that sound? Let's take water though. There are some great restaurants on Highway 1, including a fabulous health food restaurant if we want to stop and eat. First: Solana Beach, my favorite. There are wonderful rocks there that the tides keep turning and tossing. The sounds are exquisite, and rock collecting is fabulous."

When they got to the beach, Greg was amazed. "This is like a special kind of music. I love it here and get why you do too." Because the tide was out, they were able to walk the beach in silence. As they walked, they held each others hand, finally sitting down to watch the water and the way it ebbed and flowed. Greg put his arm around Venus and said, "This is beyond beautiful. To think, this is something that is available to everyone here! I love that. I don't know if you know that on the East coast, almost all the beaches are private, yet here there has to be public access to them. I wish they'd do that on the Cape, but it won't happen. It's a shame," he sighed.

As they sat there, Greg picked up a few rocks and tossed them into the ocean. "Boy that felt good. Now if only I had more energy."

"I love throwing rocks. I do it all the time," and she too began tossing rocks into the tide. "It lets out any frustrations I have. Normally I have a lot more than I have right now too. That's because you wore me out," and she blushed.

Greg pretended not to notice her flushed cheeks, "I'm with you, a few rocks will be enough today. I think we wore each other out. I seem to have no hostility left in my body. How about you?"

"Nope," she grinned. "Amazing what great sex does for the body, mind and spirit."

After about an hour there, Venus asked, "Shall we stay here or are you up for another beach?"

"Let's go."

Moonlight Beach in Encinitas was the next beach they visited. They parked on the street and Venus pointed out all the beautiful flowers lining the walkway. "The purple ones are statis – you often see them in florist bouquets. The orange ones are California poppies, and I don't remember the names of the others. Most of them will grow here if you just give the ground some water. I love that about this area. I just needed to brag about the scenery." Venus chuckled, "You know, we've only gone a couple miles from where we were and yet it so different!"

"It's amazing," Greg said.

"Yes. I figured we couldn't see them all, so I'll take you to some of my favorites today. When we're in San Diego, I'll take you to other beaches like Ocean Beach and the Cliffs and Coronado, but for this area, these are my picks."

"I've been to Coronado because of business meetings, but haven't been on the actual beach. I understand they have a doggie beach there too. Is that so?"

"Yes, it's quite big. They also have one in Del Mar. The tides wash out all the poop and pee. Sometimes you can go there and there's not much beach - it depends on the tides. Everyone who has dogs and lives near there watches the tides. Oh, there's another one at the end of Ocean Beach. It's pretty good too. The San Diego River runs into it and out to the ocean. Folks also take their dogs to Fiesta Island. You can tell Charlie all these beaches exist for doggie lovers. You have to clean up after them, but the freedom it offers the critters is really quite wonderful. Unless of course, you get a vicious dog."

"Wow, I'll share that info with him. I think his whole family will be ecstatic to hear this!"

"This beach is sort of quaint."

"Yeah, it's got a homey feeling. If you walk up the coast, when the tide is out, there are steps leading up to the street. Like you said, all the beaches here have access, and if you ride along the coast roads, you'll see the openings between some very very ritzy homes. It's that way in LaJolla too. Lots of folks are real snobby about it, but thank goodness, it's the law. I don't have steps on my property, but even if I did, I'd still be glad of the public access. Of course, a lack of steps doesn't keep out the public anyway."

They spent another hour sitting on Moonlight Beach walking as far as they could toward Carlsbad. Venus said, "Sometimes when the tide is low, you can actually walk from here to the Carlsbad beach, but you probably couldn't get back because the tide would be in by that point. If you were able to go from here to Carlsbad, you could see my house."

"I thought so. You're about what. . . quarter of a mile up?"

"Probably so."

"What about swimming?"

"You really have to be careful out here because of rip tides. They'll pull even great swimmers under and away from shore. Do you see how many life guards there are here? Let's go to Carlsbad, and you'll see clearly what I mean. In the meantime, put some lotion on; you're burning" cautioned Venus. "Good God, I'm already taking care of him" she thought to herself. "That's dangerous!"

Greg laughed, "You put the lotion on me, then I'll put some on you."

"That'll work."

Even while rubbing sunscreen on each other, both of them were totally aware of their e sexual energy.

"Boy, all I have to do is think about last night or this morning and I'm hard. Damn, you're great Venus."

Venus grinned and grabbed Greg's hand.

As they began their walk onto the Carlsbad beach, Greg said, "I can't believe the physical beauty around here. No wonder people will move to Southern California, "in spite of the earthquakes, fires and traffic," as you so aptly pointed out. Good Grief. Was it just the other night when you said that? I feel as if we've been together forever."

"Yes, it was the other night, and damn, I feel that way too," replied Venus, caressing Greg's hand.

"Why the *damn*?"

"It's kinda scary. I have never felt so relaxed and content with a man in my entire life. "I'm surprised and grateful, but I don't want to rush things. We need to play this by ear."

They sat silently for a long time being at one with each other, the ocean, and the breezes.

Finally Greg responded to her voiced concerns. "I don't want to rush into anything either, but I do know that I've never even come close to the experiences we've already shared intimately. I don't get it, and I want to see you again, if that's okay with you. But I have the weird sense you think I'm a real lady's man, am I right?"

"How intuitive of you! Yes. I did think that, but I believe my thoughts are rapidly changing. You do know that practically every single woman in my whole building is after you, don't you? That's scary! I don't want a man who is available to everyone. Furthermore, I am cautious. Nothing like this has ever happened to me, and I don't know how to handle it, or myself or you. Even when we've disagreed, it's been in good humor and consideration for one other . Remember when we disagreed about Bill's energy being so angry? Doesn't that seem like eons ago?"

Greg nodded.

"Anyway, *yes* of course I want to see you. It's *me* I'm concerned with. Don't want to fall into any old traps or fears about men. Or myself."

"I know the feeling. It is mutual. I *know* this is something big for both of us. I *know* this is no fling. Just doesn't feel that way to me and, I'm pretty sure to you either! You have absolutely nothing to worry about regarding other women. I am totally captivated and entranced by you. Do I make myself clear?"

"I guess I just don't know for how long. That's another thing that is scary. I feel like a teenager again, which is mighty uncomfortable. You know, we're both going to be fried if we don't get out of this sun soon," Venus declared, changing the subject dramatically.

"If it makes you feel any better, I feel like a teen myself. Pretty silly, but wonderful"

Venus smiled, acknowledging how he had responded to her concerns.

"I'm hungry. What do you recommend?" Greg asked abruptly.

"Do you like Thai?"

"One of my favorites. Where?"

"You really like Thai? Another thing in common. Arg. This is serious," and Venus snickered. "There are several Thai restaurants around here. I'll take you to my favorite."

As they walked off the beach, with Greg's arm around her waist and Venus snuggling in towards him, Venus had a strange feeling someone was watching them. She had had the feeling earlier in the day, but didn't see anyone she knew. She asked Greg if anyone could be watching them.

He was surprised by her question and responded, "I've sometimes had that feeling lately also, but I've never pursued it. I wonder why we both have had it."

"I don't know about you, but there is an energy I've been feeling, and the only way I can describe it is that someone is watching. It doesn't feel good."

Greg paused before he spoke again. "I do know the feeling. I have no idea what it means, but I'm going to pay a lot more attention to it, especially now that I know you're feeling it too. We'll see what we can do about it."

The subject was dropped, but Venus kept feeling invisible eyes on her until they went in to eat.

***

At dinner, Venus and Greg continued to discover how much they had in common. Venus was thrilled that Greg had a strong spiritual belief but no religious convictions whatsoever. "I think religion is made by man for man, and frankly, I think most of it is a bunch of beliefs perpetrated by some old fogies. I believe in some sort of a Supreme Being, but the rules and junk, I think are man-made"

"I'm grateful you feel that way," Venus answered. "I have a really difficult time being with someone who has strong religious convictions. I seem to let my spiritual side grow with my own awareness of how truly magnificent the Great Spirit is. Does that make sense?"

Greg laughed, "Yes it does. But I have to tell you I have gotten into more religious debates – even in college – than you could count. Fortunately Judy felt more or less the way I did. I think if Judy were enormously religious it would have been a deal-breaker even when I was in high school."

"Do you believe in intuition?" asked Venus.

"Well, the jury is still out on that. Sometimes I do when I certainly can't explain how I know certain things – like the feeling I had about you thinking I was a lady's man. At other times I'm at a loss to connect with it or even to consider what occurs as any more than coincidence. I know you're a staunch believer, so I'm sort of willing to learn."

"What's this *sort of*?"

"Well, you know, you're a scientist. How do you prove it?"

"How do you prove Spirit? You feel it. I feel intuition."

"Okay, I get that, but give me some leeway to learn from you?" Greg snickered, putting his hands in the air in a questioning mode.

"We'll see," laughed Venus. "At least you're not totally denying anything. Kudos to you. So Greg, on a less important note, what other kinds of food do you like, not that right now I could eat anything?"

"Love Southern Italian and dry red wine. How about you?"

"Dear me, exactly the same. And salads, ripe fresh fruit, freshly baked bread and of course, dark chocolate. I eat fish, and sometimes turkey. Otherwise, no meat at all. I think I could probably do without turkey too."

"That's a go for almost everything. Except I like milk chocolate better and I do occasionally eat meat."

"Well, there's hope for you. Maybe I can train you to like the good stuff or better yet, when I get a box of chocolates, you can eat the milk chocolates and I'll eat the dark. You can eat meat wherever else you want to but not at my house. I don't care about what you do outside."

"Ah, in spite of your fears you really are planning ahead, aren't you," Greg gloated as he grabbed her hand and kissed it. Without missing a beat, he continued. "Neither my boys nor their families eat meat, so you aren't alone with this. But I have so many business meetings, it makes it somewhat impossible if I show up and refuse meat all the time. I do mostly, though. Does that pass your criteria for reasonable?" Greg quipped. "My kids are absolute in their non-meat thing. How about yours?"

"I am sooo transparent sometimes, but back to the question. "My kids are vehement, adamant, and whatever else you want to call it, about no meat. I'm probably the most flexible," she observed as she kissed his hand back.

Dinner went quickly as the two of them found no lack of conversation about everything from soup to nuts and back again. There seemed to be no topic that was unapproachable – although they didn't talk about Greg's parents. The relationship was so new that she was sure that too, could be grist for the mill at a later date. After a wonderful meal,

Venus was groaning and holding her stomach at the same time. "I haven't eaten so much in forever. Good thing we did a lot of walking or I'd be fat as a pig."

"Don't forget the other exercises we were doing all night and this morning," Greg whispered in her ear.

"Believe me, I won't! And I haven't!"

As they rode to Venus' house, there was a quiet about both of them. Each seemed aware that soon they wouldn't be together. When they kissed goodbye, it was like magnets being pulled apart, and when he finally got in his car and drove away, she experienced a huge sense of loss that threw her for a loop!

After two full days of sight-seeing, talking, laughing and getting to know each other, and full evenings and mornings of making incredible love, Venus was wondering how the following weeks were going to play out. Unfortunately (or was it fortunately?) she had a funny feeling that scared the hell out of her. She'd heard others talk about love at first sight, but she wasn't sure she believed in that idea. Yet at this point, nothing else described what she was feeling and *that* was scary! "Good grief, I've known the man only two and one half days and can't find anything wrong with him except he prefers milk chocolate. I have to talk to Sally."

***

When Greg finally got home that night, he noticed the unopened envelope on the counter. It was addressed to him in bold computer-generated type. Inside was a single piece of cheap paper on which was the same type. As Greg read the words, he couldn't help thinking someone was trying to pull his leg. "YOUR LIFE IS WORTH NOTHING ANY MORE." He contemplated who might have sent that kind of letter, which was clearly addressed to him. He wondered, "What do you do with a letter like this? The police would think I am nuts. I guess it's best to say someone is just doing a sick thing they think is funny." Taking the letter and refolding it, he carefully put it in the kitchen drawer.

Sally and Venus

"Venus! Tell me how your evening went with Greg. I was out of town all weekend and just got home. Come over and let's have a glass of wine. Joe will be out till about eight tonight."

"I'm coming right over." It was times like these that Venus really appreciated how close together they lived – about a mile from each other. They both loved their homes overlooking the ocean; Venus loved the smells and views, while Sally was always swooning over the sounds. Even though they didn't technically live in the same towns, (Venus in Encinitas, and Sally in Carlsbad) they could walk to each other's places and often did.

Sally answered the door immediately and did a double-take on seeing her friend. Venus' chin was one massive beard-burn and there were marks on her neck too. Sally could just imagine all the other places they might be! "I see what you've been up to," she cracked. While Sally was pouring them each a big glass of wine, Venus sighed and said, "Oh Sally, I think I'm in trouble" and her eyes filled with tears.

"Why are you in trouble?"

"Well, you saw us leave the party Friday night. Good thing you were gone for the weekend because I definitely was *not* available."

"You mean to say you spent the *whole weekend* with him?"

"Yeah."

"Well, how was it? Are you going to tell me?"

"Fabulous, except for those few senior embarrassments. The first time we made love," Venus luxuriated in it again, "it really was making love. It was as if we had been together for eons, and I was only a little embarrassed. We were in my bedroom but I was so grateful the lights were low. Only a couple times did I feel wrinkled or droopy, but those feelings and fears vanished immediately as more important things were taking place." Venus grinned. "But it was the next morning when he wanted me to take a shower with him. . . Arg. I was stalling and totally shy again – after being made love to all the night before! It's not that he hadn't seen every square nano-inch of me, but this was in broad daylight – ya know? Scared me to think what he thought of my aging body."

"So what did you do?"

"I finally couldn't stall any longer. I'd fed OM and puttered about the bathroom trying to look busy. He called me to *please* come in the shower, so finally I dropped the towel and went in to him and hugged him. Damn, he pushed me away to look me up and down. I thought I'd die – until he started really turning me on. Oh, he also told me how beautiful I was. Did I believe it? Well, I don't know, but he certainly got my attention with the attention he paid to my sexual parts. I loved it and soon quickly lost all my inhibitions. We spent the weekend together in harmony, sexuality and comfort. How's that? Scares the shit out of me!"

"So your initial feelings were right and you fell for him big and hard. Right?"

"Yup."

"Will you see him again?"

"If he calls."

"Is there some reason you think he won't?"

"No, just old insecurities. I may need to let him pursue me; you know, men-hunters, women-gatherers. But I don't know how I'd feel if I didn't see him. And honestly, what is even scarier is I think he feels the same way. I guess I will see him, as they say, around the campus. He will be working with Will from our department for the next couple weeks. It'll be a challenge to my new self to be able to work without constantly reminding myself how phenomenal this weekend was."

"Isn't it great to know that your intuitive self knew that, from the second you met him?"

"It only knew the sexy part, but yeah, I guess so. Now I just need to relax and not lose myself to another man. He's really quite wonderful: smart, sexy, funny, gentle, compassionate, loves OM and other critters, and on and on but I don't want to bore you. And in bed, holy moly! The sparks just fly. He even told me how beautiful my old body is. Whew! I'm still not sure how I feel about all of this."

"Aside from the fact that you're cute as hell and repeating yourself, I know what you mean. I went through that with Joe the first several times I was nude with him. I kept wanting to cover myself up because, in clothes, I don't look that bad. He kept ripping off the covers and telling me I was silly and absurd. I agree with your *Argh*."

"So, you'll wait for him to call. It sounds like from everything you've told me, and the stuff you haven't said but I can see in your eyes, there won't be any question about to whether; it's just when."

"Sally," Venus implored, "do you think I ought to play hard to get?"

"Venus, my dear," laughed Sally, "you've all ready been got."

Venus and Greg at work

Venus went back to work on Monday morning slightly sore in places she had forgotten got sore, but she was managing nicely. She thought about going to Will's office to say hello to Greg, but stopped herself, only because the phone rang.

"Hello, Beautiful Lady, how are you?"

Venus' heart immediately started to pound, "Hello, Handsome Man, I'm splendid. How about you?" She heard her voice dropping and getting sexier; it seemed to do it all on its own.

"Now that I've said hello, I'm doing much better. How about dinner tonight? Will that work for you? I feel like we've been apart months."

"I hate to admit it, but me too. And yes, I'd love to. Can you leave about five-thirty and drop by my office?"

"Will do. Until then, think of me kissing you and…"

"Stop! I am already; no need to describe any more. I'll see you later." Venus blew a kiss into the phone before she hung up. "I've got it bad and that ain't good…I think that's how the song goes."

As soon as she hung up from Greg, the phone rang again. It was Bill calling. Venus was rather surprised to hear from him. He chatted with her for a while, then asked, "How about going out with me tonight, maybe a movie and dinner?"

Venus hesitated slightly, "I'm sorry, but I have plans tonight. I think maybe I should tell you that Greg and I are dating and it probably isn't a good idea for you and me to go out at this time. I guess that's the best way I can say this. I thank you for thinking of me." Venus sighed to herself and thought, "Great! Just what I need!"

Bill paused and said, "Thanks for your truthfulness. I hope you and Greg have a wonderful time, but I have to tell you, I'm jealous of Greg." He chuckled, "You should be dating me. But I'll survive. Talk to you later." And with that, Bill hung up. He was riled, upset and his insides felt on fire. He also knew there was probably nothing he could do. When Bill got off the phone he had just about reached his boiling point and he couldn't figure out why. As he paced around his office, he found himself swearing and banging things. "I don't like my current behavior and I don't like feeling explosive. What do I do now?" he questioned himself. "Jealousy sucks and so does this crazy feeling yet I want them to break up."

The morning continued to be full of surprises.

When Venus hung up, Glenda knocked on her office door and told her that Rita, from Greg's company, wanted to talk to her.

"Send her in, Glenda."

***

Rita was truly a beautiful woman. "Petite, lovely and stylishly dressed," thought Venus. "About five-feet-four inches, with a perfect figure, impeccably dressed, manicured and coiffed. She surely knows how to put together an outfit to flatter her violet eyes and bring out the best of her features. She looks in great physical shape with shapely legs, a tight butt and tiny waist. She makes it look effortless to look so stupendous!" Venus found herself somewhat envying her youth.

When Rita spoke, her voice was well-modulated and her enunciation perfect with not a hint of a Boston accent, unlike many of the people Venus had met. Not only was Rita lovely to look at and hear, she seemed to be amazingly competent in setting up the new SeaFoam office. Venus wondered why Rita had left the Boston area. "What does it take for a single woman to move three-thousand miles away?" She knew she herself couldn't do it, unless there was something stupendous for her at the other end. But then, Venus knew she was truly a homebody and never really desired to move from her Southern California home.

Again she wondered if Rita and Greg had ever had an affair and found that she was feeling a little jealous, an emotion she did not appreciate. She pushed those thoughts out of her mind as Rita began to ask her questions about what temporary services she recommended for the start-up company. Venus stared at her, wondering what she was really there for. Venus knew absolutely nothing about hiring temporary "anythings" or "anybodies;" she was a chemist and didn't get involved with that sort of thing.

Rita said, "Sorry, I was unaware you didn't have anything to do with that sort of thing. Hope I haven't bothered you."

"No of course not," answered Venus. "It must be lonely just hanging out with these guys. Have you met anyone here? Any women you might hang out with? If I didn't have my friend Sally and some other gals, I'd probably go nuts."

"No, no one yet. I've been so busy trying to get the business set up, I've gone home and crashed each night. But I am sure in a couple of days, I'll have the time. I saw you leave with Greg the other night. He's a nice man."

Venus listened as Rita spoke but as soon as she mentioned Greg, all of her senses went haywire. She felt something weird in what Rita was saying and a strange energy coming from her. She didn't know what to make of it, but she sure didn't trust it.

Rita continued, "You know he has a girlfriend in Boston, so don't get too attached."

Venus internally gasped, but kept her face unemotional while saying, "No, I didn't know about any girlfriend, but I've just met him, so I don't think that is anything I need to worry about."

"Well, it was nice talking to you. See you around," said Rita as she left the office.

***

Venus sat almost paralyzed at her desk and had to breathe deeply to keep herself from falling apart. "I will not do this again. I will not act like I'm four years old and assume everything told to me is true. I will ask Greg, and if it's true, I'll deal with it. At first I thought he might be a lady's man, but then he was so real with me during the weekend. I must stop my awful imagination from making up stories! I will simply ask him what's going on and then see where that takes me."

The rest of the morning and the afternoon dragged. As Venus filled out numerous forms and answered questions from whomever and wherever, her heart, mind and emotions kept replaying Rita's conversation.

To help herself calm down, Venus began to meditate which helped her. She was very surprised at how quickly the time had passed.

That Evening

Finally it was five-thirty and Venus affirmed, "I can handle this. I *will* handle this.

When Greg arrived, he looked at her with awe. She was wearing a sleeveless lemon-yellow shell with a pencil skirt of blues, greens and yellows. She had on blue medium-heeled sandals and her hair was pulled back in a ponytail with tendrils hanging down the side of her head. He whistled.

"Aside from looking positively gorgeous, you look upset" he said as he approached her and tried to kiss her.

"Greg, Rita was in here today asking some silly stuff."

"Rita? What does she want from you and your office? That makes no sense."

"She said, among other things, that you were involved with another woman in Boston."

"She said WHAT? That is not true. Ask any of my men. Ask my son or daughter-in-law. I'll give you their telephone numbers! I don't understand that. Why did she say that?" Greg was clearly upset at the bomb Rita had dropped on the two of them. His expression convinced Venus that he was telling the truth.

"I think she's jealous of us being together. Have you known her long? I had a funny feeling about her even before she said that."

"No, I've only known her about six months when she worked in Boston with the other office. She did a great job; very smart, quick, helpful. Came with good references."

"I think she has the hots for you and she was jealous you were with me."

"No. I can't believe that. You think she's jealous of you? You think that's her story? I will talk to her."

"Now what in heaven could you say? 'Are you jealous of Venus? Why did you tell her I was involved with another woman?' She'd have to deny she said anything like that, and then it would be her word against mine. I don't want to create an argument between Rita and me, but maybe that's what she's looking for. Don't say anything, even though I truly think I'm right on. Let's see if anything else happens. I think if she does her work well, then so be it. Just keep an eye on her. I simply don't trust her."

"I'll do as you wish, but I don't want *anyone* coming between us. Listen, Lady, I've waited too long for you. Do you understand? I want you to really get that! And now can I kiss you?"

"Yup. Absolutely!" Venus felt herself melt into Greg in a way that was delicious, sexy, and sensual. Once again, she was delighted and surprised at how well they fit.

"If we don't leave this office soon, I'll lock the door and just have you for dinner," Greg growled. "You turn me on in ways I never thought possible, but I guess I already said that to you."

"Yes, and as I already said, the feelings are exquisitely mutual. Not to change the subject, but there's a great pizza place I know of in Leucadia, the best! Whoops, forgot to ask you, do you like pizza? They have a Thai pizza that's delicious. There's chicken, peanuts, peanut sauce, cilantro and whatever other stuff you want. I sometimes get it with shrimp too."

"Thai pizza, too, this is fabulous! Thai food the other night, Thai pizza tonight. Let's go. Then I'll have you for dessert. We'll take one car so that is sure to happen!"

"Works for me."

***

It was a moonless night and quite dark by the time they finished their Thai pizza. Then they strolled on the beach, each of them feeling a profound peace and comfort. Eventually Greg took her in his arms and said, "We need to get out of here. I'm hungry for dessert."

"No objections here."

They began the drive towards Venus' house when the car jeered wildly and there was an explosion. "Sounds like a blowout, but I don't understand why or what could have caused it. These are all new tires, the very ones I bought when we first met each other. I wonder if I ran over something. Let me go out and look."

When Greg got out of the car, there, in plain sight, was one of his new tires totally in shreds. It was as if it imploded on itself. Shaking his head, he rolled up his sleeves to get his full-size spare.

Venus got out of the car and blurted, "What happened? Did you see that weird flash of light right when the tire exploded?"

"Yes, but how can that be? It's never happened before.

"Hey, I've got Triple-A - they can change the tire."

Let's not bother. By the time they get here, I will have been able to do it six times over. Oh, you can help me. In the back seat is a huge flashlight. You can shine it on me, okay? Sure glad we were driving in the lane next to the shoulder, and the flat is on that side too. Don't like the thought of having my ass out on any road in California!"

Venus laughed. "Yeah, I know what you mean. I don't like the thought of your ass out there either. You'll bring the tire back to Discount Tires tomorrow? They should replace it."

"That's exactly what I'll do. Damn, these were expensive tires. Maybe I should have gotten the cheapos. Ya think?"

"No, I don't think! I believe you just got yourself a lemon tire! You seem to have a lot of expertise in fixing flat tires. I must remember that," she laughed before stroking Greg's hair.

Grinning broadly, Greg mumbled, "Hey, leave me alone. I have an agenda here."

Eventually, the spare tire was put on and they continued their journey. When they arrived at Venus' house, OM greeted them, purring loudly. For the first time, OM looked carefully at Greg, sauntered over to him, put his front paws on Greg's legs and meowed to be picked up.

"No fair! Never have I seen OM do that to anyone, including me. *You* are something else."

"Does he always purr this loud?"

"Uh huh, that's why I call him my purring machine. But he must think you're really something. Are you usually a cat guy?"

"Yes, I've had cats all my life. And dogs. A pet was the one thing my parents allowed me. This guy is really special, but right now I have other plans," he announced as he gently put OM on the couch. "Do you have any treats for him that will appease my guilt for. . . ?"

Venus went to her pantry where she kept OM's treats on the bottom shelf. She bent down to gather a hand-full when Greg moved over to her and pushed himself into her. She felt his growing hardness and her own achiness deep within her pelvis.

"First OM! Then you! He got neglected all last weekend! "Venus laughed and turned around with a fist full of kitty treats. "Here you go big guy. OM, not you, Greg."

"Okay, Okay, I get it. OM first!" As soon as the treats were dispensed, Greg grabbed Venus, passionately pulling her to him.

"You know the way to the bedroom," moaned Venus.

"No, let's do something different. Let's have dessert on the dining room table. How's that sound?"

"I don't know if I'll ever be able to eat a meal there again without thinking of you." Getting right into the spirit of things, Venus contributed, "I have some wonderful chocolate syrup that we could play with. So yummy. Of course it isn't milk chocolate, but will that work?"

"Sounds wonderful. I'll suffer for tonight. Maybe we ought to close the blinds," Greg suggested seductively.

Venus answered in kind, "Ya think?"

An hour or so later, Venus and Greg emerged from a refreshing shower. They'd discovered it wasn't as easy to lick all of the chocolate off as they thought it was going to be, but they'd howled in delight at their messiness, slipperiness and stickiness. Not only was the sex fantastic, but it was fun too. A new thing for Venus and Greg.

"This may sound pushy, but how about if I stay the night? It just so happens I brought a change of clothing with me."

"How convenient. What if I said no?" Venus teased.

"I took my chances and figured you wouldn't. We have something going, and we're too old to play games and let time heedlessly go by."

The rest of the evening Venus and Greg cuddled and shared more of themselves, laughed at silly things they had done when they were younger, and let their hearts open more and more to each other.

"Tell me about your kids, Charlie and Ron, right? And their families."

Greg began, "There's nothing to tell except they're great kids. I love their wives and the grand-kids are awesome. Do I sound like a proud Dad and Grandpa?"

"You sure do. I suspect if you asked me that same kind of open-ended question, I'd probably respond in exactly the same way. Who is more like you? Charlie or Ron?"

"I guess Ron is. He and I respond in the same ways to certain situations, like emergencies. We both take charge. He'll do it for anyone; I do it only for those I love – like them and their families. We also laugh at the same stuff. Ron is a little more serious than I. Don't know who he got it from, it sure doesn't run in the family.

"Charlie is more of a clown with a real short temper – at least had when he was growing up. He has lighter hair and blue eyes and is probably a little shorter than I am. He is definitely the more adventuresome of the two guys, even to moving out here. Sarah is lovely and knows how to tame Charlie. She's a hot one, with a mouth and brain to match Charlie's. I think they probably fight well and make up well.

"Both the kids are smart, their wives are and their kids are. The whole family is addicted to critters of all shapes and sizes which, I might add, pleases me enormously. Sarah and Dahlia are always rescuing strays. Oh, I didn't tell you about Dahlia, Ron's wife. She is perky and bodacious. I'll show you pictures as soon as I get them unpacked. I'd compare Dahlia to you, more than I might Sarah."

"What do you mean by that?"

"You'll meet them one day and you will know instantly. Now tell me about your kids. Who's most like you?"

"Neither one looks particularly like me, though Bret has more my coloring than Toni does. He's got the auburn hair with brown eyes, and Toni has dark hair with *huge* black eyes. They are both taller than I am. Bret is a scientist like me, except with a private company. He also loves research. Toni used to be very artistic; in fact she went from fashionista to graphic designer to commercial designer of ads for companies not only in this area, but throughout the states.

The kid's partners are really cool. I love them both. Elysa is an actress who does a lot of small theater and teaches at one of the local junior colleges, and John is a CEO of a toy company. Fortunately, there are no financial worries in either family. Thank Heavens! In many ways, I'd have to say both kids' humor and loyalty are largely from me. They sometimes carry their loyalty way above-and-beyond the call of duty. But, on the other hand, they are also clear thinkers; when someone has broken their trust, they see that it no longer matters about loyalty. Does that make any sense? I'm pretty loyal, too, until trust has been broken. How about you? Do you trust easily?"

"No. That's why it's been so important that Thom moved out here with me, or should I say with the company. I would absolutely be shocked if he ever broke the trust we've had for so long.

"Do you trust me?"

"Hmm, I knew you were going to ask, and that's a hard one. On many levels I trust you more than I've ever trusted anyone. But there is still some holding back. You know, fear of *what ifs.*"

Venus sighed, "I feel the same way."

The conversation ended, neither of them defining the *"what if"* fear. Finally both of them could no longer keep their eyes open and just held each other, preparing for sleep.

"I feel safe with you," whispered Greg before he went to sleep.

"And I with you," Venus responded, realizing she was implicitly stating to Greg that she trusted him. They drifted into a deep sleep wrapped around each other.

Showering the next day wasn't nearly as bad as the first time. They laughed and talked, and Venus eventually forgot her embarrassment.

The Next Day

The next morning at work, Venus was deep in concentration when interrupted by Greg's call. "Hi Handsome," she smiled into the phone, but then heard worry in Greg's voice. "What's the matter? How is that tire?"

"I didn't get to the tire store, didn't have time. I'll drop it off after work. But a new problem has developed: two money transfers of ours never reached our vendors. We promised the companies they'd be there three days ago, and they're still not there. They were computer-generated transfers. When we tried to get into our accounts, the computer shut down. Thom, Bill, Larry and I have gone over all the data, but still can't figure out why. Larry discovered the problem early in the day and we still can't find any answers. There's over one-hundred-thousand dollars in that account and we have no idea where sixty thousand is. Bill has been feverishly working all morning on it. Finally we called the bank manager and spoke to him. He told us there was a computer transfer to a different account made the day before. . . by me! I assured him I haven't taken anything like that amount out of that account. He concluded that either I did it or someone who knows all my vital information and passwords did it. So I said, 'I didn't make any withdrawals. Someone must have hacked into our computer system. What's our next step? Do you call the police or do I? In the meantime, let me call my bank in Boston and wire the funds to cover this expense.'"

Greg continued, "We've spent all morning with the police, going over all the entries on my computer regarding our funds. I'm bone tired and no closer to an answer. The big question is, who'd break into our computer and take only sixty-thousand dollars? It doesn't make sense."

Venus was stunned, and listened quietly while Greg told her the events of the morning.

"Greg, when was the transfer made? On which computer was it done? Who knows the inside passwords?"

Greg didn't hesitate before saying, "The police asked those questions, too, and I told them Rita and Bill knew some of the essential information but certainly not enough to break into the system. I keep that information locked in a safe, and they have no access to it."

"I don't trust Rita or Bill; watch them."

"Why don't you trust Bill? I know why you don't trust Rita, but Bill? Just because he was pissed you didn't dance with him?

"No, Greg." Greg interrupted her before she could explain.

"I really don't think either of them had anything to do with this. You know how smart computer hackers are these days. Identity theft is the biggest crime around now. Fortunately, the company has an insurance policy that should cover this loss; the pain is in having to change everything and go through all the legal hassles. Now, tell me why you don't trust Bill."

"Bill called me and asked me out for tonight. I told him I was busy and that you and I were dating at this time. Then he said he was jealous of you, and honestly, Greg, I could hear and feel the jealousy and anger in his voice."

Greg instantly responded, "He asked you out?"

"Yes."

"I can't believe that, especially when I came into the office singing your accolades." Greg smiled into the phone.

"It's just his jealous streak has a bitterness to it. Watch him too."

"Good grief. I have to watch Rita for her lies and Bill for his jealousy? I guess that's what I get when I date a gorgeous, delectable, delicious. . . ."

"Yeah, yeah, yeah" Venus interrupted with laughter, "I'm the Queen of Everything, but seriously, just some gut feelings."

"Remember what I said last night, 'I've waited too long for you and *no one*, I repeat, *no one*, is going to come between us.' Is that clear? And what's with you dating me *at this time* stuff?"

Venus giggled, "Oh just a way of putting Bill off and implying that if things don't go well with you and me, maybe I might consider him. You know, a *what if* scenario."

"Forget the *what if* scenarios! You seem to forget *I* waited a very long time for you too. Let's put that one to rest."

"On the more serious side, is there anything I can do?" asked Venus.

"Yeah, be there for me to hug and crash on. Even though I love Thom like a brother, he isn't as soft to hug as you are."

"Tell me about Thom and Larry. You've told me about Bill, but never about the other two."

***

"Thom Gordon is probably my closest friend; he's the plant engineer, second in charge, and also a chemist. We've worked together for over the past twenty-five years, been friends for about thirty, and get along famously. It's as if we are on the same wave-length. We laugh at the same things, joke the same way, and think alike. Sometimes people joke that we're related, color aside. We are built alike, although he's a few inches taller than I am. Thom's also pushing sixty, and we're always fighting over who's older." Greg chuckled, "I am, by three days."

Venus had noticed Thom was a damn good-looking man. And there were those incredible green eyes again. He had a full head of black-and-silver hair, piercing green eyes, square chin, a pale mocha complexion and a great build. Greg had told her how they often worked out together until one or the other fell exhausted. And there were those beautiful green eyes again.

"What about his personal life? Is he married? Divorced?"

"Thom's wife of thirty-five years, Carrie, died three years ago in a violent car crash and he was totally devastated. Actually, so was I. The one good relationship I knew was ended by death. Broke me up. If it hadn't been for his two kids, I don't think he would have made it. But now, even they are getting on his case to begin dating again, but he still doesn't feel ready. When women come onto him - and boy, there are plenty - he doesn't extend an iota of himself. He acts just like I used to; that is, before you. Now that it's been three years, he's not carrying his burden quite so heavily. I think he's resigned himself to being alone. He adored Carrie, and she him. It's really quite inspiring: he's found it easier to be grateful for the many years they had together rather than mourn what he doesn't have now. He's kind of like I was when folks wanted to fix me up. I ignored them, pushed them aside or told them I was just fine the way I am. You and I had that little behavioral trait in common, as I recall. He's telling those match-makers, "If I see someone who turns my head, I'll be sure to ask her out. So far, there has been no one. Kindly leave me in peace. "

Some of his friends are shaking their heads and saying, "What are you looking for? Another Carrie? You're not going to find her."

His response is always the same, "I'll know her if and when I see her. End of subject."

Thom was more than Greg's right hand. He was a part-owner in the company – about twenty percent - and that, along with his brilliant financial investments, made him a very rich man. Thom and Greg solved problems as if they were diplomats from two opposing countries. People who watched and listened to them often commented that it was as if they were married to each other. Actually, they were both married to the company and delighted in presenting "devil's advocate" scenarios to each other. Their relationship had saved Thom after Carrie's untimely death.

"Thanks for filling me in, I'll make sure not to even think of fixing him up, Venus vowed. That must have been an awful time for him. Changing the subject to something a little more pleasant, do you think it's time for me to walk down the hall and give you a hug now?"

"Absolutely! There's nothing like the hug of a beautiful woman to calm my nerves and make me feel somewhat less of a dummy than I feel right now. Then Larry, Thom and especially Bill can see you again too," Greg gloated.

"Oh great! I'll just love seeing Bill and I'm sure he'll love seeing me," Venus reflected sarcastically. "I wish I were able to go through what's happened to you and still feel okay. You sound annoyed but not devastated. I would be a limp dishrag about now. Either that or throwing a fit about being violated. I'll see you in a couple minutes."

As Venus left her office, she compared Greg's calmness in a storm to her own emotional reaction to anything intense. Then she wondered what might get him emotional. Obviously this didn't do too much. All thoughts left as she walked into his office and saw the four guys there drinking coffee and looking chagrined.

"Hi guys, you all look a little peaked. How are ya?"

Bill, upon seeing Venus, lowered his eyes at first and only gradually began to look at her. She pretended not to notice, but she could still feel his anger – it seemed to be coming out of every pore in his body. She wondered why the simple refusal of a date had set him off so much. What was at stake?

Before Greg could say anything, Larry chirped in a sing-song voice, "How 'bout a hug for me and Thom and Bill too?"

***

Larry Sorrell, the marketing director, was forever the joker, the office "feel good" man. He was the only married man in the group. At age fifty-three, with medium height and build, hazel eyes and an oval face, he was outgoing, funny, witty, and everyone loved him. In fact, many of the women in the Boston office used to tell him how cute and fun he was. "Yeah, you're safe saying that cuz you know how much I love my wife," he said.

Larry had been with SeaFoam for about a year. He and his wife Nora had a great relationship except when it came to attending large social events. Nora froze in big groups; she hated them, and rarely, if ever, attended. At best, she always felt they were boring. Nora had her own software company that was rapidly growing. She and Larry had had many words about her unwillingness to be his companion at big events, but there was nothing much he could do about it, and Larry respected her for being true to herself. He just had that wonderful ability, Nora thought, of doing social chatter. She herself didn't. Sometimes she felt guilty, but Larry always was able to kid her out of it and she gladly accepted his support. When they were alone, Nora was just as witty and clever as he was.

Larry was incredibly competent in marketing ideas for SeaFoam. Greg thought he was the best he'd seen, and that was going some. It was no surprise to Greg when Larry jokingly requested not only his hug from Venus, but also hugs for the other two men.

Venus was delighted when Greg said, "Find your own hugger," and then walked to her and collected his own hug.

***

When the other three guys began to cat-whistle, Greg backed off and said, "I'm frustrated as hell, to tell you the truth. Damn! I know about computer hackers and used every precaution."

"Just goes to show that we don't know everything," Bill replied. "More new protections are being created daily. We just didn't get the right or newest technology, which surprises me a lot."

Thom said, "I think this is just one of those instances where we missed something, and that's that. Chalk it up to the times we live in. I hope someone's happy with sixty grand."

Bill was basically silent, deep within himself. Venus thought he might be uncomfortable with her there.

Greg observed, "Bill, you're awfully quiet. Have you thought of anything we perhaps overlooked?"

Avoiding Greg's eyes, Bill responded, "Like I said before, with computer hacking it's a constant effort to stay with the times, even on a daily basis. I do recall something strange yesterday when I logged onto our account; I just can't quite remember what it was," Bill looked perplexed. "I know so much about computers and now, damn it, I'm drawing a blank. Something just wasn't right and I didn't pursue it."

The four of them rehashed the events a bit more, and as Venus was ready to leave, she asked the guys if they'd mind if she gave Greg "a little tiny goodbye hug."

"Go, girl, go," Larry was the first to respond and laughed.

Just as Venus was beginning to hug Greg goodbye, Rita walked into the office.

"Why are you all here?" she inquired looking with unabashed annoyance at Greg and Venus. Rita wasn't dressed in the same pristine manner as before, and Venus wondered why.

Greg dislodged himself from Venus, and told Rita about the morning's events. Venus studied Rita and although there was not a single inappropriate expression on her face, Venus' intuition told her that Rita was lying. She didn't know what to do with it her intuitive flash.

A couple of cups of coffee later, after more discussion about the hacking, Venus finally went back to her office.

That Evening

Later that afternoon, she called Greg, basically to see how things were but also to ask him where Rita had been all morning. Greg, who was in the middle of talking to more police told her he'd get back to her. It was the end of the day when Venus was ready to leave her office, she heard from Greg.

"Let me take you to my house. We'll drop off the tire to Discount Tires then have dinner in LaJolla – lots of great restaurants - and catch up with the events of the day."

"Sounds great, but I have a request and it's a big one – at least it is for my purr machine. Either we stop at my place and feed OM, or we bring him with us to your house."

"He rides?"

"Absolutely. With my being single for so long and wanting to go places, I refused to leave him behind. I taught him very early in life about riding in the car and he's a real trooper. And, most importantly, we always have a ready-to-go clean litter box."

"You're on. Get yourself some clothes too."

"Yes, Sir! See you when?"

"About ten minutes."

By that time Venus could sense that Greg felt better about his company's situation. They drove to her house and picked up OM, who was thrilled to see Greg again and willingly jumped into his carrier - purring the whole while.

"You know, I'm lucky. My insurance is taking care of everything, so I've lost nothing except lots of hours. I can't imagine how difficult it is for individuals who have to go through all this alone! I had Bill, Larry, Thom and Rita helping me communicate with everyone, and then I personally set up the new numbers and passwords and put them in my safe-deposit box. My son Charlie, Thom and I are the only ones who have that key. And Charlie doesn't even know what's inside it; I never told him. Took all afternoon, but thank God it's done."

"You know, I'm disappointed in what happened, but I'm not the first one this has happened to. Our times are really rough now."

"Right," replied Venus, but she still pursued her earlier suspicions by once again asking, "Where was Rita all morning? She was dressed so casually, which seems to be something totally different for her. And where was Bill, for that matter?"

"We'll talk in a minute. Let me drop off the tire and find out what happened to the thing, okay? You can wait in the car with the lion," Greg laughed, as he left the two of them sitting in the parking lot.

***

In about ten minutes he came out, looking perplexed and shaken. "Venus, that was a bullet that hit the tire. I don't know how in God's name someone could aim that effectively when the car was moving, but someone did. Unless, of course, the bullet was supposed to hit something else? Good thing I wasn't going too fast or we could have had one hell of an accident. Because it was a bullet, I was required to talk to the police. The manager of the store called them while I was inside and I talked to them. Told them we had an animal with us and asked if it would be possible for them to meet us at my house in about twenty minutes. They were really cooperative."

As Greg was sharing what he knew with Venus, he remembered the long white envelope he had put away. "Should I mention it or not?" he mused.

When they got to the house and OM was settled, Greg thought about sharing the envelope with Venus. "Later," he thought.

While they waited for the police, Venus was still hashing over the computer hacking, and repeated her question she had asked Greg earlier about Rita's whereabouts.

Greg answered, "Rita told me she had several settling-in projects to accomplish, and asked if I minded if she took the morning off. I was okay with that."

"Oh," said Venus, thinking "I'll bet."

"You know, I'm beginning to think you *are* jealous of her. Trust me, you have nothing, absolutely nothing, to be jealous of," said Greg as he took Venus' hand to his lips. All of a sudden Greg blurted out, "Do you think I had an affair with her? Is that why you have this suspicion of her?"

Venus, though startled by Greg's question, replied, "It had occurred to me."

"Well, I didn't. Never had and never will. She isn't my type. You are."

"What type am I?"

"Special: soft, feminine, and for whatever reason, you exude a sex appeal and energy that I've never experienced and I find amazing, stimulating and exciting. Satisfied?"

"I guess." Venus reached for Greg's face to stroke it and asked, "What about Bill?"

"He was in the office all morning, working on whatever he works on best. I just don't see him being involved in such a small financial matter. The man is worth millions. Do you think he'd jeopardize his whole way of life for a measly sixty grand?"

"I don't know. Maybe to get back at you? He surely was angry at the two of us."

"Maybe he was angry at himself for not catching what was going on with the hacking, maybe angry at himself for caring about how he treated us. Possible?"

"I suppose so, but both those characters give me the willies."

"Have you even considered it was outside hackers? You think that's possible?"

"I'll give you that one," Venus laughed as she reached for Greg's leg to stroke.

OM pranced to the door seconds before the doorbell rang. "Wow, Venus, he really is a watch-cat."

"Lion."

Two detectives, Stan Ritter and Lee Jones, walked into the house with OM dancing alongside them. One stooped down to pet him. "That's quite a lion you have there."

Venus thought that was the funniest thing anyone could have said at that moment and she threw back her head and laughed. "Yes! You are absolutely correct officer. I was just telling Greg that as the doorbell rang."

Stan Ritter was a man in his early fifties, tall, broad and with thinning light-brown hair. His eyes were a sparkling blue, his face had laugh-lines clearly visible. Lee Jones was in his mid-forties, African American with a dark complexion and dark eyes. He was not terribly tall, maybe five-feet-nine inches but looked quite powerful with well-developed muscles. The two detectives had been partners for the past ten years and it was clear they had great respect and cared for each other. Introductions were made and statements were taken from Greg and Venus as to time and place of the blow-out, their whereabouts and why, and the speed at which they were traveling. "Did either one of them know anyone who wanted to harm them?" Both said no. "We know it was a particularly dark last night, but could you see another driver to your right who might have shot your tire?" Lee asked. "Looking at the tire, it appears as if the shot came from someone close by."

"You can tell that just from looking at the tire?" asked Venus.

"Usually," responded Stan. "Greg, did you notice anything?"

"Not a thing. I was in the lane closest to the side of the road – the shoulder, and looking straight ahead. How about you, Venus?"

"Didn't notice a thing except a flash when the tire blew out. But I thought that was from the heat and explosion. Who'd expect anything like that anyway? We were on an inhabited section of road. Any complaints last night of domestic abuse?"

"No. Well, that's all we have to ask right now. If we need you, we can call your cell phones. Any questions?"

Greg paused and cleared his throat before speaking, "I guess it might be helpful here if I told you guys about a letter I got the other day. Let me show it to you." He went to the drawer and handed over the envelope to the officers. "I think it's probably someone's idea of a big joke, but in lieu of what's happened, I thought I should show it to you."

"What does it say?" asked Venus.

Stan read her the letter, "YOUR LIFE IS WORTH NOTHING."

"Jesus, Greg, why didn't you tell me?" Venus was terribly upset.

"I didn't tell you because I figured you'd react like this, and I didn't want to worry you."

"Tell the police about the computer-hacking too," Venus demanded.

As Greg told them what he knew, the two detectives looked at each other and shook their heads. Stan finally spoke, "This may appear to be some sort of coincidence, but in order to make sure you folks are safe, we'll be treating this differently and doing a much more thorough investigation. You may have a stalker on your hands. We'll go around to the residents in the area where you were shot at, and see if they heard or saw anything. Our investigation will include your neighbors here regarding this letter. How long have you lived here, and when did you find the envelope?"

"I've been here only about three months; came from Boston to open a branch of my business. I was gone all weekend except for a few minutes Saturday when I came to pick up some stuff, and noticed the envelope stuck in the back door. I didn't read it until I got home Sunday night. You saw where I put it. Didn't take it seriously."

"You might want to reconsider your attitude especially with the computer-hacking and the shooting."

Lee added, "Regarding the bullet, it looks as if it was shot from a semi-automatic, nine-millimeter weapon, and you can use a silencer on those babies. We have the bullet if you want to see it – we know it's a nine-millimeter, but we'll have to wait for forensics to tell us whether the gunman used a silencer. Please let us know if there are any more unusual occurrences with either of you. We will take this threatening note to forensics for their analysis."

Venus squeaked, "May I see the bullet, please?"

Stan walked over to her with a small plastic bag in his hand. "Here you go."

"Wow. I've never seen a discharged bullet except in the movies. Greg, have you?"

"Yeah, I used to go to a shooting range in Boston. But for the life of me, I'd never given a thought that a bullet could have been shot at my car. Lucky it hit down low."

"A lot of police carry that particular weapon if I'm reading the bullet right, which of course, I think I am. Haven't been a cop for twenty years for nothing," Stan laughed and counseled, "If anything unusual occurs – anything - let us know immediately."

When both of the officers had left, Venus found she was still angry at Greg for not sharing the letter. "You know, I'm still pissed off at you. If something were to happen to you after I've waited so long to find you, I don't know what I do." A tear rolled down her cheek.

"Venus, honestly, I just didn't want to worry you about what I thought was a crank letter. I promise, if anything bad comes up again, you'll be the second one to know, after me. Is that all right with you?"

"Yes. I just worry sometimes." Venus changed the subject. "I'm hungry. Let's go eat."

After dining on fried calamari, jumbo shrimp, Greek salad, and a lovely red wine, in a beautiful La Jolla restaurant overlooking the ocean, they drove back to Greg's.

"This is odd," said Venus, "even though I have been to your place before, this feels like the first time. Maybe it's because I have my protective lion with me, or maybe we just know each other better. Who knows? But I do know that having OM here does bring a sense of security, especially now."

Greg came back, "Yeah, a real protector. He'd probably run if anyone strange came near him."

"No, he would not! How dare you say that about my pussy-cat, er, lion," Venus retorted.

They spent the earlier part of the evening going over the events of the day, and then Greg said, "Enough. Come here."

Venus observed wryly, "How can I come here when I'm already here?"

"For starters, you could come closer if you moved OM."

"Ah, but OM doesn't like to be moved," Venus stalled. "Anyway, you could move him yourself considering how he's draped all over you, not me." By this time Venus was giggling out loud watching Greg who had become seemingly paralyzed by her cat. "When he does that to me I try not to move so I don't disturb him. Sometimes, he even growls at me for moving. You, sir, are on your own! Did you say you're CEO and owner of a Fortune 500 business?"

"Yeah, I guess so," Greg retorted. "You have problems with that, Lady?"

"No, but surely moving a helpless thirteen-pound cat is nothing compared to the trials and tribulations you have in business. Now, is it?"

While the two of them sat on the couch laughing, the doorbell rang, and OM jumped off Greg. "Well, that's one way of getting him off me," Greg chuckled. When he opened the door, there was Rita.

"Hi," she said, "I came to drop off these papers to you. Oh, hi Venus, I didn't know you were here."

"How did you know where I live?" asked Greg.

"Oh, I asked Thom and he told me."

OM, who was watching Rita from behind the couch, ran out to her and hissed and growled.

"My God," squealed Rita, "get him away from me. I hate cats!"

"He won't hurt you. Actually he's very friendly," said Greg.

OM turned, hissed once more, then ran and hid.

"Wow, that's weird behavior from him," Venus said, startled. "I don't think he has ever reacted to anyone that way in all his five years."

Rita stayed for only a few minutes before leaving. After she had gone Greg remarked, "Maybe OM knows something we don't. Cats are pretty awesome in that way. He sure as hell didn't act that way with Stan or Lee. What do you suppose that's about?"

"Two contradictory things here, Mr. Greg. One: You think my lion wouldn't protect me? You saw that! He was protecting his interests. So there! Two: You believe cats are psychic?"

Greg defended himself. "Well, you saw how quickly your lion ran away, didn't you? I'm not sure I think cats are psychic, but they sure are attuned to things in a different way than I am. Maybe intuitive."

"Psychic and intuitive are the same things. Psychic is just a pejorative word said by people who are terrified of it. I think cats are psychic, and I think people are too. Cats know things we don't and pick up on energy we don't. At least I think OM does. After that woman lied to me, I don't trust her. And neither does my faithful lion. Something tells me to watch my back, and I know OM picked up on that."

"Yet Rita is great in the office and has helped me enormously in setting up this company. What she does outside the office is none of my damn business. I sometimes think she's a bit odd, but about business she's damn sharp and astute."

"Does she know enough to break into your computer system? Or for that matter, does Bill? Will you ask Thom if he told her where you live?"

"Venus, love, if she has that kind of knowledge, she sure as hell has hidden it from all of us. Bill, on the other hand, might know enough, but I just don't think he'd act on it. He's not that money hungry to go to jail for sixty grand. He's a multi-millionaire. I thought we'd already killed that subject. I simply don't know what to say about either one of them except that they've been great employees. I understand your concern, but I don't know how to address it. Can we not think of this anymore tonight and let me just be with you alone? Especially now that OM's not draped on me anymore."

"Yeah, I guess so. But I'd love to get to the heart of the issues, and those two are the only suspects I have. I guess I am being a pest, and repetitive too. Forgive?"

Bill

Bill, on hearing of the computer-hacking was completely disgusted with himself. He hadn't been able to be of any assistance in solving the break-in, and *that* was supposedly one of his areas of expertise. He felt he'd let down the whole company. He felt ashamed how he had treated Venus and Greg, and he was more aware of his misery regarding his behavior towards Joyce, whom he'd left in Boston. As he drove to his rented condo that evening he felt a growing dismay at himself. "Maybe another anger management course is what I need," he thought. He counted to twenty, did deep breathing and found some images appearing to him.

The first image was of his leaving Joyce, the woman he'd dated in Boston prior to coming to California. He'd been terrified of her intensity and of the depth of feelings he had for her. With that realization, he felt she really had him by "the balls." He was fearful of being involved because of what had occurred in the past. His ex-wife had accused him of domestic violence which he rationalized he didn't do. After all, he'd only really hollered and threatened. In order to prevent a trial, he was given the choice to take an anger management course or else to serve time in jail. He picked the anger management and did learn some techniques that served him well, especially in business. Yet in relationships, he ran away when he felt any consistent type of caring. He wasn't getting into any situation again to risk everything he had worked for the past thirty years. He sensed that Joyce was going to demand things of him that were uncomfortable and scary. His immediate response was to get angry at her. Rather than telling her that he felt frightened and really needed to take it slow, he opted to be sarcastic and then finally left. This was the way he'd completely denied any feelings he had.

Now, as Bill pondered his behavior, he realized that since he had been in trouble with the law well over thirty-five years ago, whenever he was angry, he either became extremely sarcastic and rude or else quickly left the scene. Going further into his memories he discovered he was terrified of becoming as angry as he had been during his supposed domestic violence as a young man. To another person, his yelling could easily be interpreted as being violent, and he finally acknowledged why he was given the choice of anger management classes or prison. Unfortunately for him, he didn't quite get how to use anger and go beneath it, or how to speak the truth. When he was very young, he watched his father being emotionally and physically abusive to his mother, to his brothers and himself. The images of those scenes never really left his consciousness; both the emotional and physical scars still haunted him.

"That was my model. There was nothing about speaking intelligently. I don't even know how to attempt to be honest in communication without sounding like a bastard," he thought. When Greg and Venus walked in, I was mortified by my behavior. *That* is a first for me. I should probably be thankful for this awareness, but right now, it's just too much to comprehend."

Bill went into his condo, changed to tennis shorts, and went to the gym where he played racket-ball. He needed to release some of the physical energy and emotions he was feeling. He found hitting the ball as hard as he could calmed him down. It was if he were slamming himself every time. "Good thing I'm playing with a young guy who can handle the strength of my slams," he thought.

After two games, he sat in the sauna wishing the ugly energy off him. "What the hell do I do with myself? Nothing is working quite right. Maybe I ought to go see a therapist. God! I don't think much of them." He went home, had a huge shot of vodka and went to bed. Nothing solved. Nothing planned. His stomach and head ached when he finally fell into a restless sleep many hours later.

Greg and Venus

On a lovely Southern California afternoon a couple of weeks later, Greg called Venus and asked if she could leave work early. "Hey, I'm the head of this department, who do you think is going to check up on me?" she inquired facetiously. "Of course I can take off early. What do you have in mind?"

"It's time to go buy a boat, and I want you with me."

"I know nothing about boats."

Greg interrupted Venus, "I know that, but I want you with me. See if you like it, if it's comfortable to you. I value your opinion. Do you have any objections?" he challenged.

"None whatsoever. As long as you know I'm just coming along with you. At least I can honestly say I know what is comfortable or pretty. But is that even relevant when it comes to boats? What's pretty in a boat, in my esteemed opinion, may be totally useless."

"I know you can't be proficient in everything, that's why you have me."

"Thanks, I'll remember that."

They traveled up the coast to Marina Del Rey and looked at some of the older sailboats that Greg might be interested in. One in particular was of great interest to him: a fifty-two-foot long schooner, built in 1924, by John Alden.

"What do you think, Venus? Do you like it?"

"What's not to like! It's beautiful *and* comfortable. I like that it's not brand new."

"In the past I always wanted something bigger and more sea-going. Now I just want to sail the various bays here and maybe take her to Santa Catalina or wherever. Speed used to be important - practically the only important thing - now it's just fun though this type of boat is fast as lightening. Wins lots of races. There was one in St. John in the Virgin Islands like it. Same builder, same size, and it won every race going with just a husband and wife doing the work. I guess I'll have to teach you how to sail, if you're up to it."

"Yeah, but you'll have to be patient. I'm not so sure about my sea legs."

"Your legs are just fine." Greg eyed her lasciviously.

"Stop looking at me like that, you're embarrassing me."

"Yeah, right."

"When will you decide whether you'll purchase her?"

"I think I already have. Wanted to wait to see what your psychic input was. Got any? Does it have good vibes?" he asked jestingly.

"Okay, Mr. Richards. I'll answer that. It's got great vibes and was dearly loved by its past owners, of whom, I believe, there were three. Can you check that?"

"Damn, I already know the answer. Yes, it was owned by three different individuals, all of whom loved her, at least according to the history I have been given. Ten points for you."

Venus, basking in her intuitive knowledge, laughed and took Greg's hand

"I know Charlie and his family will also love this beauty. So will Thom who will be part-owner. He gave me *carte blanch* to pick out what you and I liked. You know, he and I used to sail a lot in Boston." Venus nodded her head in assent. "Of course, I will change her name."

"No psychic input about the name, but a question. Why do you want to change it?"

"Cuz I have a better name than the one currently in use."

"What will you name her?"

"Venus. Any objections?"

Venus blushed a bit, turned to hug Greg, laughing. "I've never had a boat named after me. That doesn't mean I have a broad keel or whatever, does it?"

"No, silly. Your keel is just fine."

"Then wow, what an honor! Thank you. Just don't get mad at me and take it out on her." She hesitated. "Do you think Thom will be okay with that?"

"Absolutely. And don't worry. I won't take anything out on her. If I get mad at you, you'll be the second one to know. No need to bring in an innocent boat." They walked toward the salesman who had left them alone for a good half-hour while Greg explored everything on the boat. As Greg peered and pried into every nook and cranny, he gave Venus a running account. She felt overwhelmed by all the information he shared, as well as what she had taken in. Dating Greg was a real eye-opener and education!

They walked to the business office where Greg casually said to the salesman, "I'll call you tomorrow when we can further discuss price, guarantees and conditions."

Greg bought the boat and, for the next few weeks, he and Venus spent almost every waking and sleeping moment together. Taking OM, they went on beautiful sailing trips around the San Diego and Baja coastline, Venus and her cat quickly learning the "ins" and "outs" of safe and comfortable sailing. When the boat wasn't moving, OM sat at the mast or roamed about on the deck. As soon as any movement began, he raced below, where he sprawled on one of the beds, gazing at the sky and finally nodding off. Sometimes he sprawled on the counter in the galley, watching the ocean go by. No salty sea-spray for that kitty! Periodically some fisherman saw him and threw him a treat, which he gobbled. It didn't take long, perhaps a couple of weeks, before OM became the mascot of the marina as well as the boat called *Venus*. Everyone asked about "his highness" with just the proper respect. His lionesque posture was duly noted, and he was constantly rewarded with delicious morsels. Naturally he purred for everyone. Periodically, Thom took out the boat with some friends from work, most often when Venus and Greg were not aboard. Occasionally the three of them, along with OM, sailed together.

Greg teased Venus by saying, "He's still a cat, ya know! Not a lion." Venus laughed and shook her head. In spite of his words, Greg petted OM, gave him treats, talked to him and allowed him to sleep where he wished. Secretly, with just OM listening, he commented, "I know you're a wise old lion, but for the sake of Venus, I'll pretend you're a cat, Okay buddy?"

Venus was deliciously aware of how Greg treated her cat like a lion king, in spite of the teasing. She bantered, "Yeah, big shot, you sure do suck up to my little kitty, don't you?" Both of them indulged in making OM the center of their repartee.

***

As Greg's and Venus' relationship grew, they discovered they enjoyed mostly the same type of movies (except for the "chick flicks" that Venus occasionally treated herself to), the same kinds of food and even the same colors. It seemed they were able to discuss everything, even subjects they disagreed on. Each day they spent time together, both of them found growing comfort and trust in the relationship. They took long walks along the beaches where Venus had already brought Greg to, and she introduced him to others. There were short afternoon jaunts to various areas around the county, such as Julien and even Tijuana.

One of their favorite places to visit was the Self-Realization Gardens or, as known in Encinitas, Yogi's Gardens. There were beautiful walkways with a pond surrounded by exquisitely manicured flowering plants and ferns, meditation benches strategically placed in and out of the shade, and a waterfall that emptied into the pond with huge goldfish in it shaded by large trees. There were places to sit and be peaceful throughout the gardens, including those overlooking Yogi's Beach. When Venus originally decided to show Greg this magnificent place, she had been concerned that he wouldn't like it because of its religious connotations, and said so. His immediate response was, "If you love it as much as I think you do, I will too. Greg's impulse was to take Venus' hand and hold it tighter than ever before. "This is really amazing. The care and devotion it takes to create and maintain something like this is enormous. I know how much I valued my gardener back east, and my garden was more like a yard and nothing as elegant as your gardens, or this." Venus sighed with relief. Even though she felt comfortable with Greg, there was still a part of her afraid that he might, in some way, disapprove of what she valued.

"Greg," she whispered as they sat on one of the meditation benches, "I was concerned you might not like it here as much as I do. I still have to do some letting-go of Alex's judgment about what was or wasn't okay. I'm so glad I trusted myself to take you here and risk a possible put-down."

"Sometimes you are absurd. Why in God's name would *anyone* think this is anything other than a beautiful way to honor Spirit? You should know me better by now. Anything you value will never be put down by me. Oh, maybe a couple of things. . . "

"And what might those might be?"

"Maybe about intuition or stuff like that." He grabbed Venus' hands before she could pull away and said quickly, "Honestly, I'm kidding. Just needed to tease you a bit."

"It better have been teasing, because that subject is dear to my heart."

"Is there anything I *can* tease you about that you won't take so seriously?"

"Yeah. How about my being the chair of the Chemistry Department? But definitely don't tease about OM, either!"

"Now, now. I couldn't tease you about that lion of yours; he might attack and eat me," Greg snorted. "But it's a deal. Forgive me if occasionally I slip. Changing the subject, did I tell you I used to meditate all the time?"

"No. Really?"

"I guess I, too, have things I wasn't ready to share. I did transcendental meditation, you know, TM. When everyone and his brothers were doing it, I joined in and always felt much better. Actually, I think I'll start again."

He and Venus sat watching periwinkle dragon-flies alight on the flowers until almost sunset, when they reluctantly got up to leave.

"This was beautiful Venus. Thank you." Greg softly kissed her. After a scrumptious dinner of Southern Italian food, Greg took Venus home.

"Do you want to stay here tonight?"

"Are you inviting me? I forgot to put clothes in my car, I was in such a hurry this morning. If you want to take a ride back to my place, I'll grab some stuff and we can head back here. How does that sound?"

"Will do."

The ride to Greg's house usually took about half an hour; however, as they began the jaunt, an intense fog covered the land, the road, and everything else.

"I don't remember such fast-rolling fog on the east coast as here in the LaJolla region. Already, I can't see squat. I hope by the time we leave my place it'll have left as quickly as it came in."

"Yeah, this is really intense!"

It took close to an hour to get to Greg's, and they were both relieved to get out of the car for a little breather.

Greg motioned for Venus to come into the house. "We can't stay long," she said, "my lion gets upset when I'm gone too long. He won't understand how impossible this fog is."

Greg laughed as he turned the key to the house, however, when he opened the door, his face fell. "Shit! Someone's been in here. Venus, get back to the car and call 911! I don't know if anyone is still here."

From where Venus was standing she could see into Greg's kitchen. Everything was thrown from all the cabinets, and glass was everywhere. "Do you think someone is after the new formula for your foam?"

"It's possible, but why the hell would they come here to find it? Any idiot would know it'd be in some lab or a safe. Please go back to the car."

"No, I'm staying with you!"

"I really don't think anyone is here anymore, but…"

Both of them glanced towards Greg's bedroom, where someone was opening a window and leaving. "I'm going after him. Call 911." Greg grabbed a flashlight he kept by his bed and went immediately out searching for whoever had ransacked his place.

"No, Greg, don't." Venus frantically dialed the police and told them what was happening.

Amazingly, the same two detectives, Stan and Lee arrived at Greg's house. But by the time they got there, whoever had trashed the house was long gone, in spite of Greg's chase. Because of the fog, his visibility was about zero, and he could only rely on what he was hearing – basically nothing. He returned to the house about the same time the police arrived.

"Well, it's you two again. Nice seeing you. Wish it wasn't in this situation," Greg said, panting.

"What did you see?" asked Lee.

"Nothing! Damn it! How can you see anything in this pea-soup stuff? Absolutely nothing! It's still pretty dark in general and with that goop…." Greg paused, "Even with my flashlight, I couldn't see a thing. I didn't try to shine it but rather kept it down so the glare wasn't as distinct. Tell you one thing, that's one fast escape artist! Couldn't even hear footsteps. That's pretty amazing cuz I don't think he had that much head start."

Venus grabbed Greg, and in spite of the detective's being there, she said sternly, "Don't ever do that again. Let the police take care of police business. You run your company."

"Ah, Venus, I know you were worried, but a guy's gotta do what a guy's gotta do." He shrugged his shoulders and hugged her trying to appease her.

"Not going to work, Mr. Richards. I'm mad at your risk-taking here."

"Not to interrupt your lover's quarrel," said Stan, "but what might a thief be looking for?"

"The only thing I can think of is the formula for my foam." Greg explained what his company manufactured and how he was finishing up trials on an even longer-lasting product. It was intriguing that both the officers had heard of his product.

"Great idea. And, as a small-boat owner myself, I'm thrilled with your product as it is now. You say you're adding two or more years to its longevity? Good going!"

Lee interrupted, "How does the rest of your house look?"

"Bedroom is messy but not as bad as kitchen. Bathroom is trashed. But why do I even need to tell you. Go see for yourself."

Stan and Lee went through the house, touching nothing, then immediately called forensics. "At this point, Greg, you should be protecting yourself. Seriously, too much has happened. Do you have security at your workplace?"

"Yes, that's always the first thing I take care of. Our security is excellent and reliable. I've been using the same company on the East Coast for over fifteen years, and had four of my regulars and their families move down here with the rest of the staff."

"We'll be talking to them too. In the meantime, perhaps you ought to have one of them here guarding your house."

"Do you think that's necessary? There is absolutely nothing here to steal. Anything of importance is in my office and *that* is guarded."

"Just a suggestion," muttered Lee.

"Thanks, I'll take it into consideration. But what you see here isn't even my stuff – it all came with the rented house."

The rest of the investigation took several hours. Two of the forensic staff came in and went over the house painstakingly, collecting samples of everything. Greg was told there'd be more forensic specialists coming in the morning and labs would get back to Greg as soon as they learned anything.

"You were lucky no one pulled a gun on you when you entered. We think you have a stalker on your hands and an extremely dangerous situation. Is there anything else we should know about?"

"Can't think of a thing. Can you, Venus?"

"No. I just want this crap to end."

When the police finally left, Greg was relieved to be able to grab some clothes and go to Venus' house. "Good thing you invited me over. I'd have to do a major house-keeping job otherwise." Greg paused, "I assume the invitation is still open?"

"Of course, silly."

Fortunately, on the ride home the fog was not as close to the ground as it had been on their earlier trek, which made driving much easier. Both were exhausted from the night's activities by the time they arrived at Venus' house. OM was not a happy cat; he yowled at them in his frustration. Yet when Venus finally gave him fresh food, which he gobbled in a flash, he jumped on Greg and began to purr. "Nice sound to hear tonight, Big Boy. Now go to sleep, so we can."

"I swear that cat likes you better than he likes me. What a nerve. I feed him, and he jumps on you."

They both petted OM while discussing the evening's drama, trying to figure out if either one of them had missed anything or even heard anything unusual while at work. At last, they both drifted off to sleep, their limbs wrapped around each other.

***

For the police, the hacking problem played second-fiddle to the break-in. There were no answers from those investigating it, or from the insurance company, and it appeared to be a dead case. Clues simply did not exist on either the physical or the cyber-plane. Both the police and insurance companies were quick to point out that this sort of crime probably would go unsolved, much to everyone's frustration.

However, the police *were* relentlessly pursuing the break-in at Greg's house and he was constantly in communication with them. His security staff was advised of the situation and also questioned. In spite of all the forensic evidence, there seemed to be no answers for the break-in, the shooting of the tire, or the note. Whenever the various experts requested information of Greg, he cooperated fully, but for those studying the case, no answers materialized. "We'll let you know when we find out some answers." Greg was sick of hearing their mantra.

Bill

Every so often, Bill verbally attacked either Greg or Venus when he ran into them. It was clear that he was still very angry she had picked Greg over him.

"Who knows," thought Venus, "what else he's mad about." She felt his angry energy more and more, and said to Greg, "You know, I'm a bit afraid of Bill. His energy is getting angrier and angrier. Haven't you noticed it?"

"Actually, I have. But I don't have a clue what it's about. I know he is famous for his rudeness, and maybe that's the way it's coming across to us. Ya think?"

"Would he hurt either of us because of our relationship?"

"I highly doubt it. I suppose in the future I'll have all my new employees take some sort of personality test to know they're sane – if a test can actually prove that. I've been pretty lucky. Everyone I have ever hired has been great. Right now, I know you suspect both Bill and Rita of being somewhat off, but let's see how this plays out."

Venus paused before saying, "Are you upset about my perceptions? I just don't know why I get those kinds of vibes from the two of them. *You* know Bill is constantly jabbing at you, don't you?"

"Yes. He is, but that's who he is. . . I think. Yet I agree with you that it's time to have a boss-employee chat about his attitude. It couldn't hurt - at least I don't think it could." Greg swallowed, "Unless you think he'll be after me."

"Well, it's hard to trust those who lie or jab at you. Do I sound like a protective mother bear?"

"Yes, but you're cuter."

Venus, Sally, Joe and Greg

On the weekend, Sally and Joe asked Venus to bring Greg over so they could get to know him, "other than our first impression and what you've been communicating via phone." Sally paused before she suggested, "Venus, do you think this is going too fast? After all, you've just met him. You seem to be spending every spare moment together. It's not that I don't like or trust him, it just seems too fast. I myself am not sure that what Rita said about his having a girlfriend back east may not be true."

"I absolutely trust Greg. I sense he'd never do anything to hurt me in any way. I trust my intuitive part explicitly in this situation, and you know how rare that is! Don't you remember how, when you met Joe, you acted as if there was no one in the world except the two of you? Your work was forgotten, and Joe was the sun and the moon. Remember?"

Sally pondered a moment, "Yeah, I guess you're right. The major thing I remember is going to bed with Joe the first time, when I was mortified about my aging body. Gosh, I hid in my bathroom like a sixty-two year old virgin. If you had seen me, you'd have roared. When I finally managed to gather the courage to leave the bathroom, I had my robe pulled so tightly around me I thought I'd pass out. When Joe looked at me with great passion, not seeing any of my "warts" I became even more embarrassed. That he made it through all my old-lady defenses says a lot about his character.

Venus chuckled, "Hey, Joe has warts too. What's with you being the only toad around? You don't own toad-ship. Give yourself credit for being a beautiful woman. Yeah, you're not twenty-two, but think of the maturity you have." With that, Venus was laughing outright. "Maturity. Yeah. Do you ever think about how in some respects we are still like young girls when it comes to finding love."

Venus paused for a moment and said very seriously, "I think you should write a book called *Dummies Guide to Senior Dating*. You could have chapters such as 'Undressing for the First time; Sixty-two-year old Reborn Virgins - Again; Brazilian or no Brazilian or, How to Have Sex with Pubic Hair; Going Swimming Together for the First Time; Lingerie shopping; Dry Vaginas or Limp Dicks.' Oh, the list could go on and on," Venus snickered.

As Venus continued her chapter titles, Sally was howling. "I'll take that suggestion into consideration. Actually, I think it's a great idea; let's talk about it sometime, huh? When you have more time. In the meantime, my technical-writing career should be quite a help to this sort of book, don't cha think? Imagine how descriptive I could be!"

Sally got just a little more serious, "It does seem kinda funny how new relationships make you feel silly and youthful. Nothing like that love vibe! Boy! Brings out all your best and is like a shot of adrenaline! I had forgotten how smitten I was back then – not that I'm not now. Thanks for the reminder.

"You're right, I didn't get any sleep and nothing got done by either of us. We'd go places and all we'd see was one another. I guess when you're older, you don't have that much time to play the games of youth with all their absurd insecurities. Of course, you may exchange one set of insecurities for others, but game-playing just doesn't seem to make it, at least not for us. We knew what we wanted and we took it. Okay, Venus, you win. I'll simply shout my support for you and Greg."

"Now, about Saturday night. Can you two come over about seven?"

Venus replied, "I'll ask Greg and get back to you."

That Saturday night Venus and Greg joined Joe and Sally for a barbeque, and everyone was surprised by how much Joe and Greg had in common. Joe had owned a technical-publishing company and then became a computer geek in the late seventies, when he saw the momentum with computers. His business had expanded enormously over the years, with several offices throughout both the East coast and the West coast. Joe mentioned how, when he met Sally, it was at one of the few functions he attended for his publishing company - a holiday party in honor of their various authors. Joe emphasized, "For me, it was love at first sight."

Greg nodded as Joe lauded Sally's essence, and thought to himself, "Yeah, I know the feeling." When he felt enough time had passed before interrupting Joe's accolades, Greg told Joe what had happened with his computer and bank account. Joe listened carefully while Greg filled in the details, and finally said, "I think it's a great idea to make sure that all your employees are on the up-and-up. Have all their references and names gone over by the police department; they will search not only the names as you know them, but also any derivatives from them.

"Then find an expert on this type of computer problem. Police do the investigative stuff, but may have neither the time nor the resources to really stick with a case, especially when insurance is paying. The insurance company will usually spend more time looking for the perpetrators and, in your case, it will probably be worth your company's interest to pursue. If there's any way I can help you connect with the right resources, I will. I can give you the names of a couple people I know who are really into this sort of computer-hacking. Will that be helpful?"

Greg answered, "I'd appreciate any help you can give me, but I think my employees were pretty well checked out from our Boston office. I don't know if anyone counter-checked, so I will do that again on Monday morning. It's good to know we really have done everything we could, especially coming from a computer geek like you." Joe laughed and acknowledged he was just exactly that.

Greg added, "Right now we have to contend with the house break-in and the note."

"That has to be the pits!"

"Yup."

All in all, the evening turned out to be very pleasant. The four played Sexual Trivial Pursuit, and Venus and Greg lost amid much hilarity. When they left and returned to Greg's place, they found that OM had totally taken over Greg's bed.

"Hey, get off there, you big beast," Greg laughed.

OM opened one eye and instantly shut it.

Venus said, "What's yours is his, and what's his is his. He assumes that this is *his* bed and you aren't going to tell him differently."

"Just wait till I throw him off!"

"Yeah, like you'll do that," Venus smirked.

"I know, maybe if we sit on the top of the bed and just cuddle, or bounce up and down a couple of times, he'll get the hint and leave. Let's try."

Venus looked at him as if he were crazy, "You've got to be kidding. When that cat sleeps, it takes an act of Congress or a bomb to get him to move."

"How about if I just pick him up and pretend to cuddle him?"

"That's how I do it when I'm desperate. I assume you are now feeling desperate and afraid of a little thirteen-pound ball of fluff," laughed Venus.

"Well, considering the way he went after Rita, I have to keep him on my good side. Small lions are only a little less dangerous than big ones."

Venus paused a moment and said, "I still have this gut feeling about Rita that just feels bad! I know you trust her and all that, but there is something amiss, I just know it. I have to ask you, what does she know about computers?"

Greg said, "Methinks we've been through this before. Why would she come all the way out here to hack, when she could have done the same thing in Boston? I think you're still a little upset with her telling you I had a girlfriend in Boston. Furthermore, what the hell would she break into my house for? Or do with any formula if it had been there? Or shoot out one of my tires, or leave that note? Again, my darling Venus, I think you're a bit paranoid."

"Yeah! Maybe you're right. Sorry to be such a pest." She changed the subject, "I'm going to get OM a treat. That'll move him, he loves his catnip treats." Leaving the room, she suggestively bumped into Greg and huskily whispered, "Be ready for some real lovin when I get back."

"I'm more than ready."

She glanced down at Greg's pants and commented, "I guess you are."

The next day in the office, Venus scarcely got to talk to Greg. When he did call, he told her he had been called back to Boston for business and had to be gone two weeks.

"Oh, I'll miss you. Do you think it'll be all right with the cops if you leave now? When are you going?"

"Day after tomorrow. I've already cleared it with the police. They said there's nothing I can do here to assist them further and if they need me, they have my company telephone number and my cell. But, back to us: we can talk every night, even have phone sex. Want to?"

"All you ever think about is sex! Phone sex will be a new one for me, but I assume you are quite practiced in that sort of thing."

"Hell no! Never did it before in my life. Never had anyone I wanted to do that with. Anyway, I thought I'm too old for that stuff."

"Yeah, I guess I believe you," Venus laughed.

"Now that we have the important stuff out of the way, will you take me to the airport?"

"Of course. Do I see you later today?"

"No can do. I have too much to do before I leave, including a meeting with my security team and the police. But tomorrow night, definitely!"

When Venus hung up the phone, she had a sinking feeling in her stomach. To say that she'd miss Greg was an understatement. She realized she was hooked, and good.

The next two days passed quickly. Venus and Greg spent as much time with each other as they could, including quietly making dinners and breakfasts together. Greg was a great cook. One night he prepared shrimp in a butter, wine, garlic and herb sauce that was delicious and like nothing she had ever eaten. When she asked what the ingredients were, he refused to tell her his "secret recipe."

"Maybe if you're really good, I'll tell you some day."

"What do I have to do?"

"I'm not telling you that either. For the sake of harmony, dear woman, drop it."

Venus knew there was nothing she could say or do at this time that would change his mind, so she laughed and stopped the questions. She knew when to let go and gave herself credit for it.

The night before Greg left, he called Venus to tell her he had a little surprise for her. When Venus questioned him, he said, "Now it wouldn't be a surprise it if I told you. Would it? Just wait."

Venus and OM were to spend the evening at Greg's because it was closer to the airport than her house in Encinitas was. When they arrived, OM was released from his carrier, his litter box set up, and then Greg took Venus into the dining room. He had set a candlelit table with lobster and crab cocktail, wine and cheese, and fresh crusty bread. Dessert was amazing - raspberries dipped in either milk chocolate or dark chocolate. "Eat hearty my dear, for there is more to come."

"What do you mean? This is fantastic. I *love* the raspberries! Never had them chocolate covered before – only strawberries. What a phenomenal combo, much better than strawberries! Thank you for this wonderful surprise. I love it. I should have been doing it for you; after all, you're the one leaving."

"No, this isn't the surprise. Just eat and relax, I'll tell you when the surprise is."

When they had finished eating, and the table was cleared and dishes done, Greg took Venus' hand, saying, "Now, come for your surprise."

As they went towards the bedroom, Venus looked questioningly at Greg. "What's happening here?"

"Come on, just walk." He took her to the large master bathroom where there were candles and an ice bucket with a bottle of champagne in it. "Strip! I'm giving you a bath."

"What?"

"You heard me. Take off your clothes." With those commands, Greg turned on the water to fill the tub and added vanilla bubble bath to the water. When the temperature was just right, Greg opened the bottle of champagne and poured them each a glass. "Now get in, my love."

"You're not coming in?"

"Nope." With Venus in the tub, Greg picked up a soft sponge he had purchased, dipped it in the water and began gently to wash her back, her shoulders and her neck.

Venus flushed in delight. "My God, Greg, this is the nicest thing anyone's ever done for me. I can't believe you came up with this. . . I just wish you were here with me."

"Not yet. I'm not through, so just relax and enjoy." He turned her to him, wrung out the sponge and washed her face, pausing to kiss her deeply. She responded with the same depth of feeling. Then Greg took each of her feet in his hand, and tenderly, washed them, licked them and finally began to suck her toes - each one individually and then several in his mouth at the same time. Venus was trembling all the way up to her vagina and belly, her vagina pulsating in the same rhythm as Greg's sucking motion dictated. Never had she felt so delectable, sexy or treasured. And Greg continued, releasing her feet and teasingly moving the sponge over her breasts, paying particular attention to the nipples which responded immediately.

Venus moaned. "Are you stopping there?" The sensations, more than she could bear, went from the tip of her toes to the top of her head.

"You must think I'm nuts or dead if you think that," he answered. He adoringly moved the sponge between her legs, stroking her and loving the sensuality of the situation.

"This is beyond delicious, beyond phenomenal. Please come in here with me," Venus moaned, "I want you."

"First I want to watch you come as I stroke you."

"Won't take much," she cried, reaching the point of no return. As her body moved towards his fingers that were deeply imbedded within her, Venus felt herself come apart. "What is it you have, sir? Never has this sort of thing happened to me. God I love it. *Now come in.*"

"In you, or in the water?"

"How bout both?"

"Nope. Now you're getting out for a sexy massage. Think you can deal with that?"

"My God, can you?"

Greg took out a heated towel and wrapped Venus in it as she bonelessly got out of the tub. "We go to my room with the champagne after I blow out the candles."

Greg's bed was beautifully turned down. He had put candles in his bedroom too. After lighting them, he said, "Lie on your stomach and let me put some oil on your back."

In all her years of having massages, this one had to be the topper. Greg lovingly massaged Venus' back and buttocks with amazingly strong and knowledgeable fingers. "How did you learn to do this so well?"

"It's you. I'm just letting my heart lead my hands," Greg said kissing the back of her neck.

"Now turn over." Venus turned and Greg began to massage her shoulders and neck, then moved down to her breasts and nipples.

"You've got to let me touch you," Venus begged.

"Don't have to do anything of the sort. Now it's time to use my mouth, and to taste you and lick you all over. Do you mind?"

"If you don't, I might go crazy. When you're finished, you will come inside me, won't you?"

"I might," Greg said laughingly. When he reached her thighs, he said, "Spread your legs for me."

Venus came instantly, deeply, almost violently. *"Now, Greg, Now. Please!"*

When Greg saw her eyes filled with love and passion he knew his eyes reflected the same emotions. At last he took off his clothes, and his hard erection entered her. Both of them were rocked by the energy and explosion of emotions. In unison they cried out each other's names.

Venus panted, "That was amazing. God, you are so gorgeous."

All Greg could say was, "Thanks for the *gorgeous* remark, and yes it was fabulous."

"Next time I'll surprise you, except you'll know what's coming. Won't that be fun?" Venus could feel her eyes beginning to close. She wrapped her arms around Greg, pulling him into her until she didn't know where she began or ended, nor did she care.

They both fell asleep for a couple hours and then awakened when OM decided to purr in their faces. "I'm hungry, how about you?" Greg asked sleepily.

"I could eat a horse, except of course I don't eat meat. But what do you have?"

"What I'd really love," said Greg, "is a peanut butter and jelly sandwich, but only on great whole wheat bread. I know I have the ingredients – want one?"

"Of course."

"All right, I'll make them."

As they sat happily munching their sandwiches, they spoke of many things. Venus was curious about Greg's parents; it seemed they had talked about everything under the sun, except his mother and father. Finally she got up the courage to ask, "Hey, Greg, you never mention your parents. Are they alive. . . dead? Do they still live in Boston?"

After pausing to reflect just how much he was willing to share with Venus, Greg began to speak. "My parents are both alive. I have practically no relationship with them. They weren't interested in my children, just like they weren't interested in me, and that was the final straw."

"Was it *that* bad? Who did take care of you, and how did you turn out so well?"

"*Well*, you say? It's taken me way too long to come to a point of peace with myself, even, to some extent, with them. My parents were only interested in business; and a huge number of nannies were my care-takers. Because I was an only child – I guess a slip-up in birth control methods produced me - I was on my own. All I did was get into mischief and learn how to talk my way out of it. It was very painful, and I never even spoke about it until a couple of years ago."

"What changed it for you?"

"Many things; especially looking at my lack of relationships and my fear of them. What I discovered was it was so easy to blame my parents for everything and to take no responsibility for anything. I'm still learning how to trust myself and others, though I now believe that relationships *can* be loving, honest, committed and fun. I never really thought that before. You, Venus, are my test, my playing field and hopefully, my final exam."

Greg became a little more serious as he said, "Venus, I never thought I could feel about anyone the way I do about you. And what's shocking to me is that it's been less than two months!. What is it about you - besides you're being gorgeous, smart, funny, loving, and sexy that I find so appealing?"

"I think it's my auburn hair."

"Well, how about my green eyes? I think you never answered my question, whether my eyes were the type that you loved."

"Not just your eyes that I love," Venus felt shock as she realized she had just told Greg she loved him. Albeit, not directly, but she knew he picked it up immediately. And part of her was terrified.

"So, Venus, you love me, huh?" Greg whispered.

"Yeah, I guess so," Venus mumbled and looked away.

"Do you want to know if the feelings are mutual or whether you're in this all by yourself?" Greg smiled at her.

"You want to tell me?"

"Yup, the feelings are mutual. I do love you, and I don't think I have ever said that to anyone but my kids. Scary for me to say, but it wasn't quite as hard as I'd thought it might be."

"What do you mean?"

"I imagined myself saying *I love you*, and my stomach turned and flopped. I thought it was fear, but you know, now I think it was excitement. I love you, Venus Lighton."

"And I love you Greg Richards."

"Let me make love to you, Venus."

"No, let us make love to each other," whispered Venus.

While Greg's in Boston

The morning after Venus took Greg to the airport, she felt strangely empty. The feeling was so foreign to her, she didn't quite know what to do. Meditate, she heard her inner voice say. After twenty minutes, Venus felt considerably more present yet she still questioned another message she heard in her head. The essence of it was: *"Be careful."* Venus asked, "Do I need to be careful about loving Greg?" The answer was a resounding *"NO."* "Then, what?" The phone rang as she was conversing with herself. It was Sally.

"Well, did you take him to the airport?"

"Yes. God, I feel so empty. That's pretty bizarre for me, the Queen of Alone."

"It's about time someone was in your life except for OM! How is your body-awareness and self-consciousness doing?"

"I'm learning, among other things, that I am truly not my body. When I think of myself having made fun of my wrinkles or lines or whatever, I begin to recognize it's a way of not loving the real me. Now, I am definitely more comfortable in my own skin. It's taken a while, but with Greg's help and adoration, I'm on my way to becoming a blatant nudist." Venus' eyes twinkled, "Shame on me! But it's so much fun with him. When he looks at my naked body, I see him melt with love. He's *seeing me*! What's not to like with that sort of feedback!

"The next conscious challenge, when he gets back, is to introduce him to my kids. I think I'll do it individually. Not sure who will feel more nutty, me or them. Even though they have been pestering me to go out, I get this feeling they won't be quite as open towards him as I want them to be. Kids are funny when they realize their mother or father is having sex with someone new. The way Greg and I keep touching each other, they will probably groan and tell us, 'Take it in the bedroom.' That's all I need."

Sally giggled as she remembered introducing her own three kids, Jennifer, Boyd and George, to Joe. "It was hard all right. It's like they think sex is dirty or naughty if you're over fifty. And we're over sixty! Yeah, the kids couldn't look me in the eyes for fear they might notice I was a sexual being. When I used to laugh at them, right to their faces, they'd get even more embarrassed."

Venus laughed, too, and said, "Was that *all* of the kids? I thought that at least George would have been fine with all that."

Sally uttered, "George! He was the worst. That's because he was a player and he assumed anyone who might conceivably be interested in dating his mother must be a player too. Honestly, to look at me, do you think a player could be interested? I think if he were, he'd be hard up."

"Now, now, Sally. You were the one yelling at me for my lack of self-esteem and listen to what you just said! Stop doing that to yourself. You're beautiful the way you are, and no smart-ass remarks about any of your body parts! You are also *not* your body. Anyway, how were Jennifer and Boyd towards Joe?"

"Jennifer kinda smiled and giggled. Boyd moaned, like 'oh no, now what!' It took them a while, but when they saw Joe treating me like a queen, they got how much he cared for me. They were relieved when we got married; they felt it was far better for me to marry than to just sleep around. Like I really slept around!"

Venus picked up on that. "I think my kids might have been happier if I had slept around, at least based on the crap they used to tell me. 'Go out Mom. You just sit at home. You need to get out before you're too old to walk.' Ah well, kids. Who the hell knows what they want or think? As Rhett Butler famously said, 'Frankly my dear, I don't give a damn.'"

"But, to change the subject dramatically, Sally, when I was meditating this morning, I got a very strong message: Be *careful*. I asked my guidance if I was to be careful of loving Greg. . ."

"You mean you told him you love him?" Sally screeched.

"It sort of slipped out. But good news; the feelings are mutual."

"Hot dog! You think you'll get married?"

"I don't know, anyway that's not what I wanted to talk about. My guidance was very emphatic about being careful, but it was definitely not about loving Greg. I was just told to be careful. What do *you* think it meant?"

"Good God. Did you ask if it meant physically, or about your job, or anything more specific?"

132

"Fraid not. I sort of freaked when I got that message, and didn't pursue it. I'll ask again when I meditate later or tomorrow. Anyway, the very idea creeped me out."

"It would me too. But don't jump to any conclusions with just those two words. Keep asking until you get an understandable, specific answer. If you don't get a clear answer soon, call Rachael or LuAnne. They are able to tune into a lot of stuff, especially those messages. Hey, I gotta go; my business phone is ringing and I'm expecting an important call. I'll talk to you later."

Venus spent the rest of the morning deep in tasks she had been putting off during the past whirlwind several weeks. She was grateful when the stack of papers on her desk actually diminished. "Wow," she thought, "maybe Greg's going away for a couple of weeks is a good thing. Look at all the crap work I've accomplished!"

Venus called Toni and Bret and their spouses, asking them if they wanted to join her for dinner at one of their favorite Thai places. All but John were able to make it.

When Toni and Bret or their respective partners were with Venus, they simply couldn't stop looking at her and bragging to their friends about how beautiful and open she had become. In the past when the kids were with her, they often alluded to her as "Venus in Beige," or "Bunned Venus," or "My Mother the Withdrawal Queen." They fervently hoped she would remain the person who they now saw, both on the physical and the emotional plane. The woman they were to meet at dinner was a vibrant, alive young woman. How shocking!

Venus was often asked, even by her kids, what she had done to herself lately to look so good. She laughingly replied, "Nothing like letting go of a whole lot of baggage, to lift years off you. I highly recommend it." She never mentioned the fabulous, earth-shattering sex she was having, though she knew how that changed her too. She intuitively knew that her kids were aware of the sexual aspect, too, though no one had said anything.

"Do you want to meet here, or at the restaurant" Venus inquired of each.

Toni said, "I want to come by and see OM, so how about if I pick you up? Maybe I'll even pick up, Bret; that is, if he'll ride with me."

"What makes you think he won't ride with you?"

"Nothing, I was just being a smart-aleck. I will call him and Elysa, having to practically pass their house on the way to yours. Elysa, Bret's wife for almost twenty years, was adored by both Toni and Venus.

An hour later, the four of them were eating delicious Tom Yom Gai soup, roasted eggplant, curried vegetables and Pad Thai. After listening to how all the grandchildren were, and all the other gossipy news, Venus brought up Greg's name.

"Even though we've only known each other about two months, Greg is a man I am definitely into. He is just wonderful, and when he returns from his Boston trip in two weeks, I'd like you all to meet him."

"You're kidding! It's that serious already?" Elysa asked. "Then no wonder you look so good" escaped from Elysa's mouth before she could censor it. Everyone at the table knew exactly what she meant and laughed, albeit uncomfortably.

"Mom," said Toni finally, recovering some sense of propriety, "shouldn't you be more wary? After all, what do you know about him?"

Bret was next to comment, and his remark really surprised Venus. "Go, Mom, go. It's about time you got some loving and joy in your life, and don't let these women say anything different!"

A general discussion followed among the three of them, leaving Venus to listen as if she were an outsider.

"Gossiping in the present," she thought. "I'm here, but it's like I'm not. Time to stop that."

Finally, she raised her voice and said, "You know, I. Am. Here. This. Is. My. Life. I am just sharing with you, I am not here to have you dissect my relationship or analyze it into the ground. As you kids say to me when I do that to you, 'M-o-m…' Consider this conversation a role-reversal. I'm saying, 'K-i-d-s….'"

The rest of the evening was spent laughing, joking and conversing in an easy manner. When Toni finally dropped off Venus, the whole gang went in to pay homage to OM. He took his usual "king of the jungle stance" and awarded everyone with purring and individual cuddling.

Later that night, with OM by her side, Venus felt Greg's absence and it was an achy feeling she wasn't fond of. She had told Toni and John, Bret and Elysa, of Greg's presence in her life, but they had yet to meet him. Of course, they hadn't pestered her to make that happen either. They had asked all the appropriate questions, and laughed when

134

she gave them almost all the appropriate answers. It wasn't their business how hot Greg and she were sexually, even though Venus was intuitively aware that they knew already. She was also pretty sure how scared they'd be by seeing them together. Venus was, she had to admit to herself, thrilled with her physical and emotional growth and transformation. And, if she did say so herself, for a sixty-four year old woman, she was pretty great. Bret and Toni intuitively knew that now she accepted parts of herself she had long denied - her sexuality, her attractiveness, and her anger and pain – and were happy that she was dating once again. Venus herself used this analogy: I'm like a boiling pot on the stove that, now the lid is off, all the steam I've held inside can escape from the pot."

By the time everyone left, Venus was exhausted. "It's after ten o'clock," she thought, "I wonder if I'll hear from Greg." As if by magic, her phone rang, and it was Greg.

"Hello there, miss me?" Greg's voice was deep and husky.

"Well," Venus responded in a similar deep voice, "probably so, what's it to ya?"

"Oh, God Venus, you've really got me. I smile all day long, even when things are tough and trust me, things have been challenging around here."

"What's happened?"

"For some reason, I had an intense need to see my parents, and went to visit them. How's that?"

"So, *why* did you go visit your parents?"

"I don't really know, except that I realized they are still together after all these years and I was kind of wondering what kept them together. It seemed to me they had nothing in common; they seldom spoke to each other all through my life. Neither one of them had any qualms about divorce, so I've always wondered why they didn't. Christ, they've been married almost sixty years."

"Did you ever ask them?"

"Not until tonight. They actually looked me in the eye – both of them – and told me they loved each other. You could've knocked me over with a feather. I said to both of them, 'what about each other do you love?' Do you know, they actually were able to give concrete stuff.

"I finally got up the nerve to ask them if they ever spoke of love all the time I was growing up, or was it something that recently dawned on them? They were very surprised, yet appeared to be relieved by my questions. Finally, my mother, the more talkative of the two, answered, 'Well, we probably just had some revelations within the past three or four years. Prior to that, we existed on a daily basis, living our jobs and then our retirements, deriving all our satisfactions from them.'

"Then, what got me was mom's saying, 'Greg, it finally dawned on us that life is short and we hadn't been making much of it. We both felt so guilty about how you were raised, we never even spoke of it, even to each other. Then one day about seven years ago, one of our close business associates dropped dead of a heart attack. You remember Lex Russell? Well, he died suddenly. Both your father and I were shocked and deeply saddened. It seems as if from that day on, we began cautiously to talk to each other in ways we never had. When we finally talked about you, both of us were in tears and didn't quite know what to do with our emotions. We let you be raised by nannies. We were never there for you. We were ashamed and convinced you would never forgive us, so we let everything ride. We prayed that somehow we'd get to apologize to you for not having been the parents, or grandparents to your kids, that you deserved. But neither one of us is very good with initiating conversations like this.'

"My dad's eyes were filled with tears when he added, 'Greg, we were shitty parents, and we were shitty to each other, but we honestly don't know what we can do at this point to make it up to you. For ourselves, we have vowed to be open, loving, careful of our language - you remember how we were so sarcastic to each other - don't you, and to talk to each other kindly. We even want to have our vows renewed, as silly as that may seem, after sixty years.'

"I answered, 'No, it doesn't seem silly.' That's when I told them about you, and guess what? They genuinely want to meet you. Never, in my whole life, have they given a damn about anyone or anything I do. Now all of a sudden, they want to meet you! They have apologized to me; I wonder if they'll apologize to my kids. I did suggest it and they said they will initiate conversations with each of the grandchildren for exactly that purpose. It was quite an emotional scene. I'm so glad I've been with you and have carried your strength of character with me in my heart. I know it helped. I said that the next time I come East, I would bring you. I do hope you'll come with me."

"Oh Greg, I'd love to meet your parents if you don't think it's too soon. But what I really want to know is how you are handling their grand confessions and whether you can forgive them. It seems to me, folks our parents' ages weren't allowed to express emotions, so I figure that had to be quite an amazing scenario you just went through. How are you with it? And how were they when you left them? Sounds to me you all underwent huge emotional traumas."

"For a while, I felt as if I'd been kicked in the heart; what they told me shattered the reality I've called my own for so long. I'd been so pissed that I'd never noticed they were becoming kinder to each other. I had such a chip on my shoulder, it's not surprising they couldn't approach me. For that, I am truly sorry."

"Did you share that with them?"

"Yeah, I did. Man, you never get to stop learning or growing up, do you?" Greg made a kind of clucking sound that Venus heard in amazement.

"Ah, but your growth is wonderful. I know it's not my place to say anything, but honestly, Greg, I am so proud of you for hearing what they had to say and not dismissing their apologies."

"Venus, you give me the courage. Without what we've been experiencing these past two months, I don't think I could have even asked them anything, or for that matter, gone to visit them. Remember when I told you I was through with them? You just tweaked me to look deeper, whether you knew it or not. So, will you come back with me to meet them?"

"Absolutely. I look forward to it. By the way, I'm sure I'll have a million questions about your meeting with your mom and dad, right after we hang up. So if I pester you tomorrow about your conversation with them, don't be upset. Sometimes I don't think of what I want to ask or say right away."

"Fine with me. Now let me give you some news about the office. With the help of a detective, Jamie Robins, I've been busy tracing the histories of many of the staff here maybe finding out more information about who might have the skills to hack into the computer system. I still don't think it is anyone on my staff, but I'm going to leave no stone unturned. The insurance company is being a pain. . . what a surprise that is! All my employees are coming into my office and not letting me get a thing done. They all have their theories about who could have done this and how it could have been done; yet they notice there is something different in me. Talk about your energy stuff. One asked me if I had met someone special, to which I said 'Absolutely!' Before I could even continue with the business discussion, everyone was in my office asking about the woman I'd met. Would you believe that? Anyway, because they, um, love me so much, they wanted all the facts. Did I give them some!" Greg laughed, "When they told me I was smitten, I answered, 'You're damn right!'" They were actually cheering for me, for you and for us. What do you think of that, my love?"

"Greg that is sooo cute, I just love it - and of course, you. They must think very highly of you to be so interested," Venus chuckled.

"Actually, I thought so too. Getting back to the more serious stuff. Jamie Robins, the detective I've hired, says that by the end of the week we should know more. He's given me a few suggestions about upping my security in the meantime. Enough about my stressful life, what's happening with you?"

"I had dinner with my kids tonight and told them I want them to meet you when you get back. Think you can handle it?"

"If you can handle my parents, I'm sure I can handle your kids. Don't forget, I've already won over OM. He loves me, Greg gloated, "and they have to too," Greg chuckled. "Now, do we have phone sex, or do I just hang up and get a good night's sleep? I'm whipped."

"Goodnight Greg."

"I love you, Venus."

"Love you, too."

A Brush With Death

Glenda, Venus' secretary was a wonderful baker and every five or six weeks baked biscotti and brought it to the office. In everyone's words, her baking was beyond delicious, it was orgasmic. Venus was one of her biggest fans. Once a month, she asked, "Glenda, why don't you open a bakery instead of working in this stuffy office?"

Glenda always laughed and said, "This office is far from stuffy! I like it here, there's less responsibility." Practically the same words were exchanged every time Glenda brought in her goodies. Venus' two favorites were chocolate-almond and chocolate-orange, and today there were both. "I'm an absolute chocoholic and when chocolate's mixed with orange and or almond, it's swoon time."

As Glenda sat down at her desk, she said, "I left you your coffee, it's on the back bookcase."

"Thanks Glenda. I'm going to go to the rest room. I'll be back in a minute."

A few moments later, Glenda heard a crash and lots of swearing.

"Damn. . . shit! I've knocked over the coffee and it's all over the bookshelf and the rug. What a klutz!"

Glenda came running in with towels in her hand. "What happened?"

"I tripped over a pile of books I left on the floor yesterday when clearing my desk. Damn, now I have to clean up all this crap. Good thing it didn't get on the cookies," she laughed.

Glenda began to laugh with Venus, but their laughter quickly ceased, when both of them looked down where the mess had occurred.

"Oh my God. What's happening?" Glenda gasped.

Venus paled, "Shit," I don't know, the rug is dissolving. What was in that cup?"

"I put in coffee and a little cream the way you always take it," Glenda answered.

Venus' knees began to shake. She looked at Glenda and said, "We need to call the police. There is some kind of acid in there. Look at what it's doing to everything it touches. Oh my God, that could have been my insides. Jesus, apparently, it's not just Greg who's in trouble! Did someone enter the side door when I was in the rest room?"

"I didn't hear anything or see anything. Cripes, Venus. I'm calling the police *now*."

Within minutes, the police were there, and there was an almost instant response from some of the chemists in her department and the campus security. They were taking samples from the rug, the coffee-pot, the container of creamer, and the destroyed books and shelving.

"Who could have done this to you, Dr. Lighton?" asked the police officer, who had introduced himself as Detective Robert Swan.

In a shaky voice, Venus responded, "I don't know, but it sure as hell wasn't Glenda!"

"We'll question her separately. You understand we have to; she was the person who served you the coffee."

"She's served me coffee every day for over ten years; she's totally trustworthy. We don't know if someone entered the side door."

Detective Swan acknowledged her concern, told her the police were looking for fingerprints and then continued, "Dr. Lighton, has anything changed recently in your life or here in the office? Is there anyone who has some sort of grudge against you?"

"Not anything I know of. Oh, I'm involved in a relationship for the first time and Glenda knows that, but then everyone in the department knows that. The man I'm involved with has had two different, what the police are calling, 'stalking events' and a computer-hacking. Do you think they're connected?"

"Let's get back to Glenda just for a moment. Is there any possibility she could be jealous?" asked Swan.

"Look, detective, I've known Glenda well over ten years. She is not only my secretary, she is my friend. Also one of the most happily married people I know. Her husband is a doll, her family's incredible and she is just an amazing woman. I trust her explicitly. I think everything that's happening with Greg is connected to this."

"Is there anyone else who might want to harm you or even kill you?"

"Me, or Greg, or both of us?" Venus responded in complete frustration. Her stomach almost hurled when she thought, "This isn't make-believe. Someone has tried to kill me. Now what? Maybe that's what my guidance was referring to when I was told, 'Be careful.' I should call Greg, but what could he do anyway?"

Detective Swan said, "Sorry, but we'll have to ask you more questions later. You and everyone around here. We're closing off this whole floor now. Go home, relax, have a drink and talk with someone who will take care of you. You need to get out of here. Fortunately, it looks as it you had some angels who watched over you and made sure you didn't take a drink from that coffee mug. You're one hell of a lucky lady. By the way, your new relationship…Greg?"

"Greg Richards. He's had to consult with the police a lot lately."

"Greg Richards! Oh yeah! No wonder your name was familiar. You were with him while his house was being broken into *and* when his tire was shot."

"Yes. That's so. Do you think these events, um, you know, the stuff in my coffee, and his house, and the shooting of his tire, are connected?"

"It's certainly possible. When we get back the enormous amount of lab work, we should have some answers. In the meantime, we will do everything we can to make sure everyone is safe. Now go home. We'll keep actively in touch, okay?" He paused and asked in a caring way, "Do you want us to drive you home? Oh, when you speak to Greg, tell him that Lee and Stan will be working with me and the rest of forensics. Within a couple of days we should have more information."

"Okay, I'll be sure to tell him. Now can I call my friends Sally and Joe, (seeing how Glenda is under suspicion)?"

"We have to do this, understand? Call now, and then get the hell out of here. Wait a minute, I know a Sally and Joe. What are their last names?" Swan queried.

"It's Joe and Sally Parker, they're good friends of mine."

"Damn, small world! I know them," remarked Swan. "Joe and I were in the service together. A great guy. I'll tell security to be on the watch for either or both of them. You have good friends, Venus; again, a lucky lady."

"Thanks, Detective."

"Call me Bob." Now get out of here" and he lightly pushed her forward.

Suddenly Venus began to tremble. "I know that was a gentle push, but boy, my legs are rubber."

"I'll walk you downstairs and stay until they come."

"Great, I'd appreciate that Detective...whoops, Bob."

Sally arrived in ten minutes, the panicky look on her face clearly visible; she too, was white as a ghost.

"Sally, this is Detective Bob Swan. He says he was in the service with Joe. He's been kind enough to be my support system since this happened."

"Yes, I know Bob; I'm surprised you don't remember each other, having been at all our parties."

With the help of Bob, Venus explained what had taken place that morning and how Bob had said there must have been angels all around her protecting her from a very likely death. The more Venus verbalized her thoughts, the more the impact of *what-if* hit her gut.

"I don't know what to do, what to think. How could this have happened? Who would do such a thing? It's not an accident. *Poison was put there in my cup!* My God! Who did this?" Venus kept repeating herself as she shook her head. She was beginning to feel the full ramifications of what she had gone through.

"You're coming home with me and staying with us until this thing is solved. Neither Joe nor I will take no for an answer," Sally commanded. "And, by the way, your case is in good hands with Bob Swan."

"I know that now. Oh," Venus said, "OM. . . I have to get OM."

"All right. We'll get your OM kitty and pick up some of your clothes. Then it's to our house."

"Okay," Venus assented meekly. Suddenly, another thought: "I have to call Greg. I never told him about that message I got in meditation, that I need to be careful. Maybe this is what it meant? Oh, Sally, do you think I ought to tell him?"

Sally paused, "Yeah, when we get home. That should probably be soon enough. Are you comfortable with that?"

"I think so."

"Good. Let's get you out of here and in the car."

But as soon as they got into Sally's car, Venus dialed Greg's cell phone. When he picked it up, all he heard was muffled sobbing. Sally realized that Greg had no idea what was happening, so she took the phone from Venus. "Hi Greg, it's Sally." Before she could even tell Greg anything, he demanded, "Is Venus all right? What's the matter?"

"Someone put some poison or acid in Venus' coffee cup at work today. If she had drunk any of it, that definitely would not have been a pretty picture. The police are questioning everyone in the chemistry department, and right now and I'm afraid Venus is feeling the full effect of what could have happened. When she asked the police if there were a possibility that all the stuff that's happened to you could be related to this, they didn't say no."

"I'm coming home. I'll get a plane out of here in a couple of hours. Tell Venus that. No wait, let me tell her myself."

Sally handed the phone back to Venus, who said between sobs, she said, "I'm sorry I'm such a big baby. All I'm doing right now is crying, but honestly, Greg, no one ever tried to kill me before," and she let a small pathetic laugh escape.

"You once asked what might cause any emotional reaction in me, and I didn't answer. This is it, Venus. I'm leaving Boston and coming home to be with you. I'll call when I get the reservations and when I land in San Diego. You're not staying at your house, are you? I don't trust that the person won't come to your house to hurt you."

"You don't have to come home Greg. Sally and Joe will take excellent care of me."

"And," growled Greg, "I will take better care of you. I hope to see you tonight."

"I really don't need anyone to take care of me. Honestly. I'm just a bit shaken up."

Greg softened his voice as he responded, "Venus, my love, I know you're shaken, and so am I. It's not every day the woman I love is…" He trailed off as the full impact of what he was going to say hit his gut. "I love you. Now let me talk to Sally, okay?"

"I love you too," Venus replied, and handing the phone to Sally. "He wants to talk to you."

When Sally got on the phone, Greg made her promise that she wouldn't leave Venus alone, not even for a second.

"I won't leave her alone, Greg. Both Joe and I will be with her. Plan to stay here too. Let us know what time your flight comes in?"

Venus was grateful that Sally and Joe's house was not too far from her own. There, on the beautiful Pacific Ocean, it was one of the huge older homes, with two floors and staircases – front and back. There were five bedrooms, a study, library, and family room as well as living room, dining room and kitchen. It was located on one of the best pieces of property along the ocean and had privacy. Venus had always liked the way the energy of the house flowed. It was perfect for anyone to go to the various rooms or corners and not disturb others on the way. Beyond the front entry, there was a sweeping semi-circular staircase and a huge foyer. To the right of the foyer was a large dining room, and to the left was the living room. Beyond them were the kitchen and the family room, and further on were the library and study. Each of the rooms at the back had a French door that opened to a view of the ocean. The back staircase was entered through the kitchen.

Venus used to tease Sally about having to clean all six bathrooms herself, but Sally didn't mind. She loved the house and the privacy and space it provided. She gloated, "Now, Venus, you'll appreciate all the space, bathrooms, and staircases. You and Greg can sneak in and out, and we'll never know."

"Who says Greg is staying here?" Venus asked. Then she sighed realizing that her comment sounded an awful lot like game-playing. Sally and Joe's offer for them to stay there was truly from their hearts. Finally she replied, "Oh well, I suppose you're right. Greg and I get a little noisy at times, so I'm grateful for the distance between the bedrooms," Venus grinned as she sassed at her friend.

Sally retorted, "Don't forget, we're not too far from being newly weds ourselves, Miss-In-Love-for-the-First Time."

Sally and Joe had totally remodeled and refurnished the house they lived in. Both of them liked bold large, overstuffed pieces of furniture in neutral colors. They also loved an occasional accent piece that was bright and bold and mixed the colors masterfully. Their taste was eclectic. Their kitchen was huge with dark-gray cabinets, off-white counters, a bamboo floor and with yellow being the main accent color. Venus had thought, when Sally was in the planning stages of the kitchen, that it sounded awful. In truth, it was gorgeous. Venus loved the way Sally had totally agreed to change the house when she had married Joe (who had definite ideas on what was livable and what wasn't, and what was too girly for him.) Fortunately, the two of them worked well together and had created a home that was livable, warm, inviting and colorful.

Each of the bedrooms had its own bath. The bedroom she and Greg were to occupy was Venus' favorite. She had stayed there once before, when she helped Sally with a big party. It was a mint green, with a king size bed whose headboard was covered with various shades of yellow-and-green stripes. The curtains, which had the same colors but larger stripes, were pulled back to let in light and a view of the ocean. The floor was of terra-cotta tile, with throw rugs in the tones of green. The bathroom had wood cabinets of mint green and terra-cotta tiles on the counter and the floor. One wall was covered in custom-made wallpaper with the same print as the bedspread. On the bedroom walls were modern paintings, and a magnificent modernistic sculpture of a tiger took up practically the whole triple-dresser. All in all, the effect was powerful, even though beautiful, airy and peaceful.

Greg Returns

On the other side of the continent, Greg immediately went online for a ticket back to San Diego. He found the last flight leaving in about three hours, going through Chicago. If he hurried, he could be at Logan International in about an hour so he grabbed nothing but his laptop. Everything else of importance could be sent later by one of his friends.

As Greg rushed to the airport, he found himself thinking how the computer-hacking was just a little distraction, in fact, even the break in, note, and shot at his tire, bordered on annoyances. This threat on Venus' life was such a sock in his gut and such a twist to his heart he was nearly overwhelmed by his emotional reaction.

It seemed it was a long grueling flight, even though the stop in Chicago was brief and Greg's next flight was on time. Shock among shocks, he thought.

When he finally landed in San Diego at a little after eleven p.m., Joe, Sally and Venus were waiting for him. They all looked strained, near exhaustion. Greg grabbed Venus and held her to him. "I couldn't bear not be here with you and for you," he whispered, "I love you so much," and he gently wiped the tears sliding down her cheeks.

Venus thought all her tears had been shed, but these were not the same as the sobs that had wracked her body earlier. "These tears are because I am *so* grateful to have you in my life and loving me" she whispered back to him, hugging him tighter.

While Venus and Greg were hugging, Sally and Joe stood by, thankful Greg was there for Venus. Then as Joe drove everyone to their house, he explained, "It's probably a lot easier for you both to stay with us tonight. Then tomorrow, with the input of Bob Swan, the detective from the San Diego police force, who also happens to be a good friend of mine, we can talk about where you will be the safest."

"Bob Swan is very helpful, and can I have a glass of wine?" Venus asked in the same sentence. "I think I'm bushed."

Sally responded, "Yes, I'll open a bottle for all of us," then looking directly at Venus, she said, "I told you about Bob when I picked you up, but you weren't really able to hear anything. You've been to parties here while he and his wife Ester were present."

"Good grief. I wonder where my head was! When were those parties?" asked Venus.

"You missed them at the last one which was about six months ago when we had our BBQ. You didn't want to come. You were, as I recall, still sulking."

Venus let out a small chuckle that wasn't very convincing, lifted her head high and retorted, "I was NOT sulking. I just didn't like social gatherings where all my friends were either paired or else trying to fix me up. Now, where is the wine?" After pausing, Venus continued, "Anyway he didn't remember me either. But then I guess, I didn't look quite like I look now, and that's how people remember people."

Sally wisely nodded her head, saying, "Right, Venus. Who else wants some wine?"

There were no refusals and as the wine was poured, Venus said, almost under her breath, "So maybe I wasn't very present... maybe I was sulking, but just a bit."

Greg watched the two friends having their friendly banter and finally said, "Well, now that we know you're a social misfit, we seem to have more pressing problems. Or have you forgotten?"

"Yeah, like that'll happen," Venus quipped sarcastically.

It seemed to everyone that Venus' sense of humor had returned, which helped them all to relax. "Sometimes wine is just what the doctor ordered," thought Joe.

"Tomorrow I'll call Bob and see what he wants us to do, if anything, and what he wants you to do. Bob's incredibly competent and I trust him explicitly."

"Venus," asked Greg, "do you have any idea who might have wanted to do this to you?"

"That's what Bob asked me. I can't think of anyone who has it in for me, can you Sally?"

"No, unless you have just developed new enemies, I don't have a clue."

"Wait a minute," said Venus. "I hate to bring this up again, but I've told you I don't trust that new gal Rita. Nor do I trust Bill with his anger." Addressing Greg, she added, "You said Rita was okay, but I still have an eerie feeling around her, and even OM doesn't like her. Does she know anything about chemicals?" She paused, "We've both noticed how nasty Bill is to us, to the point where I asked you if he could hurt either one of us. Remember?"

"Oh come on, Venus. Rita doesn't even know you. Why would she have something against you? As to Bill, he is a loyal employee who, unfortunately has a giant chip on his shoulder and doesn't know how to relax. But I don't believe either one of them capable of doing something like what was done today."

"I know they're good employees, but the fact remains, Rita lied about you to me with an absolutely straight face and never has corrected her words. Furthermore, every time she sees us together, she glares daggers at me. Why is that? And Bill is constantly sarcastic, nasty and rude to both of us, especially when we're together. Have you talked to him yet about his ugly attitude?" Venus didn't pause for a reply. "If that's just his way, why do you want him in your company? I think they both have anger management problems. So there!" Venus said, feeling the wine and recognizing she had been pontificating.

Sally butted in, "I know this is between you and Venus but…Greg, quite often women see and know things that men simply aren't aware of or deny. Is it possible in this case?"

Joe jumped in. "Sally, you and Venus seem to think you are both psychic wonders. How much of what you predict, or think you know, is valid?"

Both women glared at Joe like he was in deep trouble. Finally Sally answered her husband. "My dear, Joseph, do you not recall the many predictions I have given you about your expanding business? Do you not recall that they came true? And, when you thought you were dying of some horrible disease, I insisted you needed to be checked for parasites. Do you recall what the doctor said? If not, let me refresh your memory. Dr. Jackson said, and I quote, 'My, my, you seem to have picked up a parasite. Have you done traveling out of the country?' And do you remember saying to him, 'Yeah, my wife diagnosed me with the same thing?' Do you remember those little examples?

"And, if we must continue," Sally was grinning from ear to ear, "what about when you sprained you finger, and I told you it was broken. Do you remember the x-rays that confirmed what I said?"

Joe looked at Sally with a sheepish grin on his face and simply said, "Busted, Greg. These women are too much, and you don't mess with them."

Both Sally and Venus hooted.

Then Sally asked sarcastically, "Joe, do you need any more examples of my intuitive abilities?"

Joe sighed, "No your majesty. How about another piece of humble pie please."

Greg turned to Venus, "Are you like her? If so, I'm not so sure I'm willing to have you know all my deep dark secrets."

"Too late," replied Venus. "Yes, I *am* very psychic, and that's why I keep warning you not to tease me about it *and* about my perceptions of Rita. She makes the hair on the back of my neck stand on end. I don't believe I was ever jealous of her, but I do believe she is jealous of you and me together. I don't know about Bill's energy either; he's just creepy."

"I think I'll check some of this out tomorrow" Greg conceded. With a silly grin on his face, he continued, "To think of women fighting over me is beyond my level of comprehension. I've always felt like such a shit around women, and jealousy is just hard for me to take in. And the same goes for another man being jealous of a relationship I have. Seems impossible."

"Well, your highness," Venus said in a cocky manner, "you'd better start believing and comprehending. I think you're worth fighting over. So there."

"Only two months," joked Joe, "and you act like old married couples – like Sally and me."

The rest of the night was spent in discussing the type of chemical or acid which had been placed in Venus' coffee cup, how Glenda might have fit in – or not, and all the ramifications for in Venus' department.

It was almost three in the morning when they all went to bed. Venus and Greg were glad to be alone, they needed that private time. Finally they both drifted off to sleep with OM trying to sneak in between them. Venus heard Greg mutter, "Not gonna happen OM, now go to the foot of the bed." Venus was amazed when he did just that.

***

The next morning Joe took Venus and Greg to the University to pick up Venus' car and to talk to his buddy Bob. The office was still cordoned off like the crime scene it was. Though Glenda was nowhere in sight, Bob told them her time had been pretty much accounted for with many witnesses, even to several having watched her fixing the coffee. Glenda was still on the list of possible suspects, however, because the police knew it took only moments to put poison in the coffee pot. There were so many questions up in the air: what the actual poison was; who put it in Venus' coffee cup; and whether the poison was in the coffee or a container of creamer from the refrigerator. Or was it something the chemistry department had on hand and somehow found its way to Venus' office? They were questioning everyone about relationships within and around the department. Was there anyone who was jealous of Venus' role as head of the department? Was there anyone who was jealous of Venus' relationship with Greg? Were there any in-house problems? The only thing everyone was sure of: *it was a miracle no one had been hurt.*

Venus was tremendously grateful that Glenda wasn't high up on any suspect list. Bob said, "I told her to go home because no one's allowed in here until we totally clean up and finish our investigation."

"I must call her and apologize for what's happened."

"What do you have to apologize for? You didn't accuse her and you still don't know if she had anything to do with this."

"I feel like I didn't do anything to help her cause."

"What cause is that? Killing you? Were you in the position to do anything? Come on Venus, this was not about you being an inconsiderate person. Your *life* was threatened, and she still hasn't been cleared. Police have to do their own investigating. Call her if you must, but I still don't trust her at this time."

Venus called Glenda, who was thrilled to hear from her. "I was so worried, Venus. I just didn't know what to do. Who would do this? I can't believe something like this happened!" Venus could feel the tears building in her friend's throat.

"Well, stay home, enjoy the day off, and make me some more biscotti. I didn't get to eat any of them, and the cops confiscated all that were left. I wonder if they ate them…"

"It's gonna be pretty hard to enjoy a day off when I know there is a totally sick person somewhere nearby. Who will they go after next?" Glenda lamented.

"Take your dogs out for a walk; it's a gorgeous day and the three of you could enjoy it. I'm pretty stuck here in the office most of the day. Oh, Greg flew home to be with me, and I feel really good about that."

Glenda smiled into the phone, "I'm not surprised. He adores you, and I can see why. You two are lucky to have found each other."

Venus knew, at that moment, her instincts about Glenda being innocent were right on target. She wished she could convince the police and Greg.

Greg tapped Venus on the shoulder which made her jump in fright. "I have to consult the detective in Boston about the computer-hacking. I'll just go into the next office. Don't go anywhere without me," he warned.

"I won't. While you're at it, see if the detective you hired has looked into the background of all your employees who are here as well as those in Boston."

"I will."

Greg was gone just a few minutes and again shocked Venus when he reappeared suddenly. "Nothing happening yet in Boston about the employees. Jamie Robins, the detective I hired, told me he probably won't be getting back to me for at least a couple of days.

I sent everyone who was still working in your department back to our new office. Now we have a waiting game. In the meantime, I do have work that did not get done when I was in Boston. How about this: I walk you to your car, you go to Sally and Joe's, and I meet you later. We can all go out to dinner together." Greg hesitated, "If anything comes up, just give me a call. I guess you're safe leaving the office."

Venus looked around her office, realized the futility of staying there while so much was going on, and finally agreed with Greg to leave. "Good, I'll take you up on your offer. Let's go." Then Venus paused, "Maybe I should ask Bob whether, if someone is really after me, I'll be safe in my car. Or for that matter, in yours. Who knows, it might have been tampered with."

Detective Bob, who had just walked into Venus' office, overheard the last of her conversation with Greg and emphatically agreed with her. "You were leaving just as I was coming in to warn you of just that. I think we should take a close look at your car before you can drive it. Maybe it might be better to take Greg's car."

"What about his car? Do you think it could have been messed with?"

"Venus, dear, they seem to be more after your life than some formula."

"You don't know that, Greg! Am I being paranoid, Bob?"

"Not really. If you wait, we'll have someone check out Greg's car, too."

"Nah, I'll just go. It's probably okay. . . I hope it is. What do you think, Greg?"

"Hey, you're the intuitive one. If you think the car is okay, then by all means, take it. I'll walk you downstairs. Then you *will* call me if anything seems weird," he commanded.

The two of them walked out to Greg's car and Venus got in the driver's seat. "Oooh, this is fun. Never thought I'd get to drive your green BMW convertible – I was happy just riding in it," Venus purred.

"Hey, you told me that your ex had a BMW. Who are you kidding?"

"He never let me drive it; never wanted to. It was his status symbol. Glad to see yours is two models down and older," she giggled. "*Status* and I had a horrible fight. For many years, status lost. Now *comfort* coupled with status has come to me, and I am happy to let this combo win out. How's that for rationalization?" And Venus floored the car, leaving Greg shaking his head in a state of disbelief.

About three miles from the university, as Venus was headed up Highway 5, (or known as "The 5" in Southern California) she thought she smelled gas. She wondered if Greg had filled the gas tank before he left, and there was still a residual smell. As she continued, she began to smell smoke but thought it was outside. But when the gas smell intensified, she noticed smoke coming in through the vent. "Oh Lord, I gotta get out of here. QUICK!" She pulled over to the shoulder of the road, grabbed her purse, and sprinted from the car-running as fast as she could up the side of the highway without looking back. When she felt she was at a safe distance, Venus pulled out her cell, punched in Greg's number, and gasped, "Greg, your car, it's on fire." Flames were shooting out from under the hood and beneath the car. As she watched, she saw the whole car engulfed. She continued to move away as she spoke.

"*What?*" Greg asked, unbelieving.

"Your car is on fire," Venus yelled into the phone. "I smelled gas and then saw smoke coming in through the vents. I got out and ran up the shoulder as far away as I could get. I don't know how much gas was in it, but I hope not a lot. Oh. . . oh!"

Greg didn't have to ask anything. He heard the explosion. "Venus, are you all right?" he shouted.

Apparently, while Venus was running away from the car, drivers of passing vehicles were calling 911. She could hear the sirens of emergency vehicles in the background, and watched as they approached. She felt as if she was watching a movie, yet she was not involved in it. She felt numb. She just watched.

Greg kept repeating, "Venus, are you all right?"

"I think so," Venus responded in a very small voice.

A CHIPS car pulled up right next to her on the shoulder of the road. A patrolman asked her, "Is that your car?"

Venus nodded sadly.

"What? I don't understand you. Is that your car or not?"

"What happened? Are you okay?" asked another CHIPS patrolman who had just came on the scene.

"No, I'm not okay," Venus managed to stutter. One patrolman looked at the other, saying, "She's in shock. Then he turned to Venus, "Lady, you must have had God in the front seat of that car with you. You are one lucky woman."

Venus, nodding her head, began to shake again, as the ramifications of what could have happened occurred to her. When one of the patrolmen put his arm around Venus, her shaking and shuddering became even greater. "It's all right, it's all right," he said. Venus just nodded and shook some more. She felt she was going to throw up, or fall on her face, or both. Her legs were like rubber, and she felt as if she were barely breathing.

"What's your name?" he asked softly.

"Venus Lighton," she coughed out.

"Can you explain what happened?"

Her eyes wide in fright and her mouth dry, Venus told her story. "I smelled gas and some smoke that I thought was outside. The smells got stronger, and then I noticed smoke coming in from the vents. I pulled off the highway, got out of the car and ran."

As the patrolmen walked Venus over to their cruiser, one said, "Good you left your car immediately. Probably saved your life. Here, let's have you sit down in our car, Venus."

Venus sat. She was in a daze. The shock of today's event, yesterday's and those involving Greg were taking a toll on her.

A short time later an unmarked patrol car pulled up, and in it were Bob Swan and Greg. One of Bob's friends on the force had heard about the explosion on the highway. Hearing Venus' name mentioned, he immediately called Bob. Fortunately, Greg was with Bob at the time.

Greg ran towards the open door of the CHIP car. But before he could reach it, one of the CHIP'S officers stopped him.

"Who are you?" he demanded.

As Greg was trying to explain, Bob Swan interrupted by showing his badge. "You go to Venus, and I'll explain to the CHIPS officers."

Greg slid onto the back seat where Venus was sitting, and tenderly, yet firmly, put his arm around her. "You're all right, that's all that counts. Don't worry, it's just a car," he added, as if to console her.

Venus shaking uncontrollably asked, "Greg, do you think someone tampered with your car? Is there a connection between yesterday's murder attempt and the other stuff?"

As Bob Swan walked to the car, the patrolmen who had heard Venus' question, looked at each other, and immediately asked all of them, "*Murder attempt?*"

Bob, after introducing himself to the CHIP officers, concurred that yesterday there had been an attempt on Venus' life. While he was explaining, Stan and Lee pulled up in a marked San Diego Police Car. The three detectives and the CHIPS men exchanged information. It was clear that someone had sabotaged Greg's car and the situation involving Greg and Venus was definitely escalating. The CHIP officers said they'd cooperate in any way they could.

In order to calm everyone down, Bob deliberately offered to Venus and Greg a simplistic explanation of the near disaster. Sometimes fuel-injection systems spring leaks or go on the fritz and cause engine fires and explosions. So let's not think the worst right now."

Greg thought, "I doubt it. I took good care of that car and had it constantly checked."

"How are they able to determine if a leaky fuel-injection system caused this?" asked Venus. "At least I assume that's what you're suggesting might have been the problem. I know absolutely nothing about cars except to put the key in, turn it and drive one."

"We'll need to wait until the lab gets here and figures it out," Bob replied.

"Damn! More waiting!" Venus burst out, having somewhat recovered from the initial shock. "We still have no answers for what's been happening at your house, Greg! I'm gonna call my kids and tell them everything that's been going on. Whoever is after you or me might go for them next!" Venus said in new-found terror.

"Let me have the phone, Venus. You're in no shape to deal with calling anyone right now, nor am I. Let's just wait a while until we are both more settled."

"When the hell do you think that will be?" Venus cried out. Someone is really fucking with me, or you, or both of us."

Greg moved closer to Venus, holding her tightly and stroking her hair. "I know you're panicked and so am I. Let's just ..."

Bob interrupted, "Greg, we'll be taking apart every piece of your car to find out what happened. This may have been an accident, but to play it safe, we will not only examine your car, but also do a thorough search of Venus' car. If someone is after Venus, maybe they knew she'd take your car. I'll take you to a rental agency so you can rent a car for the next couple of days. Rent a nondescript old car so as not to draw any attention to it. Then if you can, park the car where it won't be seen or touched. And don't worry about your car. Insurance will cover this type of thing."

"I know insurance will cover it," Greg responded, "I'm only glad no one was hurt."

After Bob dropped them off at the nearest rental agency, Greg chose a nondescript dark-green Ford, then drove Venus to Sally's house. Both Joe and Sally were shocked at what had happened.

"I want to call my kids and let them know what has been going on, Venus stated emphatically.

Sally was more cautious on Venus' behalf. "I think that's a good idea. But why don't you let them know that you and Greg are okay. Then Joe and I can fill them in with all the serious information. If they want to talk to you again, we'll give you the phone.

Joe added, "Greg, why don't you call your kids and tell them too. I think all members of both families should be told. This is not something to keep secret."

"God," Venus said bitterly, giving a weak excuse of a laugh. "What a way to meet each others kids, what a way to go for introductions."

"Yeah, a really good way." Greg answered sarcastically. "But let's look at this positively. Everyone is going to rally around us, and that's a good thing,"

"You've got something there," said Joe.

"I have another idea," said Sally. "Why don't we invite them all here?"

"What will be the excuse? It's not like this is something to celebrate," Joe said acerbically.

Greg paused before saying, "I don't think that will work. . . but then maybe it might. If I call Charlie and his family, and you call Bret and Toni and their families, maybe we could all meet."

"Too much trouble," Venus countered. "They'd want to know why the rush; you know how kids are."

Sally shook her head. "If we invite them over, they can make sure you're both all right, and then ask whatever questions they might have forgotten when they were talking to us. I think that might do it,"

"You've got some valid points, Sally. Okay, I'll call Toni and Bret and tell them I'm okay, then you can fill in the details and invite them over for pizza. Greg, you call Charlie and talk to him, and then put Joe on to fill in details and invite him and his family here too. But tell him no dogs here. Don't forget His Highness OM is still here."

Greg smiled, happy to see Venus returning to herself. "I'm in."

After all the kids were spoken to and had agreed to come, Bob Swan arrived with a few more questions to ask Venus and Greg. The afternoon passed so quickly that they barely had time to call in the pizzas, when Venus' daughter Toni and husband John, were at the door.

"Sally, Joe, I'm so glad to see you. Where's my mom?"

"She'll be right down. She's upstairs changing. Where are your kids?"

"John and I thought it might be best to leave them home for tonight. When we learn more, we'll clue them in. Bret and Elysa aren't bringing their boys either, for the same reasons."

"Probably a good idea for now," said Joe.

No sooner were Toni and John in the house then the doorbell rang again. This time it was Elysa and Bret. They were assured that everyone was fine and that their mom would be down in just a moment. But before that moment was up, the doorbell rang again. This time it was Charlie and his wife Sarah, who introduced themselves to Joe and Sally, and all the others.

As if making a grand appearance, Greg and Venus picked that moment to waltz down the steps. All their kids gawked.

"What's the matter with you all?" queried Joe, not having missed everyone's panicked stares.

All at once, everyone started talking. There were many moments where Greg and Venus knew they were getting the once-over from each other's and their own children.

Greg then took control. "Now that you've all met, in rather unusual circumstances, I admit, do any of you have any questions?"

Everyone spoke at once. But eventually all the questions were answered and pizza was delivered. At first, no one wanted to eat, but when Greg and Venus began, everyone joined in.

"So, what is the next step, Dad?" asked Charlie.

"Don't know. We have 'San Diego's Finest' working on the case - or should I say, cases. We'll do what Bob, Lee and Stan tell us to do; we'll wait for all the information from the labs and from Jamie Robins, detective back East."

John asked, "Do you think all these incidents are related?"

"Don't know," answered Greg, "Could be some connection; we'll have to wait for the various test results and detective reports. Although I gotta say, whoever is doing this shit has some incredible knowledge and has been doing some amazing planning. Hopefully, this is the last attempt from that crazy person."

Venus sat still, watching the kids interact. A sense of peace and calm overcame her, much to her surprise. "Wow, this is really some extended family. I could get used to this," she thought.

Toni and John were the first to get up to leave, but before Toni left, she said to John, "I want to talk to my mom for a second, I'll be right out."

She took Venus' arm, brought her into the kitchen, hugged her and said, "I like him. He's a keeper. That's all I have to say. Love you, Mom."

"Love you too Toni," Venus smiled, "and yes, I know he's a keeper."

Elysa and Bret were the next to say they had to leave, and Bret, in his usual way of blurting things out, said, "We approve."

Venus, blushing, said, "Thanks."

Charlie and Sarah chimed in together, "We approve too. It's unanimous."

Greg and Venus stood grinning at their kids and Greg put his arm around Venus and, pulling her closer to him, said, "We're glad you approve because we approve too."

***

It felt like forever until they were alone. They were exhausted. Yet, as they lay talking, Greg's growing erection indicated that he was not as tired as he'd thought. And Venus seemed to be right along with him in desire and willingness.

"We're like young bunnies, for goodness sake," laughed Venus as Greg pressed himself against her firmly and kissed her. She responded by firmly kissing him back. "I thought we – notice, I said we – were too tired for any of this," she giggled.

"You know the saying," chuckled Greg, "use it or lose it."

"I'm surprised my *it* wasn't lost a whole lotta years ago" Venus retorted.

"It's just us together," whispered Greg. He took her breast in his mouth and gently nibbled on it, feeling her nipple get even harder. She sighed in delight. But before she was going to let him run the show tonight, she would have some sexy fun with his body too. Pulling her breast from him, she began to kiss and lick his neck then continued to lick her way down his shoulders to his chest. She stopped briefly at his nipples, and heard a groan escape from him. When she got to his erection, she gently took it in her mouth and sucked him, then ran her tongue up and down the shaft. She held his balls gently in her hands, then began to lick them too. All the while, Greg moaned in bliss.

Watching him as she gave him pleasure made Venus hotter. She saw the intensity in his eyes, and sighed from her love for this beautiful man.

Suddenly Greg pulled Venus up on top of him, asserting, "Stop! I don't want to come this way. I want to feel all of you, on me, around me, inside of you. Come here."

Venus stopped her carnal assault only momentarily to allow Greg to kiss her. He opened her mouth to suck her tongue, mimicking the rhythm of intercourse and, with his thumb, reached down to her clitoris and stroked her until she thought she was going to explode. "Oh. My. God. Don't stop, please."

"I won't, I want you to come." As she reached her orgasm, she cried out Greg's name. "Please come inside me. Now."

"Ah. . . yes." Greg pulled her on top of him so she could slide down on his erect penis. As he entered her, he stroked her hair and face, then he reached for her buttocks, moving slowly and with as much control as he could muster. He guided her into a rhythm of thrusting and withdrawing, whispering to her, "Venus, I love you with all my heart."

With each stroke of Greg's penis her, Venus could feel her own excitement building again and the love they shared taking over her whole being - body, mind and spirit. "I love you too," she gasped.

The intensity, passion and depth of their lovemaking had increased, along with their love for each other. Their contractions, their waves and waves of sheer pleasure, were astounding. They felt a new unity in their relationship.

"Lord! I didn't think it could get any better, but it does," Greg panted.

"I know." Venus kissed him and sucked his upper lip. Then they lay together, just holding onto each other until sleep claimed them both.

More News

The following morning Bob was the first to call, asking to speak to Greg, who put his phone on speaker-mode. "Bob, Venus is on the phone, too, so she can hear."

"Excellent. I hate to tell you this, but yes, as you suspected, your car was tampered with. From what our investigators could see, the fuel line going into the fuel rail was punctured in several places. The fuel line, in case you don't know is metal and - although there was an explosion - the metal pipe still showed evidence of having been perforated. The hose that's attached to that pipe was pretty much destroyed, but there seems to be some evidence that it, too, was pierced. As a result, the gasoline sprayed all over the motor, and then - when enough gas was present with enough heat - an electrical charge ignited the motor. That's why Venus smelled gas and then saw smoke. She was lucky to get out."

Greg and Venus weren't terribly surprised, but *thinking* and *knowing* something are two different things. Venus asked, with only the tiniest bit of hope, "Could there just have been wear and tear, or some internal weakness in the hose, instead of its being deliberately destroyed?"

"No, I'm afraid not. We also found a GPS device on the car, magnetically attached to the underside. Its data downloads to a USB port. Not real complicated, but definitely useful for someone who wants to know where you are!

"We'll continue to analyze what we have, to rule out any possibility that it could have been an accident; but we highly doubt that. In the meantime, we need to look at your car, Venus. Should be able to get to it this afternoon; I'll call you when we have the results. That okay with the two of you?" Bob asked.

Greg answered for both of them, "We guess it'll have to be okay. Thanks Bob."

Sally and Joe were apprised of the new information and offered to take Greg and Venus anywhere they needed to be.

Greg said, "I'll take the rental car to my office building and park it in a safe place. I don't want to be gone any length of time. I'm not too happy leaving you, Venus, so why don't you come to my office with me?"

"First of all, how do we know that someone hasn't screwed around with the rental car? Furthermore, what in hell am I going to do at your office while you're working? Greg, you don't have to baby-sit for me. I'm a big girl," Venus growled.

"Number one: The car has been in Joe and Sally's garage, so I am confident that no one entered it and put another GPS on it, or did anything else destructive. Remember, the garage can't be entered unless someone crawls over the fence and then the motion-detector lights go on, along with the security systems screaming, awakening anyone who's not dead. Secondly, to respond to your other inquiry: You could just be with me so I'd know you're safe. I'm *not* trying to baby-sit you, I just don't want anything more to happen to you. I love you, damn it," Greg snarled at Venus.

Joe and Sally, still at the breakfast table, were actually tickled to hear the little spat and, if the conditions had been any different, they would have laughed out loud.

"I have an idea," Sally said. "Why don't we call Toni, Elysa or Sarah to go shopping with us? That way we'll be out of the house and occupied. Shopping would give us something else to think about."

"Neat idea, Sally," answered Venus, "but what if we're followed? You know what, I can stay here and do some paper work from the office. Maybe later, I'll call the kids and have some sort of snack brought in."

"Sounds like a plan," said Joe. "I'll be home all day working on some marketing ideas. So, you'll have company."

"Fine, Joe."

Venus and Joe went to separate areas in the house to do their respective work, and Sally went out grocery shopping. When she returned, she found both Joe and Venus in the kitchen, having coffee. "Perfect timing," laughed Joe. "Venus and I were just about finished with our homework when you came in."

"Yeah, Ma, we've been good," Venus laughed. "You know, it's hard to believe I can even laugh, considering everything that's been going on. Either I'm a sicko, or I have good coping skills."

"Hey, laughter is a great tension reliever! Don't knock it," said Joe.

As Venus and Joe helped Sally put away the food, the doorbell rang. All three of them froze. Venus asked, "Do you expect anyone?"

"No. Let's see who it is, huh," said Joe.

Standing at the door were Sarah, Elysa and Toni. Upon seeing them, Joe visibly relaxed his shoulders. "It's okay everyone," he called out.

Toni blurted, "Sorry not to call, but we knew you'd be here. And you're all right, right?" Toni was so excited that she babbled on, "Guess what? Mom, you'll never guess! Sarah, who we didn't know before last night, is our new neighbor. Remember I told you the house next door had sold, and the folks who moved in were from Boston? Well, it's Charlie and Sarah. I am so excited, and thought you and Greg will be too. We're just sorry we didn't go introduce ourselves to the new neighbors earlier. But then, you know how snotty we folks in Southern California can be - 'good fences make good neighbors?'"

Venus grinned. "Now you know that's not true – about the fences, that is."

"Where's my father-in-law?" asked Sarah.

"He went to his office in the rental car. I expect to hear from him momentarily. He was only going to stay the morning, and here it is lunch time. Have you ladies eaten?"

"No," replied Elysa. "We thought maybe we could take you and Greg out for lunch."

"Why not? Let me call Greg, to meet us at the restaurant."

"Did they find out anything about Greg's car?" asked Sarah. Without pausing for a response, Sarah continued, "He's so cool and Charlie and I are both so excited to see the two of you together."

"Unfortunately, they did," said Venus, and then repeated the scenarios.

"Hey, everyone," hollered Greg as he walked in surprising everyone.

"We were just going out for some lunch. I assume you must be hungry too," Venus said.

Perplexed, Greg asked, "Hey, how did the three of you get here?"

This time Toni told Greg about how she and John were Sarah and Charlie's neighbor.

"Forgive the cliché, but it sure is a small world," he grinned, then continued in a more serious tone. "Yup, I'm hungry, but first let me fill everyone in. When I got to the office, I called Jamie Robins in Boston and told him about the explosion of my car. He is already working day and night on who my employees were in their past, before they were SeaFoam folks. He said he should be able to get back to me by tomorrow. There may be someone who is intent on stealing the new formula for SeaFoam. That's what Lee and Stan felt. Who knows? I should've been a cop I think.

"About Venus' car, we should be hearing from Bob this afternoon. We realize you're all scared, and so are we, but honestly, we're doing the best we can, and we have no other information we can give to you. But consider: Police on both coasts are working on this case. Now, that's all I know except I'm really hungry."

Elysa made a suggestion, "I know a great Ethiopian restaurant not too far from here." Addressing Sally and Joe, she asked "Have you been there? The atmosphere is just okay, but the food is to die for. Whoops, maybe I shouldn't have put it quite like that," she laughed. And everyone joined her, releasing some of the tension from the situation.

Sally said, "I've never eaten Ethiopian food, how about you Joe?"

"No, but I'm willing to give it a try," Joe answered, and everyone else nodded in agreement.

"Hey, maybe the guys can meet us," suggested Toni.

With a few cell-phone calls from the wives, John, Bret and Charlie were reached and, quite amazingly, were all available to have lunch with them.

At the restaurant, the foods were new and unusual, so the owner helped them order. "Fabulous stuff this is" exclaimed Joe and Sally. "I love that it's all eaten with our fingers. So much more delectable! We'll come back here again really soon." Most impressive was the large (twenty inches or more) sourdough flatbread made of a fermented teff flour. All the diners shared it, scooping up their various spicy entrees. Scrumptious!

"Wonder if they have take-out," mused Greg.

Venus said, "Yum! Let's come back tomorrow." In everyone's opinion, Elysa's suggestion was brilliant.

After lunch, after the kids had left, Venus and Greg were laughing with Sally and Joe about how each of their kids was falling all over the other. Sally commented on how they'd watched with delight and amazement. "Nice families you two have," Joe declared.

"Man, do I know that! Oh, I forgot to ask Charlie if he'd called Ron and told him what's been going on."

Venus turned red as she replied, "Whoops! Yeah, I forgot to tell you. . . scatterbrained as I am. Ron wanted to call last night, but Charlie told him to wait until morning. Hasn't he called you yet?"

"First my love, you're not a scatterbrained person. I am *just* as forgetful as you are at this stressful time. No, Ron hasn't called and that's unusual for him," Greg mused.

As if by mental telepath, the phone rang. "Dad, it's Ron."

"I know who it is, guy. When have I failed to recognize your voice? What's up?"

"Well, it's what's down. Dahlia and I just landed in San Diego and we're renting a car and driving to…"

"You came all this way? I'm impressed and honored. Who's staying with the menagerie and the kids?" Greg's voice softened and his eyes glistened.

"Dad, tell us where you are and approximately how much time it will take us to get there."

Greg laughed. "Travel on Southern California Highways is not measured by the miles, but rather by approximate times. Don't try to rush, just proceed with caution and remember to *breathe*." Greg gave Ron directions to Sally and Joe's house and, when he hung up, he heard Venus chuckling.

"Another thing we have in common: You also tell yourself and others to breathe."

"You do that?"

"Certainly! How do you think I was able to go over to you when we first met? I had to give myself a *huge* pep talk, stop my legs from shaking, get my feet on, and tell myself continuously, '*breathe*.'"

Sally and Joe looked at each other and laughed out loud, both of them remembering the scenario Venus was describing. Sally chirped in, "She's not exaggerating, Greg. Venus was the most nervous wreck I've ever seen – much worse than how she's taking this stuff you're all going through now."

"As an aside, Greg, I agree with Sally," and both Sally and Joe laughed again as Venus sadly shook her head. "But changing the subject, I'm doubly impressed that your boy, or should I, say man, flew out here to be with you," Joe said.

About one hour later, the doorbell rang and Greg ran to get it. "Ron, Dahlia, how great to see you both. I'm so glad you're here." Greg hugged each of them and then, holding their hands, brought them in to meet everyone else. "We just finished having lunch with Charlie and Sarah and with Venus' kids. Now I want to introduce you to our friends Sally and Joe and to the love of my life, Venus."

"Yeah, Dad, I hear you two are a hot item," said Ron, looking at first one and then the other.

"Ron, stop it," remarked Sally, "you're embarrassing your father and Venus."

"Not me," said Venus and Greg at exactly the same time.

"On a more serious note, what's happening?" Ron asked.

Greg again explained all the known facts and complained that they were waiting for calls from the four detectives.

"Where are you two staying, and how long will you be here?" asked Venus.

"We already made arrangements with Charlie and Sarah to stay there for a short while and if we like it, we may extend our time here in California. I need a break from Boston and the cold. Actually, since you moved, we've been thinking about coming out here too. Mom won't be so happy about it, but. . ."

Venus' cell phone rang.

"Hi, it's Bob Swan here."

"Hello, Bob, how's it going?"

"Well, I have more stressful news for the two of you."

"Let me put the speaker phone on, so Greg and the rest of us can hear."

"Sure."

"What's up?"

"Well, you guys, unfortunately I have more news that isn't very good. Venus, we found a GPS device on your car too. You remember what that means, don't you?"

"Only from stuff like CSI or police shows: Whoever put the GPS on can know exactly where both the occupants are when they are driving the car. No wonder I've felt as if someone was watching me!"

"You got it about right. It's the same type GPS used on Greg's car, and whoever put it there has tracking-key data that includes where you were, your speed, your arrival destination and so forth. It's a rather amazing little gadget and not even too expensive; I've seen them priced for a little over two hundred dollars."

"But there's more: We found punctures in your gas tank too and in your gas line. Whoever is doing this has some sort of a vendetta towards you and/or Greg. I hate to be the bearer of bad news, but we really need to keep you two under close watch. Someone, or some ones, are after you, and we can't take any chances. "

Greg recovered quickly, "How are you going to assure us safety?"

"Well, you're not to go anywhere without our knowing exactly where, and with whom. Also there will be an officer either with you or tailing you, for the next couple of days, or until this case is solved. At this point we know that whoever is after you will stop at nothing! We are still waiting to learn more from both your Detective Robins and our labs."

Venus sighed. "More waiting is just what we need. Hope you have some interesting games to play here," she said sarcastically.

After that phone call, everyone began to talk at once until finally Greg yelled, "BE QUIET, EVERYONE! There is nothing we can do at this moment so why don't we just relax as much as we can with a nice glass of wine." Looking at Ron and Dahlia, he continued, "I'm sure you could use 'coming down' after your flight and after what you've just heard. As it happens, I brought a couple of bottles in with me when I arrived, so I'll just go open them now."

Joe jumped up, "Hold it, Greg. You stay with your family and I'll do the honors. Tell me where you put the bottles."

"I left them on the kitchen counter when I came in. I'd be honored if you were the official steward."

Joe went into the kitchen, with Sally right on his heels, giving the others time – even if just for a few minutes – to be together.

Greg, smiling at Ron and Dahlia, went up to them again and held their hands. "Hey, thanks for coming out. As Venus always says, 'Welcome to Sunny Southern California.' I think Charlie and Sarah will enjoy your visit here, in spite of the circumstances. I hope you're planning all sorts of touristy things to do."

Ron answered his father with sternness in his voice that, in Venus' mind, duplicated his father's. "We're not doing anything except being supportive for you two until this thing comes to its happy conclusion."

"Ron, as much as I, or should I say, *we*, appreciate your concerns, don't you think we have this pretty much covered by everyone here?" Greg replied.

"No, Ron and Dahlia said at the same time.

Dahlia went over to Greg, laughed as she pinched his cheek, and said, "You know we have to take care of you, don't you?" Dahlia seemed to be more comfortable than Ron looking for humor in the situation.

When Greg had first met Dahlia, he knew instantly that she was the right woman for Ron. It was as if they had an invisible thread between them, one that bound them but allowed for movement on both their parts. They raised two great kids, Eric and Shanna. Not only was their invisible thread still operative, but Greg knew it had strengthened. He was very proud of them, especially when seeing the love they shared. "Sort of like mine and Venus'," he thought.

Joe reappeared with the wine bottles and glasses, saying, "Let's have a toast: Let safety and love be the outcome of this situation."

Everyone joined in the toast, and soon even Ron looked more relaxed. Venus watching Ron observed, "Ron's not only like Greg in behaviors, voice tones, and the way he carries himself, but in his looks too." Ron had Greg's build and height (he may have been a few pounds heavier), Greg's dark hair and his exquisite eyes. He also moved with the same sensuality. "Lucky Dahlia," thought Venus.

Dahlia was dark-haired and petite with huge hazel eyes that shone with intelligence and caring, also a perky attitude that sparkled. Venus could see why Greg called her "bodacious." She watched as Dahlia moved, and saw the same sensuality in her movements that she saw in Ron's. "What a couple," she thought. "Wish I'd had that when I was younger...but I have it now. Lucky me!" And she smiled to herself.

Greg caught the new-comers up to date with everything that was happening, and Venus, every so often, added a few details of her own. As the whole story was retold, Venus thought, "Poor Joe and Sally have to listen to this again." After the retelling, when all the questions were satisfactorily answered, there was no lull in the conversation for the rest of the evening.

"So tell us, Dad, how did you meet Venus?"

"Well, that's a funny story," said Greg. "How about if I let Venus tell you?"

"Only if you fill in the details," replied Venus.

The two listened, and saw Greg's heart blossom as he added his flourishes to the story Venus was telling, until finally Dahlia could no longer remain silent. In her playful manner, with a big grin, she remarked, "Wow. You two sound like Ron and me."

Sally, barely able to get in a word edgewise, practically hollered, "Even Joe and I weren't quite as absurdly crazy in love and passion as these two have been. And now you're telling us that you and Ron were the same way? Or is that too much information for us to hear?"

Though Ron looked embarrassed, he finally conceded, "Yeah, I guess we were like that and still are. Right Dahlia?"

Dahlia nodded her head and smiled at her husband. "You bet!"

***

The next few days passed slowly but pleasantly, considering the stressful conditions. Both Venus' and Greg's families were in and out with determined regularity, insisting on bringing in meals and on amusing them, even while watching them like hawks.

At the end of the second day of surveillance, with nothing happening, Venus pleaded, "Good Grief, you guys. Why don't you go home and get some rest? We appreciate your concerns, but honestly, we'll behave. Promise!"

"Yeah, we'll call you." Greg added.

Finally everyone left, and the four of them were alone. Greg volunteered, "Not that I don't love our kids, but I felt as if they were babysitting us."

"Aha! Now you know how I felt when you wanted me to go to the office with you, Mr. Richards. Remember you said it was because you love me? Well, they love us too, even though their love right now is smothering."

"She got you, Greg," laughed Joe.

It was a good thing Sally and Joe had a big house; each person able to go to separate areas to be alone and do whatever they wished to do. They all valued their individuality and separateness; only OM walked from room to room, rubbing himself against each person, shedding magnificently, and purring. In his way, he was telling them everything was going to be fine.

At Joe and Sally's

Day three in isolation began very early with the abrupt ringing of Greg's phone, waking him from a deep sleep.

"Hey, Greg, Jamie Robins here. Did I awaken you? Of course I did, I always forget it's three hours earlier out there. Sorry. But I think you'll be interested in what I've found out."

Greg immediately sat up. He rubbed Venus' shoulders to waken her, and then he put on the speaker-phone.

"Yeah, I'm sure I will be interested."

"I've already called Detective Swan, giving him the same rundown I'm giving you. Ready?"

"As ready as I'll ever be."

"Almost everyone on your staff checked out to be who they presented themselves as. . . except for two.

"*Two*," Greg asked in surprise. "Who are they?"

"Bill Dewart was once arrested and made to take an anger management course. He was in his mid-twenties when this happened and, to our knowledge hasn't been in any more trouble with the law. Seemed he and his wife were involved in a domestic-violence scene. Everything about him checks out okay now, including how much money he's made and how he's made it. There are persistent stories of his unpleasantness, but no police incidents. It is pretty clear he still has some trouble with his anger," Jamie laughed. "But, on the positive side, I certainly wouldn't mind having him advise me on my financial portfolio - such as it is."

"Do you think Bill could be responsible for what's been happening?"

"Hold on a minute, Greg, till I give you more information."

Greg was feeling impatient, and demanded, "Tell me who is the other one?"

Jamie paused before saying, "This is strange: There's a woman working for you by the name of Rita Connolly, who changed her name about ten years ago from Emily Baxter. My impression: she's a weird lady."

Venus looked at Greg with an "I told you so" expression.

"What's with her?"

"First, does the name Emily Baxter ring a bell?"

"Sort of, but I can't place it." Greg paused. "Oh wait, yeah, now I remember. I think that was a woman I went out with about. . . yeah, ten years ago. But that must be a coincidence because the Emily I went out with, if I remember correctly, looked nothing like the woman calling herself Rita Connelly. Tell me more."

"This Emily, or Rita as she is now known, has had numerous mental breakdowns. We traced her family and, from what we could tell even without a thorough investigation, they are a strange lot. Her mother seemed like a space cadet, possibly on heavy drugs. She basically refused to talk to us and gave the phone over to her husband. He was evasive, yet protective of everyone. Something just isn't right there.

"When we spoke to some of Emily's friends, they were evasive too. They didn't like us asking questions and knew nothing of her family. Seems she avoided that topic with them. Like I said, at first they didn't want to talk to us. We managed to get through to them that there was some dangerous stuff happening out in California that Rita might be involved in. They finally told us she has had periodic psychotic episodes where she'd threaten to harm folks she felt had insulted, rejected or abandoned her. You know that show on TV, My Name is Earl? Earl makes a list of everyone he has hurt or cheated or in some way harmed during this lifetime and, by his actions, atones for each of them. Well, Rita, or Emily, also has a list, but it's a 'hit' list of those she feels have harmed her. When she is on her medication, she acts appropriately, according to her friends. But it's like she has split personalities; one part of her remembers every nuance of perceived negativity ever tossed her way, and the other part seems quite reasonable and normal.

Rita's family completely denies she even needs meds, in spite of her episodes every couple years, ignoring the many ramifications. Nothing serious has happened yet, probably because her friends were able to intervene and literally protect her. It also appears to me that each episode becomes more and more dangerous. They found a copy of her list, and you, Greg, are on it."

"But that still doesn't answer the question that I posed. Rita doesn't look anything like Emily – at least the way I remember her. How could that be?"

"Let me continue, Greg. There are several very interesting facts here. First: She is quite brilliant. She's studied chemistry, computers, forensics, and even electrical engineering. We think she applied for a job with the Boston Police force's forensic department, but they didn't hire her due to poor references - including mental instability. We're still waiting confirmation on this, which should be later today. Second: She has an amazing mind with a photographic memory. She basically learns anything and everything in a flash. We know she's studied a variety of chemistry subjects, as I mentioned. And, according to one of her professors that we were able to track down, she had a deep interest in acids and poisons. She claimed she wanted to work in a poison center so she could be helpful saving kids' lives. The professor gave her all sorts of information not commonly found in books. Every time he gave her something, she devoured it and asked for more; he thought she was a brilliant student. Third: No matter what she wants to do, she prepares herself with extensive study. Too bad she's not using all her skills for good purposes; she'd be an amazing FBI agent!"

"So she's the person who's done all of this to Venus and me? Computer-hacking too?" Greg was stunned.

Venus muttered, "Wow. She is quite a piece of work!"

Jamie continued, "At first, I was following a hunch and going out on a limb about her. I began asking questions of people who knew her as Emily, and knew what she was like between and during episodes. I inquired why she changed her name."

"So, what did you find out?"

"Give me a chance, I'll get to that. According to affidavits, she was an angry, vindictive woman who did anything to get even with anyone she thought didn't care for her or in any way rejected her. She seems to have a few loose screws. As a matter of fact, as Emily, she was fired from many of her jobs. She got enraged when anyone suggested a way of doing things different from what she was doing. She also was nasty to other employees and - finally, inevitably - she was always canned.

When she changed her name, she vowed she was going to get even with those she felt had harmed her. She underwent a series of operations to change her appearances: a nose job, liposuction all over, a

172

boob job. Then she got colored contacts and a total makeover. When she was Emily, she was a brunette; as Rita she is a blonde. When you knew her as Emily, she was a size ten; she is now a size two. Anyway, the changes are difficult to recognize Emily as Rita. She even took voice classes, learning how to modulate her voice and ridding herself of her Boston accent.

"We suspect that she has been responsible for a number of mischievous happenings to folks who were on that list."

This was almost too much for Venus to bear.

Yet Jamie continued. "Her friends begged her not to leave the Boston area, but to continue with the psychiatric help she had begun. She refused. They're worried about her, but can't imagine she would do anyone the kind of harm you have - fortunately - avoided. In the past, they've gotten her out of trouble.

"Her family, on the other hand, has stopped seeing her. Some of her siblings are worried about vengeful behavior towards them. They say she can act in a way that looks pretty regular, but then flies off the handle in fits of rage and goes ballistic. Among other things, her abuse and rage has extended to small animals. Frankly, I think the whole family is cuckoo. The mother seemed like she was in another world, the father was self-righteous and pompous, and the rest of them were evasive as hell. Don't know what they did to each other or her but it can't be good."

"I can't imagine this is the Emily I knew," Greg said quietly. "Could she actually be holding a grudge from over ten years ago? Because I told her I didn't want a relationship with her?"

"According to everyone we spoke to, she could and would."

"I just *knew* something wasn't right with her," Venus added. "She'd look at me with vacant, wide eyes that gave me the creeps. It was like she wasn't even there – certainly not seeing me. And then, periodically, she'd look Greg and me. I saw what I can only call, intense jealousy and rage. I told Greg that, but he didn't seem to see it."

"I think you were right, Venus," Jamie affirmed. "Unfortunately, we have no evidence at this time to link her with all the events that have gone down, only circumstantial stuff. Her list is probably the best evidence we have, so we've faxed it over to the San Diego Police Department. We'll leave the rest to them. But, be careful!"

Greg stretched and sighed. "Thanks Jamie. I don't know what the next steps are, but whatever you still have to do, do it." Then he muttered with some sarcasm, "I bet Bob Swan loved being awakened."

"Nah, he was perfectly okay with it. I sometimes think cops and doctors sleep with one ear on the phone, yet amazingly they're able to fall right back asleep after taking care of business. I know I did when I was a cop. Now as a PI, it takes me a big two minutes to go back to sleep. Hey, anyway, I know the news isn't so hot, but at least now you know what you are looking at and so do the police. Take care of yourself, and I'll talk with you again if anything else comes up."

With a huge sigh, Venus inquired of no one in particular, "How is *anything* going to be proven?" They haven't found anything to implicate Rita, or should we call her Emily."

"Not yet, but all the lab work hasn't come back. She may be brilliant, but she'll have slipped up somewhere. At least I hope she has."

"And I hope we're both not dead before she does."

Greg tried to soothe her. "There are probably some tests they're doing that we have no idea about. In a way, I am anxious to see Rita again, wondering if I can remember who she was. Right now, I don't see any resemblance to Emily. Come here, Love. We've got a while to just snuggle together and keep out the world."

"I'm here," Venue said, stretching to make full body contact with Greg, putting her arms around his neck and pushing her body against his. "Purr, purr. I'm a cat. Did you know that cats purr when they're scared too?"

"No, I didn't."

"Whenever I have to take OM to the vet, I hear his motor. The other day I read an article about it: they purr for all sorts of reasons. Something to do with their breath. In direct answer to the question you haven't asked, I'm purring because, among other things, I'm scared to death."

Greg sighed heavily and said, "I guess I'm not as brave as I used to think, or as liberal. There has never been anyone, except my kids, I felt I'd kill for. But I'd kill for you too. That makes me question the whole role of pacifist or peace maker. Eh? But I guess that's a whole other discussion."

"No, it's not, but I don't know where to go from here. Defending yourself and the ones you love is a lot different from starting up a conflict from a greed perspective."

"Let's go back to sleep. You purr if you want, while I stroke and hug you. . . ."

***

Two hours later, Greg and Venus woke up at exactly the same time, but for different reasons. Venus sat straight up in bed and was breathing heavily when Greg opened his eyes.

"What's the matter?"

"I just had another dream. This time it was about Rita. Do you remember the past-life dream I had about us? When a neighbor of yours murdered you because she thought you two were to be together? Well, this time, I dreamt the same dream, but the person was Rita. I think the three of us have some sort of karmic number we're playing out here. The dream just now was basically the same as before though this time Rita was screaming at both of us that she'd sooner we die than that she be embarrassed again by you discarding her."

"Discarding?"

"Yeah, that was the word I heard. Do you think Rita remembers the other lifetime?"

"First of all, I'm not sure I buy into any of that past-life stuff. Second, I didn't discard her. . . at least not this time. . . that is, if I were to believe in it."

Venus stated adamantly, "I *do* believe in it, and I am going to tune in to see how this can play out."

"I'm not totally denying anything like this could occur, but I'd need more information. Right now I need to get dressed and go over to the office. Do you want to stay here?"

"Yes, I think so. You'd better call Bob, or. . . who was it we were to call if we went out of the house? Anyway, I want to really meditate, and then maybe call a couple friends who are really good with getting to past-life stuff."

"Let's eat some breakfast first," Greg suggested.

When they went to the kitchen, they found Joe and Sally awake and preparing coffee. "Yay! I need some of that," said Greg.

"Coming right up," Joe replied. "Hey, we heard the phone ring real early this morning. Is everything okay?"

Greg related what Jamie Robins had told them, and then Venus shared her dream.

"Sounds like you two have had a busy morning already" exclaimed Sally.

"Sure seems that way. Next I'm going to meditate and then talk with Rachael and Luanne about this past-life stuff that keeps coming up. Perhaps they can clarify some of what has happened, or for that matter, what *is* happening. What do you think, Sally?"

"I'm with you, girl."

When everyone had finished breakfast and Greg had finally left, after checking in with Bob Swan and getting his okay, Venus took a few moments alone to contemplate how the past-life dream and this life seemed to be running together. "Well, thank God for friends who know more about this stuff than I do," she thought.

After Venus had set up a time for the four of them to meet, she got dressed and sat with a cup of tea, feeling her heart fill with wonder and love for the beautiful people in her life. "Oh dear, I mustn't forget my dear sweet fuzzy OM," she thought and giggled to herself, still surprised at her ability to stay somewhat calm.

The phone rang and Sally answered it. Then she yelled to Venus, "It's Bob Swan on the phone for you."

As Sally listened to Venus' side of the conversation, she felt her stomach drop.

Venus hung up the phone, whispering, "There was a small bomb set to go off five minutes after the car was turned on. I don't know the technicalities of it all, but if I had driven it, I'd be, once again, a dead woman. Good God." Venus let out a huge sigh. "They didn't tell me earlier because they needed more specifics."

When Sally saw her friend totally spaced out, she said, "Venus, come back! Did you find out if Bob called Greg about this?"

Venus recovered enough to say, "Yes, he knows too."

"What's the next step here?"

"Don't know. Oh Sally, how could this have happened?" When Venus' stomach calmed down, she called Greg. "Now what?" she asked glumly.

Greg, trying to seem more at ease than he actually was, replied, "Don't know. We keep waiting for whoever's doing this to slip up. We can't blame Rita or Bill for what has happened, at least not yet."

"Were they both at work today?"

"Yes, but Bill refused to look me in the eyes when I specifically engaged him in conversation. He just didn't want to be anywhere near me. Even Thom noticed and asked me if perhaps Bill could have done these bizarre, awful things. When I told him that Bill had taken an anger-management class many years ago, Thom was really concerned for our well-being and ready to fire Bill without proof. Fortunately, Thom is now my own special watchdog. Like he said, 'No way will someone angry and sick hurt you or Venus.' We have good friends, Venus."

"Then there's Rita, who's a whole other story. When I looked at her today, I saw, for the first time, the crazed look you were talking about. I took aside the other three guys in the office individually, and asked them questions about Rita. That's when Bill became so defensive. His defensiveness carried out to the main room, where we were just chatting about boats. Actually, Thom hadn't noticed anything until I started to make references to it then his brilliant memory was able to fill in details of weirdness – on both Bill and Rita's parts. Only Larry seemed to have noticed anything unusual with Rita's behavior. So do we know anything special? Probably not, but let me clue you about what was noticed."

Before Greg could begin, Venus butted in. "What was that?"

"I'm getting to that. . . patience, my love." Greg valued and acknowledged Venus' scientific mind and her wanting to know every detail. But for him, it was easier to tell what he knew in a sequential fashion. "Rita was asking about where we parked our cars. Thom thought that was strange, even though she quickly covered it up by telling him she was supposed to put something in my car. Thom didn't check with me because that was before the crises with the cars occurred."

"Greg, had she ever put stuff in your car before?"

"Yeah, once in a while if she were going out and I was still in the office. I wonder just how long she has been aware of my every move; probably since we came out west, or even before," Greg speculated. "So, yeah, you were right. We were being watched. Damn, are you never wrong?"

Venus chuckled, "Aside from sounding a bit paranoid like I do, I'm rarely wrong." Venus added with a hint of sarcasm. "And that's probably how Rita knew I was at your house a couple of months ago."

"When was that? I was probably so smitten with you I didn't remember anything," he said, trying to put some levity in the conversation. "Not that I'm not smitten now."

"Good thing you added that last little piece, my dear. Don't you remember when OM hissed at her?"

"Oh, Yes. . . And I actually remember when she came to the door. Did we ever tell Swan about that?"

"Don't think so," replied Venus.

"I'll give him a call. Now I've got to go. I'll see you later."

"Take care. Stay away from Rita and Bill. I love you."

"Love you too. I'll be back really soon."

Venus called Rachael and LuAnne, and briefly explained what was going on, and invited them to lunch with Sally and herself. When they arrived, Venus felt some immediate relief. "Maybe now I'll get to a deeper place with their help," she thought.

Before lunch, Venus disclosed how Greg and she had narrowly missed serious injury or death. Venus shared everything she could, Sally occasionally added a comment. Then the women discussed in depth what had been happening.

Rachael commented, "Well, aside from all the shitty stuff, really, Venus, your relationship has progressed rapidly and beautifully. The energy of you and Greg together is awesome, surrounded in a pink aura of love. How cool is that?"

"I see the same thing," said LuAnne, "but also there is something trying to harm you. It's already accessed your energy field."

"That's what I want to delve into. I know that and Greg knows that. The main question is: What do we do about it? Do we need to know *how* we are part of this drama?" Venus asked.

"I don't feel that Bill is the culprit; he's probably just a case of bruised ego. However, I do feel you have to watch out for Rita. I think the police are onto her and will be able to stop her, but it might be helpful - and healing - if you knew more about what led up to this whole thing. You know, there are no accidents," said Sally.

The women spent the rest of the morning tuning into what was going on with Greg and Venus, meditating, and doing relaxation exercises to access Venus' unconscious. By the time they finished, they felt they had a really good handle on the past and how it was showing itself now.

"Will you stay and wait for Greg to get back so we can explain what we've been doing?" asked Venus.

"Of course, I'm not missing this for anything," said LuAnne. "And I'll be delighted to meet the man who finally got to your heart."

"I agree," said Rachael, then added sarcastically, "and I'm not at all pissed about your not introducing us earlier."

"Well, you shouldn't be pissed," Venus said, "I've just been so busy with new love and work. In fact, I was planning a wonderful party when this stuff hit the fan. Greg and I had even talked about it. Do you believe me?" She pleaded.

"Well, ya, I suppose," laughed Rachael.

"How about you, LuAnne?"

"I'll take it under consideration only if you tell me when this party/shindig is happening," LuAnne grinned as she spoke to Venus.

"Let's have a glass of wine with our lunch and catch up with other stuff. It feels like it's been a long time! I'm grateful to you all for being here with me during this stressful time. Please accept my undying gratitude," Venus said emotionally.

"Normally, I'd say you were such a drama queen," said Rachael, "but I guess you have a reason now. Your gratitude is accepted," and she laughed. "Here's to you and Greg and a happy lifetime, this time around."

"Here, here!" they all chimed.

Rita and Greg

After talking to Venus and telling her about Thom's observations and Bill's avoidance, Greg had the opportunity to go out to the front office where he was somewhat alone with Rita (if you count a security man and a plain clothes cop a few feet away being alone.) Greg didn't like all those guards around him, but realized their presence was for everyone's good. Although Rita knew about the security man, she didn't know that the other man was a cop. He had been introduced as a graduate student in business management and was studying how their office ran and the different ways each of the "big wigs" in the company utilized their time and influence.

As Greg approached Rita he thought, "I have to say *something*." As the other members of his staff roamed about doing their work, he began to talk with her. "Rita, I know all about your work - and you do an excellent job - but I know nothing about you personally. Why did you leave Boston and come out here with the company? It seems like a huge move. Do you have family here? Tell me a little. . . ."

Rita didn't look Greg in the eye as she began to speak, "There's really nothing to tell. I wanted a change and decided to take the risk, even though I am getting up in years." She tried to shift the conversation, saying, "You know, you've made a big change too."

"But surely a nice looking woman like yourself had a boyfriend - or several - back there," he prodded.

"No, It's just that I needed a complete change, kind of like you did. And I wanted to be able to use all the skills I've acquired during the past ten years."

"That's very commendable. What skills are those, and while I'm asking, what do you still want to learn?" asked Greg.

"I just love learning, so I have all sorts of skills - probably not enough to ever be proficient, but enough to get me by." She hedged, "A little of this and a little of that. . . I've taken tons of courses on all sorts of things."

"What kind of courses?" asked Greg?

Rita replied smoothly, "Once I wanted to be a cop, but I couldn't pass the physical strength requirements. I studied everything else, and am a great shot with any type of weapon. I was really angry at myself for not having the upper-body strength that was required."

"Really, why?"

"Because I was overweight and never took that part of the training very seriously. I vowed to lose the weight and try again."

"I'm impressed," said Greg. "Well, did you?"

"Lose the weight? Or try again?"

"Either or both."

"I lost the weight, had a personal trainer to build my upper-body strength, but didn't try again. Instead, I decided forensic science was more interesting, and got involved in that."

"What kind of stuff did you learn there?"

"Too much to talk about right now. But I loved it. Couldn't get a job though."

"Why not?"

"Oh, I don't know. . . I'd love to carry on this conversation, but I have tons of work to do. Maybe some other time? By the way, how are you and Venus getting along? It looks like she drools all over you. Not very attractive, if I do say so. See you later."

By the time the conversation was over, including Rita's snide remark, Greg's insides were shaking. And it was as if a light bulb had exploded in his brain. "I know what Venus senses is right on, but how in the world are we going to prove it?" he contemplated. "The vacant look in Rita's eyes is eerie, almost as if she's on drugs. And, unlike the guys, she hasn't said a thing about being sorry any of these near-tragic events happened. That is very weird. Still can't believe she's Emily, but I sure believe she's a nut! I should be glad she didn't take some sort of shot at me here, in spite of the guards and cops."

Life Continues

Before Greg left SeaFoam for the day, he called Bob Swan asking how to search for a GPS and/or bomb in his rental car. Within minutes, Bob sent over one of the officers with an electronic device which would quickly find one if it were on the car. Greg's shoulders dropped a few inches with relief when told the car was free from either of those two devices. After having a cup of coffee with the officer and thanking him, Greg returned to Sally and Joe's house, where Rachael and LuAnne were introduced. "About time we met you," Rachael muttered loud enough so Greg could hear her.

"Hey, it's not my fault," he laughed, defending himself and pointing to Venus.

"Yeah right, Greg, like you've been up for meeting my friends instead of being alone with me. Right!" Venus smirked.

"Yes, I most assuredly have." His face had a wide grin on it. "But not so much in the last couple of weeks with all that's been happening. Glad to meet you both, I've heard lots about you." Greg turned to Venus, "See, I can be nice." Everyone laughed at Greg's flippancy. Having broken the ice, he could get to more serious topics – like the conversation he'd had with Rita.

He related their talk and his feelings about it. As they all listened, he conveyed his surprise that Rita seemed to *want* to talk about her background. But she mentioned nothing about what was happening to the two of us. Doesn't that seem unusual? But then, she's nuts," he said to no one in particular. "Furthermore, I did *not* recognize her," Then he said, as if thinking out loud, "What if I take her out for dinner tomorrow, or whenever she can make it, and just talk to her? See what comes up. I could keep fishing for information."

Everyone jumped on him with their misgivings.

It was Venus whose voice prevailed. "Yeah, you'd have to watch everything you ate, or she could poison you without your even knowing you were had. Well, maybe if you tell me and the San Diego Police Department where you are going, and when. . . Tell the Army, Marines and Navy too; maybe they'll all watch over and guard you." Then, in all seriousness, Venus added, "It's also a good idea to inform Swan of everything that you intend to do. I just don't like it or think it's safe at all, even with all the backup. So I veto the whole thing because of my love and concern for you. How's that!"

"I don't think I have anything to worry about, but – like the coward who refuses to fight so that he can live another day - I will honor your comments and the agreement of your friends to can the whole idea. I know business, I don't know crime – or in this case, insanity. And that's the bottom line."

While they were still in their discussion, the doorbell rang. Once again they were inundated with all their kids, their spouses and grandkids. "Good God. Don't you guys trust us enough to let you know what's happening?" Greg mumbled with a big smile.

"Did we hear from you today?" Toni challenged. "We waited until a respectable hour!" She glared at Venus and Greg while a chorus of Yeah's punctuated her comment.

"Let me begin to apologize for us," Venus responded. "Um, I guess today we haven't been so great in communicating, have we? Um, we'll tell you all we know at this time. Greg, you start. Later I'll have the chance to tell everyone about my session with Rachael and LuAnn."

Greg informed the group about the GPS devices on both cars, the bomb in Venus' car and the facts from Jamie Robin's call. The kids and grandkids sat mesmerized. Finally one of them said, "This is like a movie. Except it's real and scary."

"That it is," echoed another.

After a pause for everything to settle, Venus said, "Now it's my turn to tell you about past lives." She proceeded to tell about the two dreams she'd had, and how she felt there was some connection to what was happening now. "The cells in our bodies remember throughout life-times. If you don't believe in past lives, then consider this: Quantum physics suggests that all time is simultaneous, that we are doing everything *right now*." Venus turned to Charlie and Ron, the wives and kids. "Rita wanted to be with your dad a long time ago and she felt that he used and discarded her. Now she wants revenge and, by getting rid of me, she can deeply hurt him. If she can't get rid of me alone, then she wants both of us dead. At least I think that's what she wants. Either way, she wants to make Greg miserable. Striking out at me creates pain for him. That's the same thing she wanted in another lifetime when she perceived that he had discarded her for me, and she thinks the same thing is true now."

Venus continued to explain how past lives can, negatively or positively, affect who we are in the present. "If we learn what they are attempting to teach us, it's wonderful. If not, we repeat behaviors over and over until we do understand and embrace the lessons." She gave many examples so that everyone could at least understand her view of reincarnation, which didn't mean they had to agree.

"But how is all this reconciled?" asked Bret. "I mean, assuming it is all past-life stuff that has bled into this lifetime."

Toni commented, "She is nuts now, and if she's brought forth all this anger and hatred from then, she was nuts then too."

Venus said, "I totally agree. Then she went on to explain. "Rachael, LuAnne and I believe we all come onto this Earth to experience certain lessons: The experience of having mental problems is one that Rita chose. She has also consistently chosen vengeance. Perhaps, either within her deep unconscious or her small ego-self, even before she came onto the physical plane, she chose it. Of itself, that is neither good nor bad. What she does in the here-and-now, is what counts. She can decide to take her meds to keep herself on an even keel and actually feel better, but she is choosing not to. That act, in itself, which put the ball in her court, denies she is a victim. What happens from here, based on her behavior, is just what it is. There is nothing *we* can do to change her behavior. When we feel strong, we can see Rita as whole and complete, recognizing the divinity within her, but that may not do anything to the outward manifestation of her behavior. And, it's pretty hard to do when you know she's trying to kill or harm you. I sure haven't advanced to that point yet," Venus gave a sad sigh.

"What did your session with LuAnne and Rachael produce?" Sarah asked. "I mean, aside from what you just shared."

"It seems that Greg and I have already had a couple of lifetimes together. Each ended before we were able to be together for any length of time. This present lifetime and the first dream I had were more dramatic than the second dream; or at least it seems that way. Who knows, if we had gone deeper, we might have found out more."

"How did you do this? Hypnosis?" asked Ron.

"You could call it a form of that. Any hypnosis is really a deep, deep relaxation technique that accesses the subconscious or unconscious.

In this case, we were seeking information about Greg's and my lifetimes together. After I was totally relaxed, LuAnne asked the right open-ended questions, and we were lucky, we found out lots. I was actually surprised at some of it! There are also other ways to access such information, but most take a lot longer; for example, programming your dreams, going on shamanic journeys and visions. What we did today is the fastest.

You see, it's really not important *how* we get to the information; what *is* important are the patterns as they show themselves. And plenty have showed! When a situation is not taken care of properly, there is a repetition until it is. Our situation was not dealt with in a healthy and loving way, and so it continues to be repeated. It seems that neither Greg nor I, in those other lifetimes, acted so very well ourselves. In one of them, Greg cheated Rita, and in a way, *did* discard her. In the other one, I lied to her to get what I wanted, and somehow that also involved Greg. As I mentioned, that third lifetime is still unclear."

"All this from a woman of science," Greg muttered sarcastically.

Venus felt her temper flare and asserted, "You're darn right! You know how I feel about this subject! I know there is much more than science that makes life go around, and I totally believe in intuition and past lives. I believe in energy and I know it doesn't lie. I believe in Spirit and Love and all sorts of things that science says it can't prove. Not yet, but maybe one day it will. So when this whole dream thing came up, I almost immediately knew one dream was a past life, although I said nothing to you. The other was precognitive, and a warning. We *can* change our reality. So there, Mr. Greg," She strutted over to him, hands on hips, and stuck her face right in his, daring him to challenge her.

"I don't know anything about what you said," Greg replied sheepishly, lowering his green eyes to the floor "but I do know you were right-on about Rita, from the start. I still wonder where Bill fits in. Is it just his bruised ego?"

"Don't try to get off the hook so easily with your disregard of my intuitive beliefs," Venus growled, with the tiniest hint of a smirk.

"Who. . . me? My Love, I grovel and beg forgiveness."

"That's better," replied Venus haughtily.

Rachael intervened. "Back to Bill. Yes, it is his bruised ego, and he has some other issues he needs to work on."

185

As Rachael was answering Greg, Dahlia and Ron were watching and giggling at Greg's deflated response to Venus. Ron whispered to Dahlia, "They're like we are. That's what you do to me, see? Hope they're as happy as we are. He's met his match!"

In response, Dahlia grabbed Ron's hand and grinned as she whispered back, "I know that's what I do to you, and I too, hope they're as happy as we are."

"What are you two doing?" demanded Greg knowing they were talking about something that had to do with him.

"Nothing much, Dad. . . just laughing at how you respond to Venus the way I respond to Dahlia, and how those two women try to keep us in our places. Venus has got you good, and we can't be happier." The rest of Greg's family began to laugh, nodding their heads.

"All right, so what," he laughed. "Let's get back to my question about Bill. Ego *and* issues?"

LuAnne and Rachael together stated, "Yes!"

"Oh, simple as that, huh? I should know about men and their egos." Turning to Venus, he said, "If you had picked Bill over me, I probably would've pouted for the next hundred years. I guess that's considered ego. So, what are the issues?"

"Irrelevant at this time," Rachael replied.

Everyone in the room laughed, once again, breaking the tension.

Greg continued, "Anyway, my Love, you had no way of knowing anything about Rita *or* Emily, so based on that and the fact I love you, I'll accept what you say. Maybe you'll even teach me something about intuition and all that stuff. A possibility?"

"Absolutely," said Venus and hugged him. "That's what I like, a man who can admit ignorance." She paused, "And defeat." She laughed, then added, "And moreover is willing to do something about it."

"Getting back to the drama at hand," said Sarah, "where does this leave us now?"

"The police have been advised of Rita's unusual past, and her vengeance list, and are supposedly with her now," replied Greg.

The whole group sat and discussed everything that had been happening with each other, every so often asking Venus, Rachael or LuAnne a question. Finally, the company left, and the two couples were alone again.

186

"How much more of this can we take?" Venus asked, flailing her arms dramatically.

"What do you mean? ... The life threats? Or all the family?" countered Joe.

Greg smiled, "The families, of course. Never thought I'd see the day when all these kids and grandkids constituted a separate police force to watch me... and you, my dear – Queen of the Humorous Stage."

"Okay, I get it. I'm a drama queen. But I do have nice hair." Venus said patting her head. "I think we are all keeping things in good perspective, and I love that in emergency, we sort of... sometimes... keep our senses of humor. Sense of humors. What *is* the correct phrase?"

Sally laughed. "Don't know. I'll look it up next year."

Joe said, "Bless comic relief! Now, let's go to bed. Hopefully, tomorrow all of this will disappear. But, even if it doesn't, tomorrow is another day. Good night, Venus. Good night, Greg. Let's go, Sally."

Sally added, "Good night, see you in the morning."

"Yay! Off to bed, Mr. Greg. Coming?"

Back in their own private quarters, they held onto each other while laughing at the absurdity and the danger of their situation. Never did I think I could be in such a weird kind of drama," said Greg. "But there is something else I thought of," he said, getting serious. "If I didn't see you anymore, you wouldn't be in danger. I think we ought to stop seeing each other until the police have found out the truth. I hate putting you in harm's way. If I am what Rita really wants for her vengeance, at least *you* will be safe."

Venus pulled away from Greg and stood with her hands on her hips. "THAT. IS. SO. NOT. GOING. TO. HAPPEN. Forget it! Don't think about it! No Way!"

Greg, upset and protective as he was feeling, had to laugh to see her so. "What is *this*? Oh, self-righteousness, caring, and the ferocity of a mama bear." Then smiling meekly, he said, "You have me around your little finger, Venus Lighton. But I'm not sure how much of this I will take. Just remember that!"

"Good, I thought you might see it my way" she growled. "Now come to bed before the mean-old-mama bear bites you."

Questioning Rita

Just as they were ready to turn out the light, the phone rang. It was another call from Bob Swan. "Listen Greg. . . oh, please put on Venus too. I have some more bad news for you."

"More?" moaned Greg.

"Yes. Remember I said we were going to question Rita later this evening?"

"Yeah," Greg replied.

"First we tried the office because you said she often works late. She'd already left. Then we went to her house, and she was there. She behaved in a totally sane manner, allowing us to question her, even to look around her apartment. We didn't show her the 'hit' note; we thought we'd get to that later. She was pleasant and calm, offered all sorts of suggestions about who, when and where. But when we asked her about her problems with taking medication, she basically had no answers. She literally shrugged her shoulders. We were just about to take her down to the station for more intense questioning, when she asked if she could use her bathroom. Because there was no female officer with us, we accompanied her only to the door. Hate to tell you, but she split from us."

"What? How?"

"It took us a moment to realize she was gone and we high-tailed it out of her house to find her, but no luck. Don't know how or where she went. It was an incredible disappearing act, she must have practiced it for eons. It's like she became invisible.

A few things we know for sure. One: She is after the both of you; make no mistake about it. Two: She will do anything she can to accomplish this. We think she's going to make an intense move right now, on either or both of you. Please stay put and don't open the doors for anyone. I think we have a real lulu here. Oh, and three: She carries a gun – with a permit - and from what I hear, she's an expert shot."

"That pretty much solves the problem of the tire!" Venus said.

"Bob, I'm a pretty expert shot myself, and I have a permit to carry a weapon. Up to this point, I haven't. I'm thinking now might be the time to take that precaution. What do you think?"

Venus interrupted, "Greg, I don't want you carrying a gun. It scares the shit out of me."

"Don't worry. I'm a safety freak."

Then Bob remarked, "On second thought, Greg, that might not be a bad idea. Rita is loony! Lock all your windows and doors, and be on the lookout for her. I wish I knew what to predict, but with a fruitcake like her, who knows."

Greg and Venus could hear the frustration in Bob's voice when he said, "Mostly I'm pissed off at myself for allowing her to go into the bathroom! Damn, I should have known even though she was acting totally sane and responsible. Been in this business long enough! We'll be watching the house every moment. We've called in several more officers, and even a dog."

Rita

Even Rita (or Emily) thought her childhood life resembled a very bad hyped-up for television movie. That it was true - all of it - sometimes in her saner moments shocked her. Emily was the third youngest of seven children. She had three older brothers, one older sister and two younger sisters. Her parents married when they were extremely young and immediately began having children. Clearly, they couldn't cope. In Emily's earliest memories as a child of almost three, she often heard screaming and gagging that made her hair stand on end. She tried to hide – anywhere - mostly under her "big girl" bed. Although she didn't know why, she knew the awful noises had to do with her father. It was only a few months later that she found out what was occurring in her small world. That was when her father began to go after her and to sexually abuse her. She learned to freeze.

The whole household was filled with tension, distrust, and anger. Everyone walked on eggshells whenever her dad was near. As she grew older, the tension increased.

Ironically the whole family attended church every Sunday under threat of brutal beatings, which were often administered anyway, depending on her dad's mood. He felt it was important to present a good face to the rest of the world – "the family who prays together stays together" kind of reasoning. Emily's father, George, was a functional alcoholic, and had even been diagnosed as psychotic. He held a fairly good job but, when he got home, he drank himself into a stupor and became a mean drunk. Whoever was closest got the brunt of his anger and frustration. Each member of the family, including Emily's mother, Maureen, was regularly abused. But even in his drunkenness, George was careful so that any bruises he inflicted, were always covered by clothing. He sexually abused Rita (as well as each of his daughters) when she was not more than three-years-old, and threatened her with her life if she was to tell anyone. Emily's mom, who knew what was happening, was terrified for her family but felt totally impotent. There was nowhere she could run; all her relatives refused to help her or the children and their attitude was, "You made your bed; now lie in it." When Maureen threatened to leave and take the children, her husband raped and beat her, leaving her bleeding and weak. The last two children she bore resulted from rapes. Sometimes George even locked her up or put her in handcuffs so she couldn't run away. She became more and more a walking shell of a woman, living in constant terror for herself and the children, until the terror finally turned to hopelessness and increasing degrees of numbness. When she went to a confessional with a priest and told him her dilemma, he ridiculed her - an additional shock for Maureen. What was worse was that the same priest told her husband, and then there were more beatings, more verbal abuse, more rapes.

Emily could still remember the utter shame and terror she felt when her father, in his more brutal moments, made the girls and her mother strip and stand in front of him. Then - systematically - he beat or sexually abused them while the others were forced to watch. After many years of continuing his criminal behavior, Maureen was able to disassociate from whatever was going on. She was truly isolated and alone. Her survival, such as it was, relied on numbing every part of herself. Sometimes, when she had a flash of awareness, she knew she was losing her mind and wished she could die.

Any money Maureen had was taken away permanently. All clothing and household necessities, including groceries, were purchased when George took her and/or the children to the store. It was very important that his family look respectable. Meals were prepared by duties assigned by him after church on Sundays. No one had the nerve to poison George or even to hurt him, although each of the children wanted to. Maureen's life was a living hell; she was a walking zombie. The one shining light in her life was when Emily graduated from high school and announced that she was leaving. George threatened her, but she left in the middle of the night.

Emily had begun "acting out" quite early in life. She would find a puppy or kitten and beat it till it was a bloody pulp. She took her anger out in the school yard, where she became a notorious bully. When school authorities questioned her mother, she was too frightened to tell anyone the truth. Emily's bullish behavior escalated until she was always in trouble. Being a brilliant young girl, it finally occurred to her that if she just played the game right, she could get what she wanted easily and without negative repercussions. When her behavior began to change at school teachers mistakenly attributed it to parental guidance. Wrong!

When Emily reached her early teens, she found she could avoid her drunk father with relative ease. Her younger sisters did not learn that lesson but, in her mind, that wasn't her concern. In her own fight for survival, Emily didn't share with her younger sisters *how* she managed, even though she saw them consistently being assaulted by their sick and cruel father. "I have to take care of me" she thought, "*and I will.*" When she left home she was just about eighteen, vulnerable to any softness of the world, but hardened and tough to the rest.

"I'll get even with them all," she kept telling herself. "Never again will anyone ever treat me with so little regard."

Prostitution offered Emily almost a year of making some good money. She was a very attractive young woman and saved as much as she could, living on the streets or in cheap motels for that year. It didn't take her long to figure out that there was much more she could be doing with her life. One day, on a whim, she walked into a junior college, filled out some papers and found herself, to her delight, totally immersed in the educational system. Finding a couple of roommates, she shared an apartment until she got her first associate degree in - psychology. From there, she found a job at the welfare department, where she loved the power she wielded. She studied everything and anything; always with an eye towards making her life successful *and* towards getting even. Her job selling chemicals to Greg's company, SeaFoam, came when she was about thirty, having learned the necessary skills with alacrity.

Nothing was ever forgotten by Emily. In the past, she had gotten even with many who had wronged her, but Greg Richards was another story! She really thought she loved him and mistook his kindness and caring in his business contacts as meaning he loved her too. Greg was going to be her savior. When he refused to be with her, it was as if all the years she had been angry and holding onto her pain exploded into shards of glass. When she finally located him again, after her major outer transformation, she was single-minded in gaining access to his life.

"I'm getting closer to my goals," Rita schemed. "I have worked on this so long, planning each step as intricately as humanly possible. Every person who ever threatened or demeaned or discarded me will get their fair punishment. About time! When this is all over, I'll leave behind my diary and how I planned everything, including my big escape."

***

Rita had planned the escape for months, just in case a situation ever arose in which she were suspected. She'd even rented *this* particular condo, knowing the bathroom window was on ground level and, if need be, she could quickly exit. So when the police suggested she go down to the station for more questioning, she agreed without protest. When she asked innocently if she could use her bathroom, they said yes. Playing sane without drugs was part of a game, and she knew she could do it easily and with conviction – as she had proved to herself by working in Greg's company. When she entered her bathroom, she quietly opened the window in preparation for her escape. She took rubber gloves from one of the drawers and quickly put them on. Then she covered her shoes with plastic bags and took out a hidden key for her car. She flushed the toilet and then turned on the faucets before climbing out the window of her condo with ease. No one was taking her anywhere!

Outdoors Rita took extra precaution by running back and forth on a large plastic bag placed on the ground behind the window, confusing any scent. She moved with amazing definitiveness and speed. Quite sure that she was suspected of the events of the previous weeks, Rita was unwavering in her resolve to get away. "I've planned well for this," she thought. "I'll beat them at their own game!"

A car had been rented under her parent's name with a phony credit card she had taken from them, and a counterfeit driver's license had been easy to purchase. The car, an older model dark-blue Ford, had been parked on the street and the police hadn't bothered to notice it. There was, after all, nothing suspicious about the car; in the area of her rental property, people always used the street for parking. She quickly made her way around the back of the house to the car, got in, and drove off. She was not seen.

It was several minutes after Rita escaped that the police realized she was gone. They went out back but found no clues. They proceeded to question her neighbors, asking if anyone had seen her, but no on had. Nor had anyone seen any suspicious car.

Rita had big plans. "The San Diego area and North County," she sighed, "are so easy to hide out in. This is almost too easy – even for a newcomer like me." She had donned a brown wig, taken out her colored contacts, and dressed in nondescript jeans and a T-shirt. Rita felt confident knowing she would not be recognized. She barely recognized herself! She freely went into restaurants, stores and wherever else she wished. She even checked the post office to see if her picture were on the wanted list. "All I have to do is bide my time and then make my move."

After two days of doing nothing, she found her internal tension building. "I need to get this over with!" By the end of that day, Rita could feel her insides coiled tighter than a spring. Her head ached, and voices that had been somewhat reasonable to listen to were screaming at her all at once. She could not quiet them. They accused and judged her for everything that had occurred in her life: It was *her* fault her mother was a zombie, it was *her* fault everyone was sexually abused, it was *her* fault everyone was beaten, it was *her* fault her father was a drunk. She began to talk to the voices, pleading with them: "No, it wasn't my fault, it was Greg's." Soon the voices began to agree with her. Then they added, much to Rita's delight, "It was Venus' fault too."

Four Friends

"Another day, another drama. Rita is really after us, Greg. What now?"

"Like Swan said, *stay put*. Let's go tell Sally and Joe the latest."

"We might wake them up."

"Hey, we can't sit with this all night!"

"Yeah, I suppose you're right."

They both walked over to Sally and Joe's bedroom, dreading what they had to tell them. Even though this was an emergency, they felt guilty for bringing more trouble to their gracious hosts.

"Joe, Sally," Venus called as she knocked lightly on their door. "Are you awake? We need to talk to you."

After hearing a grumpy sigh, they could hear Joe getting up. "This better be good," he said with a growl.

"Oh yeah, if you call being told that Rita has split and there were threatening notes all over her apartment, then it's good."

"Shit. What are the police doing about it?"

"They have an APB out. Several men and women are assigned to look for Rita and to watch your house. They know she's got a couple of screws loose."

"That info won't save your life if she decides to come here," said Sally who had appeared, sleepy-eyed.

"No, but Swan told us not to open the door and to be on the lookout for her. She has a gun and knows how to use it."

"Does Rita know where you guys are and where we live?" Sally asked, terrified.

It's not too hard for her to look up our address," Joe said as he put his arm around her shoulder. "She's a whiz in resourcefulness. We need to check *everything* and tell the kids *not* to come over. If Rita's as nutty as we think she is, she could attack one of the kids."

"I never thought of that," moaned Venus. "Let's call the kids —
now!" All the kids were soon apprised of the situation and told to stay
away until they heard further.

"It's the four of us now, and I feel badly for getting you guys
involved. I think you should call your kids too, to tell them not to drop
in. God knows what she's capable of."

"Good thinking, we will."

"Now, can we try to get a couple hours of sleep?" Greg looked at
the three others with a droopy-eyed expression.

"Best idea yet," exclaimed Joe.

***

For the next two days, the four friends sat on pins and needles
waiting for something – anything - to happen. Nothing did. They played
games, talked, debated politics, watched TV and made phone calls.
Boredom was soon added to the intense frustration and fear everyone felt.
These four were accustomed to being active in body, mind and spirit, and
now each of them was feeling like a caged animal. Only OM was happy
with the situation; he had company all day.

Venus often sat with her legs crossed, swinging one and then
another; then she got up and paced. Finally she could take it no longer
and said to the other three, "I think I'll run up and down the stairs just to
get rid of some of this excess energy. Anyone want to join me? The
staircase is certainly wide enough. Thank God for your big house!" For
the next ten minutes everyone watched Venus as she went up and down
the stairs. Greg started to laugh. "You certainly are working up a sweat
on those great legs of yours."

"Want to join me?"

"No, I'll pass for now."

"You know, patience is not one of my strong points."

"You're not telling me something I don't know. And just for
your information, it's not one of my strengths either."

"We really don't have many options except to wait this thing
out," Joe grumbled.

Even though Swan was in constant communication with them, he seldom had anything to offer in the way of information. There was absolutely no trace of Rita; it seemed that she had disappeared from the face of the Earth.

Bill

After the first car tampering, Bill became obsessed with how badly his life was going and how he had let down those who trusted him. Among the strongest of his regrets was how he had treated Joyce, followed by Venus and Greg. "I've got to get help with this," he concluded. After many sleepless nights and after talking to a few doctors, he found a referral to a therapist he could trust and began intensive therapy. The difference in his attitude this time around was he *wanted* to get rid of his anger and pain. When he was in his twenties, he thought everyone else was at fault. This was the first time in his adult life he could remember owning responsibility for his behaviors, words and thoughts. "In a way," he mused, "this taking responsibility stuff actually frees me. Wish I had known about this sooner." Another part of him answered, "You didn't want to."

Bill's therapy was fast. His therapist didn't allow him to wallow, judge or become either a victim or a perpetrator - to himself or towards others, most notably to his father. Bill was ready.

During the third week of his sessions, and with the agreement of his therapist, he called Joyce and apologized to her for his previous horrible behavior. "Please listen to me before you say anything, okay?"

He explained how, when he felt he was beginning to care for someone, he panicked and turned off all feelings. He went on to tell her about his childhood and first marriage and the anger he felt. "Pain, Joyce, it was all pain that I turned into anger. I was terrified of the pain! Now I'm getting rid of the old demons. I don't want to live like this anymore. I care about you deeply but was too terrified to get in a relationship. I understand that now. I have been releasing more pain than the mighty Pacific Ocean can absorb. Please forgive me."

He was grateful that she didn't ride him or question him. Instead, listened and said, "That must have been so horribly painful for you; I can't even imagine it." Bill could feel walls collapsing around him. He stifled a sob and quietly acknowledged what she had said.

After several minutes of near silence, he asked tentatively, "Would you be interested in coming out here to visit me? I really want you to come. But if you're not interested, I totally understand."

There was no hesitation on Joyce's part when she responded, "Of course I will come. When do you want me to book my ticket?" For the first time in Bill's life, he felt his heart smile and knew he was on the road to recovery!

"Today, tomorrow, when can you?"

Two days later, Joyce arrived on the West Coast. Bill couldn't believe how joyful he felt; he was a man walking on air, a man clearly in love. When he saw Joyce come out of the gate, he was floored. She was much more beautiful than he had remembered, with her long shiny black bob, trim body and gorgeous brown eyes. "I think I'm in love! Wonder if she is too." With tears in his eyes, he kissed her. He took her hand in his and, for the first time in his life, felt peaceful, comfortable and secure.

"Is it too soon to tell you what you mean to me?" he asked quietly.

"Not if it isn't too soon for me to respond," she answered.

"I think I love you; I think I've known since I left Boston but was afraid to admit it. I told you I'm a little nuts and I want you to come with me to my therapist. I believe he can help me. . . help us. . . have a great relationship. That is, if you want."

"Bill, I loved you from the get-go and of course..."

Joyce didn't get a chance to finish her statement because Bill took her and practically danced around the airline gate with her. He had wasted no time in being real because he felt he had a lot of catching-up to do. With Joyce, he knew life was going to be open and real. He was (finally) really truly in love! He couldn't wait to share Joyce with everyone at SeaFoam, especially Venus and Greg. Because he had been so focused on Joyce, he had taken time off from work and spoken to no one else. He was totally unaware of the drama unfolding at Joe and Sally's home.

More Waiting

On the third morning of the interminable waiting, while Greg and Venus were showering, there was a knock on the door. "Joe, can you get the door, I'm not dressed?" called Sally.

Before Joe opened the door, he cautiously looked to see who was there. Outside stood Rita. He raised his voice and asked her what she wanted. He was *not* going to open the door.

"I want to see Greg. I need to see him. Now!" Rita snarled.

"What makes you think he is here?" asked Joe,

"Don't play games with me! He told me where he was and that he was with Venus. I need to tell him something about his car."

"He did not tell you where he was. Why couldn't you just call him?" asked Joe who was witnessing Rita's vacant dark stare and knowing full well her motives.

"I already told him I was coming over here," she said, making no eye-contact.

Joe knew she was lying. And he felt the desperation and anger in her when he said, "That's not true. I'm sorry, I won't let you in. We're not dressed and whatever you need to say to Greg will have to keep."

With that, Rita pulled out a small hand gun and shouted, "Open the door. NOW! Or I'll blow the lock off this damn door. I *am* an excellent shot; if I do say so myself," she cackled.

Joe wasn't quite sure what to do, but knew the house was under surveillance – at least he hoped it was. He decided it would be better to open the door than to have the door blown to smithereens which would allow her to get in anyway. He slowly opened the door, just a crack. Rita instantly pushed it open enough to get through, and began waving her gun wildly in the air while yelling for Greg.

Sally came out immediately when she heard Rita's voice. When she saw the gun, she tried to back away quietly. But Rita saw her and threatened, "If you don't want to get hurt, come back here."

"What are you doing?" asked Joe. "You're not going to get away with anything. The police know what's up with you and are just waiting for you to slip. In fact, they're watching the house."

"You have to be kidding with that line," she sneered. "I was with the police several hours a few days ago, and they don't think there's anything wrong with me or the situation. I had to leave because they wanted to take me away. You think I'm crazy? Well, I'm not. I'm a great shot too, in case you don't know. I know what's going on: You're all trying to make me look insane and crazy. That's not the way to treat people. You think I'm a piece of garbage to discard?" Her voice rose several octaves, "I will not be discarded or degraded by you, your ugly wife, that miserable Greg or his whore. Where are they? Tell me now."

Joe was carefully observing Rita as she repeated herself and her gaze went wild. He wasn't quite sure what to do and only hoped neither Greg nor Venus would show themselves. Maybe he could talk Rita down?

Just then, Greg appeared, hair still wet from his showering with Venus. He started when he saw the gun, but said, "What do you want, Rita?"

"I want you and your whore to suffer like I've suffered."

"How have you suffered?" Greg asked quietly.

"You damn well know. You gave me up for her. The ugly whorish red-head. You loved *me* before *she* came into the picture. You were going to take care of me. I want you back and, if I can't have you, she can't either."

"Emily, that was over ten years ago. Surely there have been other men who wanted to have a relationship with you."

"How dare you call me Emily! I wanted you, and you didn't want me."

Joe and Sally were watching as Greg tried to calm Rita. They could see how confused, fearful and angry she was. It was as if she were in a time-warp where she couldn't discern anything in the present. Joe tried to signal Sally to sneak out of the room and call 911. But Sally was paralyzed and didn't pick up on what Joe was trying to convey.

Rita demanded, "Where is that bitch?"

"If you mean Venus, she's not available. You'd have to either kill me or maim me before I'd let you near her." Greg paused, noting that her pupils were fully dilated. "You are such a beautiful, smart woman. Why don't you just give up on this whole thing? I knew you as Emily. Do you remember how I told you we were just going to be friends, that I wasn't ready for a relationship? Do you remember any of that?" Greg questioned her, stalling for time until she might let her guard down.

Instead Rita became more agitated. "You only wanted to be my friend. I wanted more. I told you that. You were mean. You wouldn't even sleep with me. You thought I was ugly and stupid. You thought I wasn't worth shit." By this time, she was yelling. Her eyes were black with rage and pain and her hand holding the gun was shaking.

Greg, Sally and Joe were praying silently that Venus had heard the commotion from where she was in the house and had contacted the police.

Several more minutes passed while Emily reiterated how abused she had been by Greg and how she had planned the computer-hacking, the poisoning and the car tampering. "I watched the two of you. I knew where you were. I tried to get you away from that bitch, but you didn't pay attention. She is no good for you. She should have been dead. If only that damn coffee cup hadn't spilled. Nothing worked right. She should have been dead!" Rita screamed, "And you too! I was so much better for you, but you lost that chance! Did you see that? No. You were too wrapped up with her. I tell you, she's bad. And so are her friends. After I'm done with her and you, I'll get rid of everyone who means anything to either of you. This will be the last time I'll be discarded by the likes of you." Rita was hysterical at this point.

As she continued to rant, she occasionally slipped into a sing-song tone of voice and rambled about nothing that had to do with what she claimed she was there for. All three of her would-be victims let her rant knowing that the longer she was distracted, the more time the police had to act. It was quite apparent that Rita was having a total mental breakdown - unable to discern who she was or what she was doing there. Only her rage didn't change. Her eyes were vacant shells and her body shook, but still she waved the gun around.

After what seemed like hours, but was only about fifteen minutes, there was a loud knock on the door. Rita became more cogent and told all three of them to get into the corner and not say a word. "Ignore the knocking. If you don't, I'll pull the trigger, and let me remind you once again, I'm an ace shot," she whispered menacingly.

Everyone remained silent while the pounding on the door continued. After several minutes, whoever was at the door seemed to be gone, and Rita asked again, "Where's the bitch? I want to see you go down together!"

Greg shook his head and said, "It's not going to happen, Emily. This madness isn't going to bring about anything for you except your own death. Is that what you want?"

"I told you what I want," she screamed. "Where is she?"

At just about that moment, the back door and the sliding door to the deck opened simultaneously and four members of the SWAT team charged into the room, guns drawn.

At first Rita stood there in shock, but then she dropped the gun. As the police handcuffed her, she screamed continuously, sometimes shouting obscenities and other times non-intelligible comments.

Sally, Joe and Greg heaved sighs of relief.

"How did you get in?" Sally and Joe finally asked. "Those doors are locked."

Venus came into the room, her face white as a sheet and trembling. She managed to run over to Greg and hug him, saying, "I heard her and called the police. I told them I'd open the back and side doors while Bob was banging on the front door, hoping that Rita would be distracted by the banging. Thank God for the layout of this house that made it possible." Venus sighed a huge sigh before saying, "That no one got hurt is a miracle."

Bob Swan called for an ambulance to be dispatched so Rita could be taken to the nearest hospital that had services for the criminally insane. As they were waiting, Rita began to scream at the top of her lungs, "I hate you all. You're all works of the devil. I'll get even, just wait. I'll kill you. You big ugly cops, you're evil. If you knew the whole story, I could turn you around and you'd be on my side." She continued to rave until the ambulance pulled up and she was forcefully put in a straight-jacket to prevent her from harming herself and others, and then taken away.

The police took statements from everyone and finally, after a few hours, finished their investigation.

Bob was the last to leave. He addressed Greg and Venus, "Well, it worked out successfully this time. I wish they'd all work out like this. We were sure grateful to Jamie Robins in Boston who found Rita's hit list. Incidentally, I can tell you now: You *were* next on the list. Anyway, good meeting you folks." Turning to Joe and Sally, he said "We've got to get together again; might even invite those two, nodding to Greg and Venus. Let's make a date to meet with a more pleasant agenda. Huh?"

All four nodded in agreement, and Joe volunteered to set up a six-some for dinner.

Finally, the two couples were alone.

"Whew! Thank God that's over. Now we can all go home, and Sally and Joe can have their privacy back," Venus murmured.

Then Greg strongly suggested, "If we don't call the kids, there may be some other threats of murder in the near future. I'll call mine: Venus, you call yours."

All their kids were fully informed of what had occurred and they insisted on visiting immediately. This time the scenario was one of relief and joy.

When the doorbell rang, Joe answered it. With a huge grin on his face asked, "Don't you guys ever work?"

In one way or another, they all chimed in with a version of "Being here was more important than working." Now, they all felt - with clear consciences - they could go back to their lives. Except for Ron and Dahlia, who enjoyed being tourists in the area. When Greg asked them how much longer they planned to stay in California, he was elated with the answer he received.

"We're debating about moving here. Mom will kill me, but oh well, I'm a big boy. Dahlia has cousins here, though her family lives in Chicago. For them, it's a ride either way. And yes, we've mentioned it to Charlie and Sarah. I miss my nephews, nieces, brother and sister-in-law. Dahlia's an only child, so there is no one around anyway and she loves company. Also you Pop, and now Venus. You, my dear Dad, picked a winner."

"You know, you could have a job at SeaFoam any time you want."

"We'll see," replied Ron.

When everyone had finally gone their separate ways, Greg took Venus and OM back to her house, and Greg helped her bring in her things. "You *will* marry me Venus Lighton. There is no answer other than yes that I will tolerate. The only question that remains is *when*. How about tomorrow?"

Venus laughed. "I guess after all this, I have to. In the meantime, wanna come here and stay with me and OM? I know he'll miss

204

you…. You could even get rid of your rental house, if you want." She paused. With a giggle and her arms around his neck, she said, "I don't think I want to be without you for even a night – unless of course, you have to make business trips. And I trust there will be *no* funny business, happening, and that girl friend in Boston is not to be seen." She giggled some more while pulling herself even closer to her love. "Imagine that, I actually said I'd marry you. Just don't expect me to change at all!"

"You? Change?" Greg laughed and kissed her. "I don't want you to. Yes, I will be delighted to be here with you until we decide whether we want to have your house become our house, or to create another one!

***

After a few glorious, relaxing days together with no threats of any kind, Venus and Greg headed back to work. For Greg, work began to normalize as everyone in both the DelMar and the Boston office was given the details of what had occurred. SeaFoam employees were shocked and amazed at the events from the past two weeks. The Boston office, feeling very protective, called Greg several times a day under false pretenses just to see how he was. Finally Greg had to tell them to stop.

Venus was treated like a goddess at work until she finally had to tell everyone to stop acting as if she were fragile and waiting for her death. After sharing the complete story with everyone who clamored around her, she brusquely told them all to get back to work.

A most surprising and wonderful event occurred two weeks after the drama with Rita was over. Bill came to Greg's office, holding a woman's hand, and announced, "Greg, I'd like you to meet my Love, Joyce."

Greg smiled at him (How could he help it seeing the big grin on Bill's face?) and said, "Happy to meet you. Are you settling here?"

Joyce looked at Bill, "I believe so."

Bill looked at her with love in his eyes, "I damn well hope so." Then he turned back to Greg, "We were wondering, could you and Venus have dinner with us tonight? That is if your wedding plans allow you some free time."

"I'll call Venus and see."

That night the four of them went out to dinner and Bill apologized to Venus and Greg for his treatment of them. He explained briefly how he was in therapy and learning why he had behaved so poorly earlier on, why he'd been so jealous of what they had together. "I couldn't even look at you two; it about broke my heart. I have been terrified to commit to anyone my whole life – until now." Bill paused before continuing, "I am no longer afraid, and I have the love of my life sitting right next to me. I knew it when I met her, but I just didn't have the balls to deal with me. . . my issues. I thought I'd had a heart attack when I left Boston; to protect myself I was ugly, nasty and uncivil to her." He looked down for a moment, "I'm working on our relationship with a diligence that I've only used when working on fiscal demands. I want Joyce more than I've ever wanted anything in my life. If it meant losing every red cent I had in order to keep her, then so be it!"

Venus, who had loved Joyce the moment she met her, got up and went over to Bill and hugged him. "Bill, I am so glad you have taken the bull by the horns and have found peace. I think I can speak for both of us when I say we are both so happy for the two of you. And of course we forgive you."

Epilogue

Two months later, Venus and Greg were married. Three days before the wedding, Greg's parents flew in from Boston. It was love at first sight between Venus and them. Greg's mom, Adele, took one look at Venus and, with tears in her eyes said, "I know why he loves you. I can see your essence; it is magnificent. We are so thrilled to be here with all of our family, and yours, too, Venus. Thank you so much. My heart is indebted to you and the joy you've brought Greg."

Venus, immediately tearful as Adele hugged her, began to cry softly. "Thank you," she said.

Before she could continue to speak, Greg Senior made the hug three-way, putting his arms around his wife and her.

Then he called to Greg, "Come over here and let's hug as a family. Let's make this how we are." Greg was thrilled.

The wedding was held at Sally and Joe's house. Their home was perfect, with the beautiful semi-circular staircase for Venus to descend. Joe walked her down the stairs, Sally was her matron of honor, and Thom was Greg's best man, followed by OM with his tail held proudly in the air. After all the excruciatingly long days and nights they had been through, Greg and Venus, Joe and Sally, had truly formed a life-long friendship. They were even kitty sitting for OM when Greg and Venus went to Cancun for their honeymoon. That was true friendship!

All members of both families were at the wedding and Greg delighted to see how well everyone got along. He was particularly elated to see his parents really *being* with his kids and grandkids (and even with Venus' family and Joe and Sally's brood.) This truly was a time of festivity.

After Greg and Venus' wedding celebration was completed, Greg raised his champagne glass and tapped it with a fork to silence the group. "I have a surprise for all of you. My parents want to renew their vows at this time. Could we have silence at this time, please."

Greg Senior and Adele walked to where Greg was standing and, without any fuss or any clergy, stood together looking into each other's eyes and holding hands. There wasn't a dry eye in the house when Greg

Senior said to Adele, "I will continue to love you for the rest of my life, with everything I have. I will talk to you with love and respect and joy, and never leave a stone unturned when we have differences. You are my single love. And I promise all this before God." He then presented Adele with a single red rose.

Adele responded, "I will continue to love you the rest of my life, with everything I have. I will communicate with you in truth and respect and harmony. You are my life. I am so grateful we found each other again after all those years. I am overjoyed to be renewing our vows of love. And I promise this before God."

"What a beautiful thing to do, huh Greg?" Venus closely held the hand of her new husband. Both of them had tears in their eyes. "Think we'll be like that in twenty years or so?"

"I don't have any doubts," said Greg, kissing her on her neck.

It was a joyous event, with lots of dancing and singing. Among the guests were LuAnne and Rachael; everyone from Venus' department; Glenda and her husband Ralph and their children; John Paul and Simon; and many of the old employees from SeaFoam. Larry even got Nora to come! The newly-weds were tremendously pleased that Bill and Joyce attended and they announced their upcoming wedding in three months. There were new employees from SeaFoam; Bob Swan and his wife Ester; and a variety of police officers who had helped during Venus' and Greg's ordeal. His majesty OM walked about greeting everyone with his tail and head held high. He was an enormous hit.

Aside from the gift of being surrounded by their parents and friends, the wedding gift from Bill Dewart was the most precious and dear to them: a magnificent video of the wedding, and a framed picture of the two of them holding OM.

While Venus and Greg were dancing, Venus looked at her friend Rachael and remarked, "I think there is something really *big* going on over there with Rachael and Thom. Just look at them! What do you think?"

Greg laughed, "Yup! He's looking at her the way I looked at you. And I know Thom, even though I've never seen this part of him. They're in for quite a ride. Shall we congratulate them now, or later?"

Venus laughed and said, "Shhhh. They'll find out for themselves."

***

To reach Nina, go to

http://intuitiontalesbyninaedd.com/blog/

CPSIA information can be obtained at www.ICGtesting.com
Printed in the USA
LVOW081419301211

261783LV00001B/160/P